Calling on Quinn

BLUE SAFFIRE

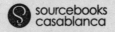

sourcebooks
casablanca

Published by Sourcebooks Casablanca, an imprint of Sourcebooks
P.O. Box 4410, Naperville, Illinois 60567-4410
(630) 961-3900
sourcebooks.com

Printed and bound in the United States of America.
OPM 10 9 8 7 6 5 4 3 2 1

CHAPTER 1

SHOULDN'T BE

Quinn

RUSHING THROUGH THE AUTOMATIC DOUBLE DOORS OF the hospital, I feel the acid rising in my stomach. I swallow hard as the cool air of the emergency room blasts me in the face. It's like I can taste my emotions. When I drag my hand across my sweat-soaked forehead, I can't help wincing against the burn of the salty sweat that enters my wounds.

I'm not here for my injuries, but my injuries are a result of why I am here. My baby sister is somewhere in the walls of this hospital, and that's just not right. Erin is the sweetest soul you'll meet. She takes care of family and keeps to herself.

My brothers and I have always been the troublemakers. If there's a fight, we're at the center of it. The four of us—Kevin, Trenton, Shane, and myself—we've spent our lives running into the line of fire. Receiving a call that one of us is riddled with holes wouldn't be a surprise. I'd be just as livid, but not surprised.

Ach, this isn't right.

I've been repeating those words in my head the entire drive here. I look down at my smashed phone. My screen is destroyed. I'm not able to text my family to find out where they are.

When my mum called to tell me that Erin and her dumb-as-fuck husband, Cal, were shot up in front of their home, I blacked out. When I came to, my phone was ruined and the back window of my truck was smashed out as I flexed my busted fist. I have a bit of a temper. It's best for me to keep my world under control so I don't lose it.

This is completely out of my control, and I'm not coping one bit. Scanning the space around me, my eyes are unfocused and my head buzzes with too many noises and unfiltered information. Crying babies, a drunk slurring, the walkie-talkies of security—all shit I'm not composed enough to block out.

Get it together, Quinn. First, find the desk. Second, ask for Erin Kelley. Third, get to Erin and the family.

With a clear list in my head, I start to gain a minimal grasp on my focus. It's enough to move my feet toward the desk to start barking out questions. Turning, ready to get answers, I take a step, but my attention is drawn when my name is called.

"Quinn," my younger brother Shane calls.

I whip my head in the direction of his voice. I turn to find an identical expression to mine on a face that's just as alike. The Blackhart genes are strong. We all have the same green eyes and dark red hair, with the exception of Trenton. He is the only one of us that has my ma's dark brown hair and freckles.

From the look on Shane's face, things aren't going well. My insides start to coil tighter. I wish I'd carried my baoding balls with me. I need a way to channel some of this energy.

"Aye, how is she?" I grumble once I reach my brother's side.

My Irish accent is a bit thicker than usual in my ire. My siblings and I were born and raised in New York, but you don't live in a home with Renny and Teagon Blackhart and not retain some semblance of an accent.

I received my fair share of teasing in my school days. My siblings are better at hiding the brogue than I am. It could be that I don't much care to. I'm right proud of who I am and where I come from.

"It's not looking good. She's still in surgery. It's been a few hours," Shane replies.

"Fuck," I seethe. "How did this happen? What the fuck is going on?"

"Have no fucking clue. Whoever did this knew enough to cut the cams on the house. There's nothing during the time of the attack. Those cameras should've been working. I did a check of all the systems about a week ago," he says, a deep frown consuming his face. His accent is showing a wee bit as well.

"Ya checked the neighbor's cams?"

"Oul man Nelson's cams are grainy as fuck. It will take me a while to clean up the images to see anything. I've tried. While we've been waiting, I've been working on it," he says in frustration.

"Where's Ma?"

"Ya know Da. He raised hell until we got a private waiting room. Everyone's in there. What happened to yer hand? I thought the job went smoothly," Shane says, while pointing at my busted knuckles.

I ignore him, like I'm ignoring the throbbing in my hand. I'll see to it later. First, I need to get to my family.

"Where were the wee ones?"

My heart squeezes. My nieces and nephew can be a hand-ful, but I love each one of them. I couldn't ask my ma about them on the phone. Knowing Erin was clinging to her life was enough to keep me unhinged on the two-hour drive here.

I had finished my assignment. I'd planned to head up to my cabin for the weekend. I was halfway there, only stop-ping for gas, when the call came in.

"They were with Ma and Da. It was their game night." Shane pauses to run a hand through his hair and blow out a harsh breath. "Christ, I keep thinking about how they could have been there."

"Thank God, they weren't. Where are they now?"

"The twins are with Ma and Da in the waiting room. The wee ones are with the O'Connors," he grumbles.

"Grand, they'll be safe. Thomas is retired, but he's still sharp," I say of my father's best friend and neighbor.

"Aye, but I'm more afraid of his wife," Shane says with a wince.

I would laugh under different circumstances. Mrs. O'Connor used to give Shane a good lashing with her broom. Always with good reason.

"Where ya headed?"

"To get snacks and drinks for everyone. I needed to get out for a bit of air."

"Point me to the family," I say.

"Aye." He nods, understanding me enough to know I need to stick to my plan.

"I'll walk with ya," he says.

We walk to the waiting room in silence. My head is still swimming with so many thoughts. Anger is lying on the surface ready to boil over.

"Quinn," Ma nearly sobs as we enter the room.

She rushes forward into my arms. My mum is not as tall as my da, but she's still tall. She's no small woman at all. However, in this moment, she seems tiny.

I embrace her tightly. Her shoulders shake with her tears. I'm at a loss. I don't know what to say to make this better. It's killing me because I'm the fixer in the family.

I look at things from the angles no one else does and figure it out. My family may act annoyed at times when I have to have my lists to organize everything, but they appreciate them when I'm fixing their problems. Yet, I can't think of a task to start the path to fixing this. I don't know what to say or do.

"What's the word?" I say to my da, who looks as lost as I feel.

"We wait," he says gruffly.

"She has four babes to be here for. She has to be okay," Ma chokes out through her tears.

"Erin is tougher than she looks. All her life she had to be, to survive the lot of us. She'll pull through. She's a Blackhart through and through, she is," I murmur in my ma's ear.

"Aye, I hope yer right. She's still my wee un. My little lass."

"I know, Ma. I know. She'll pull through, and we'll get to the bottom of this," I reassure her.

"Ach, the bastards will be sorry, they will," she fumes.

"Aye."

I don't say anything more. Now is not the time for my anger to take over. I keep my composure as I rock my ma in my arms and hold on to see what comes our way.

"This is good. We need to wait out the night, is all," Kevin says as we step out into the hallway.

The doctor just came in to say Erin is out of surgery and stable. It's been four hours since I arrived. We got news about two hours ago that Cal has been moved to ICU.

"Aye, it's good. But we know what I want to talk about. What the fuck has Cal been working on?" I grunt.

"I don't know, but I'm thinking like you," Trenton says, sounding more like a New Yorker than any of us. "He had his hands in something he let blow back on his home."

When together, most of us have a muddled version of our parents' Northern Irish accent. Trenton, on the other hand, only slips when extremely pissed or trying to hide his words from outsiders. It's clear he has had some time to calm himself, unlike me. I'm still fuming beyond measure.

"Aye, I would say so," I reply.

"They picked the wrong fucking door to come knocking on," Trenton snarls.

"First, get a couple of guys here. I want round-the-clock security. We'll rotate as well. We don't know what we're dealing with."

"Got it covered. I've woken a few of the boys to have them come down," Kevin replies.

"Second, I want to know exactly what the fuck Cal was working on. I want to know where he's been going, who he's been with. I don't care what ya have to do to find out. I need answers," I say.

"We're on it, Quinn. Don't ya think it's time to get that looked at?" Shane replies.

I look at my hand. He's right. My ma fussed until I put an ice pack on it, but I refused to leave her side until now. My da got ready to roar for someone to come tend to me, but I stopped him before he could get worked up.

Ma needed us both. My da on one side, me on the other. Together we kept her from falling apart.

"Aye, I'll go. Get me what I asked for."

"Aye, aye, captain," Trenton teases.

I narrow my eyes at him. "I'm not in the mood for yer faffin'. Just do as I say," I snap, turning to walk away.

"One of these days he's going to clobber ya," I hear Shane say as I saunter in the direction of the nurses' station.

"As long as I don't end up like his truck," Trenton says.

"His truck?"

"Aye, window is blown out. Saw it when I went out to make a few calls, put two and two together," he replies.

"And ya want to tease the man?" Kevin snorts. "Eejit."

"I'll show you an idiot," Trenton grunts.

"Get to work," I boom over my shoulder.

I keep moving as they shut their gubs. They're all eejits, but I love them. I'm going to find out who did this to our sister, and we'll all make them pay.

CHAPTER 2

CRASH COURSE

Quinn

I POUND MY FEET AGAINST THE PAVEMENT, SENDING A welcome burn up my calves. Sweat is pouring from my face and back as the sun beams down on me. It's going to be a hot one.

My morning run is a needed part of my daily routine. Normally, I would talk to my sister for the first five miles. It's our thing.

There is something soothing about talking to my little sister as I start my morning. After we hang up, I usually take the time to focus myself and get my lists in order. Although, there won't be a call this morning, and there hasn't been one for two weeks now.

There's a lot I want to get done today, which requires I get myself organized. First, I want to head over to the police station to talk to Dugan, the police chief. He's been a friend of the family for years. Not many on the force know he's my godfather, and we've always kept it that way.

I need answers from him. I'm not getting what I need from his detectives. I know there's some bad blood between Cal and the force, but that should have nothing to do with my sister.

Second, I have a few cases that I need to give my attention to before the end of the day. We've fallen behind in the
office. I can hand a few security jobs off to our staff, but my
brothers and I handle most of the private investigations.
That will have to change for a bit. Cal is a part of the PI
team whenever he's not off getting his nose into shit that
blows up in his face.

"Fucking melter," I release a growl as my thoughts turn
to my brother-in-law.

He's looking a hell of a lot worse off than Erin. I don't
know whether to be happy she's going to be widowed or
pissed off at him for leaving her with four babes to take care
of. Honestly, I pray they both pull through. My nieces and
nephew don't deserve this.

Maybe this will finally teach Cal that a hard head makes
a soft behind. I know none of this has come from any case
I've assigned him. If I find out he's been getting into something illegal, I'm going to pull the fucking plug myself.

I pound my feet against the ground harder, allowing the
burn to spread up my legs. Locking back in on my list, I bear
down on what I need to get done. I'm almost back at the
house. After getting some work finished up, I'll head to the
hospital. I'll need a list for that. I have some things I need
to take there.

Fresh flowers, something to eat for Ma and Da, a music
dock—Erin loves music, that will be good for her—a picture of the kids for her bedside. Last on my to-do list for
the day, a beer and a steak on the grill. It'll probably be late,
but I've been craving meat and potatoes. I have to have that
steak today.

Satisfied with my list, I slow at the walkway of my home.

I start to stretch my tight muscles. I'll have my shake, take a shower, get dressed, and head out. I can call my brothers on the way to the station.

My phone rings as I map out my next steps for the morning. I frown, pulling the device from my arm strap. My frown deepens when I see it's my ma.

I flex my still healing hand, remembering my reaction to the last call my ma made to this number. If this is bad news, I'm going to have to hold it together. I just got the pickup back yesterday. The back window was replaced. I hadn't realized the dent I put in the same door. It had to be worked out as well.

"Hello, Ma," I say into the phone.

"I need yer help," she says in greeting.

"Aye, what's up?"

"Mckenna has a driving lesson this morning. I need ya to go with her," Ma says.

"She's sixteen. Legally she can drive with the driving instructor," I reply.

"Aye, but this is different, Quinn. Her mind has been on her ma. Erin gone with her to every lesson. I think someone should ride along."

I groan. This was not on my list. I just finalized my list. Everything will have to shift now. I wasn't ready for this today.

"Ach, Quinn. Spare me yer damn list this morning," she snaps.

"I didn't say anything about my list," I mumble back, like a wounded child.

"Who do ya think yer yarn to? I've been yer mum all yer life. I know yer thoughts before ya do," she retorts.

"I know who I'm talking to," I reply, feeling like a chastened five-year-old.

I hear her sigh and shift on the other end. She sounds tired. I've been meaning to help out more with the kids. Shane is the best with them, which is why I've allowed him to take over there.

"The chisellers need a sense of normalcy. This has all been a lot to take for them. I need ya to do this for me," she says after a beat.

"Aye, I'll have my shake, a shower, get dressed, and head over to yer house to ride with Mckenna for her driver's lesson. I'm on it, Ma," I relent.

"Sounds good," she says, relief clear in her voice. "And Quinn?"

"Aye, Ma."

"Don't scunder the poor lass." She chuckles.

"How would I embarrass her?"

Her laughter rings out, but she hangs up without an answer. I frown at the phone. I've never embarrassed Mckenna. She says I'm her favorite. I walk into the house, muttering to myself.

Alicia

Pulling up to the row and section I've been dreading, I park and shut the car off. I smooth my hands over the leather of the steering wheel and blow out a breath. I know I need to do this, but it still hurts.

"We're here for you," Aidan says beside me, reaching to cover my hand. "You can do this."

I hear more than see Tari slide forward in the back seat to place a hand on my shoulder. I pull from my best friends' strength. Their presence alone helps to soothe my aching heart.

I look out at the sun rising in the distance, and I think about the sunsets I'm here to mourn. I'm not ready to get out of the car. I'm stalling.

"I need a minute," I murmur.

"Ali, I loved your parents like they were my own. This day kills me as much as it does you. Your mom and dad were something special. When you guys moved in next door, you all changed my life," Aidan says.

"Yeah," Tari says from behind me. "I feel the same way. It hurt like hell to lose you guys as neighbors."

I give a wistful smile. The day I moved away from the old complex, leaving one set of friends behind, I gained a new friend in my new neighborhood.

I love these two. I didn't think there would be a day they would manage to get along. I was Aidan's new best friend, and Tari refused to share the first two months after I moved and she started coming over for weekends.

Things were so different back then. There were four of us in those days. I shake away the thought before that darkness can creep in.

"I hate this day." I sigh.

"Yeah, but we're here to change that," Tari whispers.

"Remind me how that's supposed to happen again?"

"I don't know how she managed it, but that heifer knew what she was doing last year. I promise you she did. I'm going to fuc—"

"Tari," Aidan warns, turning to look at her. "I feel you,

but that's not helping." He turns back toward me. "You're stuck, baby girl. We see it and you see it. Breaking things off with Gio was the right thing to do, but you seemed to stop there."

"As your friends we're just being straight with you. We can't explain it, but your freedom starts here. You know?" Tari adds.

"Yeah." I turn to look out my window at the row of graves that my parents rest in. "Yeah, I get it. A part of me is still here."

"I think so, Sweets," Aidan chokes out.

"All right, give me a minute by myself," I say, pushing the door open and stepping out of the car.

I move forward, feeling my heart sink as the heels of my ankle boots do the same inside the moist soil. Memories of the last two times I was here fill me. I reach up for the locket my father gave me the day we buried my mother. He told me she picked it for me. It was the last gift she purchased for me.

A year later, I added his picture beside hers as I had to place his body in the grave next to hers. Same day, same place, only a year in between. I finger the locket, wishing it held some magic to turn back the hands of time.

"Hey, Mom. Hi, Daddy," I whisper.

I lift my eyes to the sky to collect myself. This has been a long time coming. I haven't been back here since laying my father to rest.

"I think Aid and Tar are right. I left a piece of me with each of you. Oh, and Mommy, you were so right about that fast-ass little girl." I snort. "She tried to ruin my entire life. I…I thought she was my friend.

"Daddy, it's been thirteen years. Why haven't I gotten my life together? Why does this day seem to hate me so much?"

I fall to my knees. I push a hand into the front of my hair.

"I'm so damn lost and angry. Do you know I have roommates? I'm thirty with roommates!"

Aidan and Tari drop to my sides, each wrapping an arm around me. "Hey, Mr. R, Mrs. R."

"Hey, guys," Tari sniffles.

"I knew you two wouldn't mind your own business," I mumble.

Silence falls over the graveyard as the three of us sit and stare at the two headstones before us.

I don't know how much time passes as we all sit quietly. I breathe through my grief, searching for...I don't know. Yet, I think I'll know the moment I find it.

In my mind, I wrap my arms around my parents one by one, giving them each one last hug. The wind picks up even as the warm morning's sun kisses my cheeks. It's as if my hugs are being returned.

Live.

The word carries on the wind to my ears as if my daddy were saying it out loud to me, just as he would on one of our weekends when it was only the two of us. My lips turn up.

"I think it's time for me to get my life together," I say as I open my eyes.

"Good, because you ruined your pants and those heels. We're going to have to stop at the house before going into the office," Aidan says.

I look down at my knees then my boots. *Shit.* I check my watch. *Double shit.* I groan.

"Let's go. I have a pair of jeans at the office. I can change when I pick up the car. I have a lesson this morning," I say as I push to my feet.

Aidan dusts my butt off, causing me to look over my shoulder. "Oh please, I'm making sure you don't get dirt in your car," he says when I give him a teasing frown.

"I know I'm your girl crush," I toss back.

He rolls his eyes, but grins at me. "If I didn't fall in love with you as a little sister first, maybe," he replies, wrapping an arm around my shoulders to give a squeeze, and kisses the top of my head.

"And this is why I *always* feel like the third wheel," Tari pouts.

"Come here," Aidan says, tucking her under his other arm, looking down at her pretty brown face. "You and I both know, I'm trying to fix her so we can drink and be merry in peace."

"So true," Tari sings, nodding her head.

"I'm throwing you both out."

"Not a chance, baby girl! Today we all start fresh. I promise there is life waiting for us," Aidan says gleefully.

"To life," Tari cheers.

I smile at my friends.

Yeah. To life.

Quinn

"What time was your lesson supposed to start?" I ask Mckenna, looking down at my watch.

I got here as soon as I could. When I texted my niece,

she said her lesson should've started at ten this morning. It's ten minutes after.

I'm already tight on time. My schedule has shifted enough. I don't need this guy messing up the rest of my damn plans. I need to get this day back on track.

"Relax, Uncle Quinn," Mckenna sings.

"I'll relax when he gets here," I grumble.

She giggles, looking up at me through bright green eyes. My heart squeezes a little. She looks so much like her mother when she was her age. I remember when Mckenna and her twin, Conroy, were born.

They were these wee little things that wouldn't stop crying. The first time I held Mckenna, I thought I'd break her, much like when I held her mother for the first time as a wee lad. When Mckenna looked at me with those same bright eyes, she took something with her. I've been wrapped around her finger since.

I reach to pinch her nose between my fingers, causing her to giggle more. Drawing her to me with my other arm, I tuck her into my side. She places her arms around my waist and locks me into a tight embrace. I squeeze harder, sensing she needs it.

"Ach, who plays their music so loud?" I frown as a car turns up the street blasting "Ironic" by Alanis Morissette.

"I love that song," Mckenna chimes.

"What would ya know about that song?" I ask, lifting a brow.

"I heard it at Uncle Kevin's house," she says with a shrug. "That's Ms. Rhodes."

"Ms. Rhodes?"

"Come on, Uncle Quinn, keep up. My instructor isn't

a man. Ms. Rhodes is my driving teacher," she says, rolling her eyes.

"Ah, fuck me," I mutter under my breath.

Mckenna bounces over to the driver's side door. The woman inside lowers the music, but she's slow to step out. I squint to look through the windshield. I can't see her face. Her hair is covering it as she looks down in her lap.

I mutter to myself as I go to the passenger side door. Aye, my ma raised a gentleman. I open the door and wait for her to get out and make her way around.

"My uncle Quinn's riding with us today," Mckenna says as the woman steps from the car.

"Oh, okay," the lass says.

Brushing her long sweeping bangs from her face, she turns to look at me and does a double take. Her pretty eyes go wide and her full lips part. I know that look.

Aye, at six three, 250 pounds, I'm a big lad. Then there's the red hair. I get that look all the time.

What I'm not expecting is my instant attraction to the lass staring back at me. She's gorgeous. A wee thing, no more than five eight. Her dark hair is cut into a shoulder-length asymmetrical hairstyle that frames her face and complements her rich brown skin.

The actress from those movies I watched with Erin and Mckenna comes to mind, *Ride Along*. Tika Sumpter, that was her name. I remember Erin saying she knew someone who reminded her of the actress.

Those lips, they're full and enticing. I'd love to know how they taste.

You're losing it, Quinn.

I shake my thoughts clear. It seems Ms. Rhodes does the

same as she makes her way around the driver's side door. Her curvy body comes into full view. She's thick in all the right places. The white button-down dress shirt and light blue jeans wrap a perfect package.

My gaze travels down her body to the heeled ankle boots on her feet. I take back three inches from her height. She's no more than five five without those heels. I guarantee it as she edges her way around me like she'll catch fire if she gets too close.

I narrow my eyes when she moves to the trunk of the car. She pops it, retrieving a pair of runners. I snort. She's late and still not prepared. I bite my tongue to keep from embarrassing Mckenna as my mum suggested.

She takes her time, dropping the sneakers to the ground, seeming lost in thought. My restraint slips. I don't have time for this. I have to get to the rest of my tasks for the day.

Those thoughts float right out of my head when she bends over to unzip her boot. First, I tilt my head as I notice the dirt caked on her heels, next something entirely different draws my attention. My jaw tightens, but I can't tear my gaze away, which is the reason she catches me with my eyes glued to her bum.

She turns fully to give me a quizzical look, but doesn't bust my balls for it. I'm grateful. My cheeks already feel warm with embarrassment. Eyeing me with caution, she makes her way back to the car door I'm still holding open.

"Thank you," she murmurs as she climbs inside.

"Aye, you're welcome," I say.

Closing the door, I get into the back seat. Ms. Rhodes moves her seat up, but I'm still too big to sit directly behind her. I angle my body and sit across the seats. Strapping myself in, I say a prayer. I love my niece, but Erin has had a few stories to tell about Mckenna's driving.

"We'll go a little longer since I was late. I'm sorry about that," Ms. Rhodes says in that soft voice of hers.

I ignore how it raises the hairs on my arms. Instead, I focus on the words she just spoke. I shake my head.

"No, we'll stick to the original time," I speak up.

"Uncle Quinn," Mckenna whines.

"Sorry, lass. I have things that need to be done."

"Oh, I'm sorry." The instructor clears her throat. "I can make it up during your next lesson then. No problem."

"Fine," my niece pouts.

"Okay, girly, show me what you got," she says gently to Mckenna.

"Ach, ya don't have a checklist or order of operations for her. Just…show ya what she's got," I say.

"Ugh, why me?" Mckenna groans from the driver's seat.

"Excuse me?" The instructor turns to look back at me. "She's taken several lessons already. She knows what to do. I watched her go through every step she's been taught, without me prompting her."

"Ya should still give her a refresher," I say tightly.

There's a blazing fire in her gaze. Her full lips purse. It's like I'm watching the lid getting ready to blow off a pressure cooker.

"Would you like to take my seat? You can feel free to give this lesson if you like. Clearly, my six years of experience as an instructor mean squat," she tears into me.

My mouth falls open. I wasn't expecting that to happen. I'm also stunned into silence as I'm drawn into her brown eyes—so pretty up this close.

I'm caught in them as they lock on my greens. Yet, the tears that start to well and the sadness in them stirs my protective side. I know in my gut she's not only pissed at me. I want to know the cause of the pain I see in her depths.

"Where's your mom?" She turns to Mckenna when I don't reply to her.

"She's in the hospital. She won't be around for lessons for a while," I say.

I want to kick myself as soon as the words are out of my mouth. I see my niece's shoulders sag the moment they fill the small space. Reaching to unfasten her seat belt, Mckenna opens the door.

"I think we should reschedule. I don't feel so good," she says.

"Ach, love, get back in the car. We'll do the full time slot."

"It's okay. Can we go to the hospital?" She looks back over her shoulder to ask.

"I had to shift some things. I hadn't planned to go this early—" I cut my words off and roll my lips. "Sure, we can go if ya like."

"Thanks, Ms. Rhodes. Sorry to waste your time."

"You're not wasting my time, sweetheart. I didn't know your mom was ill. We can reschedule whenever you like," she says tenderly to Mckenna.

We all exit the car. The soft-spoken wee lass stands in front of me, glaring daggers. If only she knew how cute she is. Not intimidating at all, not the way I think she intends to be.

"You're an insensitive boor," she snaps. "You all are."

With that, she storms around me. I watch as she wraps her arms around Mckenna, giving her a tight hug. My niece clings to her, causing me to tilt my head and study this wee instructor more closely. When she releases Mckenna, she reaches up and rubs a hand over the young lass's hair and smiles at her before turning to hop into the car.

The music cuts back on and starts to blare. This time Wu-Tang's "Triumph" spills from the speakers. My lips twitch and I nod appreciatively. She pulls off, and I'm left staring after her.

"Well, damn," I mutter, rubbing the back of my neck.

"I've never seen anyone silence you, Uncle Quinn," Mckenna says.

"The lass is something," I admit.

"Ma's going to kick your butt. She likes Ms. Rhodes."

"Aye, when she can, I'll welcome it, love," I say with a small smile.

"Yeah, me too."

I pull her in and kiss the top of her head. "How about you drive to the hospital?" I offer.

"No, thank you," she says warily.

"Ach, why not?"

"Because you'll freak me out. I'm not ready for that kind of pressure," she replies.

Even I have to laugh at that. I see a twinkle in her eyes, and I'm glad for it. She's a tough one. Like her mum.

CHAPTER 3

HELLO

Quinn

"Quinn, did you hear me?"

I lift my eyes to look up at Kevin. He's staring at me expectantly. I frown. I haven't heard a word. I haven't been able to get the chocolate lass out of my mind.

I've been distracted with thoughts of her all day. It doesn't help that I never got my day on track the way I planned to. I've been on edge and circling the same image in my head—Ms. Rhodes.

My gaze scans around the kitchen area. The wee ones are at the nook table, swinging their feet as they eat pizza. The twins are sitting at the kitchen island on either side of me. My brothers are spread out among the small circle we've formed.

Shaking away my thoughts, I turn my focus back to Kevin. He's still waiting on my reply. I try to search my head for the question he just asked, but I come up with nothing.

"Sorry, what did ya say?"

"Can ya help out at the Golden Clover? With Ma, Da, and…ya know. The place needs eyes and a few extra hands until things get back to normal," he says.

The restaurant and pub crossed my mind a few times

this week, but I hadn't had the time to head over there. Erin has helped my parents with the place for years. She keeps it a well-oiled machine. Although, Da prides himself with running the pub.

I nod. "Aye, I'll help out. I can work from Da's office and pitch in when needed."

"Great. I was hoping ya could look at the inventory as well. Make sure everything is the way Da would leave it. Yer the best for that task," he continues.

"I'll get it in order. I'll take this weekend's shift," I offer.

"Grand, I have something I want to look into," Shane says. "I wouldn't be able to do it."

"Ya stay on top of the case," I say. "I'll handle the Golden Clover."

"I can help out," Mckenna offers. "Mom lets me waitress for the restaurant costumers."

"You just want to go and stare at Baker Jones," Conroy teases.

"The rawny lad with the blond hair?" Shane snorts.

"Yeah, that guy. She's always drooling over him," Conroy replies.

"He is not skinny, Uncle Shane," Mckenna pouts before turning to her brother to hiss. "Shut your mouth, Con. I don't say anything about the girls you chase after."

"What can you say? Every girl on my roster is A-one," my nephew crows.

"Will ya listen to this? He plays his own fiddle, he does." Kevin bursts into laughter.

"Right, he does," Shane adds through his own chuckles.

The laughter that fills the house is genuine. It's much better than the long faces that arrived a few hours ago. It's my turn to keep the lot for the night. I get the feeling my brothers intend to crash along with them.

Looking around at the kids again, I can't help but wonder when they all grew up so fast. At sixteen, Conroy and Mckenna think they're adults. The two wee ones, Molly and Kasey, still see the world as babes. They don't fully understand what's going on.

"Conroy, my boy. Is that a mustache coming in, or did you forget to wash your lip?" Trenton taunts.

More laughter rumbles through the kitchen. Conroy's cheeks pink, and he puffs out his chest. The kid is a handsome lad and he knows it.

"Whatever, Uncle Trent. Tell your girlfriends to stop hitting on me. I know I'm the better-looking version of you, but I'm too young for them. They'll have to wait," Conroy tosses back.

"That's my boy," Kevin calls out.

Kevin walks over to Conroy, placing him in a headlock as he messes his shaggy hair. Shane pats our nephew on the back. All the girls giggle. The wee ones are laughing, more so as not to be left out of things than truly understanding what the fuss is about.

"Don't be encouraging him," Trenton mutters, with a small proud smile in the corners of his lips. "You do know I'm going to kick your little ass later."

Conroy makes a muscle with his arm and flexes it. "Bring it on," he replies.

"Don't be writing checks yer ass can't cash, lad." I chuckle.

"I can take him," Conroy says, a frown taking over his face.

Reaching to give his shoulder a squeeze, I offer him a smile. Con always wants to prove himself to us. He needs to slow down and enjoy being a kid.

"One day," I say to him.

"Bullshit," Trenton scoffs. "You name the day."

"When Ma gets home, I'm going to take you down. You'll see," Conroy challenges.

"I'll give you my Camaro the day you kick my ass," Trenton goads.

"Yes!" Conroy cheers.

I see the twinkle in Trenton's eyes. I already know he's planning to let the lad best him. He's been talking Erin into letting him give the kid that car for months. She relented a few days before the shooting.

"I want to see this." Kevin chuckles.

"Kasey, ya want more pizza?" Shane calls over to my little niece as she stares longingly at the box on the table.

"Yes, please," she says with a gap-toothed little smile.

More banter fills the space as Trenton teases all the kids and my other brothers. Laughter rings out like a normal Friday night when we get together as a family. This is the way these four should be. Happy and taken care of.

I flex my injured hand as I think of the fact that there's someone out there who tried to take that from them. My mind starts to make a list of priorities.

One, find the source of the attack. Two, keep the kids safe, out of trouble, and happy. Three, help out at the Golden Clover. Four, make Alicia Rhodes mine.

Whoa!

I frown, not knowing where that last one came from. Images of those eyes invade my head. I don't date much, and my usual type is nothing like the wee instructor. Yet, I haven't been able to think straight since she drove away.

"You're more quiet than usual," Trenton says as he turns his attention to me.

"It's probably because he has a crush on Ms. Rhodes," Mckenna says with a cheeky grin on her lips.

I narrow my eyes at my niece and she giggles. I groan as all three of my brothers hone in on me. I should get up and leave, but I'm not one to run from anything.

"Ms. Rhodes? Who's Ms. Rhodes?" Trenton says with a shit eating grin.

"Alicia Rhodes, actually. She's my driving instructor," Mckenna chimes.

"Aren't ya full of information," I mutter.

"She's hot. I was totally bummed out that I already learned to drive," Conroy says.

"Mind yer manners," I rumble.

"Ach, what's this?" Trenton says with a sly grin. "Quinn, you have a glad eye for the lass? Oh, wait until I tell Ma. She may get those grands out of you."

"Shut yer gub."

"You should have seen it. She had Uncle Quinn speechless," Mckenna gushes.

"Is that right? Tell us more," Kevin coaxes.

"He couldn't take his eyes off her. And when he pissed her off, she gave it to him good. Uncle Quinn just stared at her," she blabbers.

"You, Quinn, didn't take control of the situation?" Shane asks skeptically.

"The wee lass looked to be on the verge of tears. I didn't want to push her over," I say.

Mckenna scrunches up her face, cupping her chin. Her thoughts are racing across her pretty features. The twins are both observant. I can only imagine what will come out of her mouth next.

"You know she didn't look like herself today. And I've never seen her lose her patience like that," she finally says.

"So ya finally find someone yer interested in and ya run her off?" Kevin chuckles.

"It was his damn lists, wasn't it?" Trenton adds, humor lacing his words.

"Sort of," Mckenna says, her cheeks turning red.

"Right, lass. I want my burger and the ice cream back. Yer lips are looser than change in yer grand's purse," I mumble.

Folding my arms across my chest, I grimace as everyone around me laughs. I let them all have fun at my expense. It's nothing new.

"So what do ya plan to do, big brother?" Shane asks, his teeth showing in a full grin.

"Mind my own business."

"Five hundred says he finds her number and address before the night is over," Kevin says.

"I'm in, but I think he has it already," Trenton replies.

They both turn to look at me. I stare back at them. Shane's smile grows as his eyes twinkle.

"Kev, you best hand over that money," he chants.

"No way, Uncle Quinn. You didn't." Mckenna gasps.

"I don't know what the lot of ya are talking about, I don't," I respond, taking a sip of my beer.

"Yes, you do," Trenton pushes back.

"So what if I do?"

"I knew it." Shane barks with laughter.

"This should be good." Kevin snorts.

"Please don't embarrass me, Uncle Quinn. I like her. She's patient with me," Mckenna pleads.

"When do I ever embarrass ya?"

"Seriously," she deadpans.

I wave her off and grab another slice. In between bites, I grumble to myself. Yes, I ran a search to get Alicia's number and address.

I may or may not have done a background check to find out more. She rides around with my niece in a car. I have a right to check her out.

I think back to what Mckenna said about the soft-spoken instructor. Her behavior was out of character. I have questions rolling in my head that need answers.

"He's going to call her." Trenton's voice breaks into my thoughts.

"Aye, never questioned that for a second," Shane adds.

I flip them both the bird and get up from my seat. I snatch my beer then I head to my office to get some work done. I can at least try to catch up for a few hours.

"Don't scare her off, Quinn, my boy," Kevin calls after me.

Alicia

"Love is a Battle Field" is blaring through the Bluetooth speaker that's connected to my phone. Pat Benatar is singing to my soul. I've stripped out of my clothes and locked myself in my bedroom with a bottle of wine. I'm in my panties and a tank top as I get lost in the music.

I shake my shoulders and wiggle my hips. I let all my sorrows and this day from hell pour out into every move. It's the most freeing thing I've done in forever.

I need this more than I could have known. When Tari and Aidan both said they'd give me space as we locked up the office for the night, I nearly rushed home to be alone. My head has been buzzing with thoughts from this morning.

Erin Kelley is a gorgeous redhead. I'm very fond of the mother of one of my sweetest students. I would even say we've become friends.

What I wasn't expecting was to look up and find a huge male version of Erin. None of the soft features his sister possesses, but just as gorgeous if not more so. There's no mistaking the relation.

The man is stunning. Those thick but well-groomed red brows, placed over startling green eyes with equally thick fanning lashes. His full lips framed sinfully by that sexy beard.

I squeeze my thighs together mid-dance as the echo of his voice slams into me again. I shiver. The memory of it is as delicious as it was to hear it in person.

Damn.

"That man is my type to a T," I say aloud as I continue to dance.

I shake my head. He's everything I know I need to stay away from. He's the kind of guy I drool over but would never have the confidence to date.

"Not with these scars. At least, not yet."

At this point, he'd only be a smooth distraction from the fact that I need to get my life together. That's what my ex was. A huge distraction, one of the biggest mistakes I've ever made. Good looks and a little charm had me trusting a man who wasn't worthy at all.

"Ugh, Ali. So much damage was done from your dependency on that relationship," I say to myself. "Nope! Never again."

It's my promise to me and my sanity. When I was twenty, I thought that was what I needed. A guy to love so I could fill the void and not feel so lost.

No man is worth the hurt and pain I've been through. I'm still licking my wounds and can taste the salty soreness.

Besides, I'm here obsessing over a man I both don't know and am positive hasn't given me a second thought. I'm annoyed with myself for being so invested in thoughts about someone who irritated and turned me on at the same time. Honestly, I'm seriously questioning my sanity.

"What in the world is so sexy about a huge, brooding man? Ugh, get a clue, girl."

I grab my wine, emptying the glass. I place it back down and let my dramatic side take over. Backing up to the beat of the music, I toss an arm in the air and let a yell rip from my lips. It's cathartic, like a deep cleanse that I need more than anything.

"That's it. Dance it out, Ali," I cheer myself on.

I break into the choreography from the video. I smile, feeling it take over my face. Throwing my hands in the air, I shake my head back and forth and lose myself.

"Crap."

I stumble as the music is interrupted by the ringing of my phone. Moving for the device, I frown. It's too late for bill collectors or solicitors.

I don't recognize the number at all. I think about

ignoring it, but my curiosity wins out. I hit accept, but it connects to the Bluetooth. I fumble, trying to switch it off so I can put the phone to my ear.

"Crap," I murmur again.

"Ach, I thought we got off to a bad start, but I don't think I deserve that greeting." That thick, sexy accent from this morning fills my bedroom from the speaker.

I swear my knees buckle. I reach for the dresser to catch myself.

Images of the man that voice belongs to invade my head. The way his gray T-shirt clung to those bulging muscles. My face heats with thoughts of his well-worn, well-fitting blue jeans.

"Ho-how did you get my number?" I stammer.

The business line that comes through to my phone redirects to the company voicemail at seven in the evenings. During the day, it rings me through a service. If he were calling through that line and someone in the office failed to answer, I'd still have to accept the call on my cell first. This is a call straight to my personal line.

"Tricks of the trade. Don't worry yerself. I wanted to say sorry," he starts.

All thoughts of my attraction to him fly out of the window. I jerk my head back. Warning bells go off as my deep-seated trust issues roar to the front.

"If I ask a question, I would like an answer. Avoiding means lies. I don't like liars. How did you get my number, please?"

Silence greets me. He's still there. He just doesn't reply.

"My office hours are from nine to five. If Mckenna wants to reschedule, you can call the institute during those hours," I say.

"I would not be calling yer personal line if I wanted to reschedule a lesson for my niece. I'm a private investigator by trade. Getting yer personal information is as easy as lacing my own shoes," he says.

"What?" I gasp. "Yo-you…I can't even get it out. You investigated me? Why?"

"I told ya. I want to apologize," he says, his voice holding a note of frustration.

"I don't think this is appropriate," I reply.

"Yer an adult, I'm an adult. I don't see what's inappropriate," he retorts.

"Excuse me, Mr. Kelley—"

"Ach, Blackhart," he says, making a disgusted sound in the back of his throat. "Blackhart is my sister's maiden name."

"Oh, right." I slap my forehead.

Way to make yourself look smart, Ali.

I shouldn't care what this man thinks, I chide myself. Digging into my life isn't the best way to earn my trust. *Trust.* That word terrifies me on so many levels. I don't give it away half as easily as I used to. I can't afford to.

Throwing my shoulders back as if he can see me, I dig up the nerve to tear into him. I totally shocked myself when I did it earlier. That's so unlike me. I'm usually the last person to react in frustration or anger. I blame it on the day.

Yet, I think I may need to find that courage again. Who digs up peoples' phone numbers to call them randomly?

"Alicia," he says my name like magic.

I mean, it rolls off his tongue in a musical way that rumbles right through me. He says it just right—Ah-lees-ee-yah—the way my mother intended. Not the common Ah-lee-sha version.

I can't help it. I cross my thighs and squeeze. His voice should be illegal. I want to be childish and start singing, *la-la-la-la*, to block it out. Does anyone see the silly crap this man has me thinking?

Yes, I'm shy, but I've never had a man unnerve me the way he does. Even when I was totally pissed at him this morning, I wanted to tug him forward and inhale his cologne. From a small distance, he smells like heaven. I can only imagine burying my face in his neck or against his chest.

"Mr. Blackhart—"

"Quinn, ya can call me Quinn."

"Mr. Blackhart, you don't owe me an apology. Maybe your niece, but certainly not me," I say into the phone.

"Mckenna understands me just fine. Ya don't. I want to fix that," he says with that warm, honey-dripping voice.

"Why would I need to understand you?" I blurt out.

Feeling my face crunch up more, I rub my forehead in confusion. I should've hung up on him by now, but there's something about him that's drawing me in. I can't seem to force my finger toward the button.

"I want to take ya out on a date, lass. I can't have ya thinking I'm an asshole if I want to woo ya," he replies.

Aww.

Oh, no you don't. Don't you start melting. Not for the accent and not for how cute he sounds. Don't do it, Ali!

Right, I'm so right. I will not turn to goo no matter how adorable his words are. I can't get sidetracked. I have to focus on me. I need to get my life together, not fall into another relationship I can bury my head in. Been there done that. Not going back.

"I'm sorry, but that's not going to be possible," I say.

He groans. I can hear the phone shift as he curses in the background. I roll my lips, trying not to laugh.

My heart tugs a little for him. Again, I tell myself not to bend as I chew on my lip. He doesn't need the mess that's currently me. No one does.

"Alicia, I'm tryin—"

"I'm sorry. I have to go. Thank you for the call. You have a good night," I say quickly and hang up.

I stare at the phone after the call ends. I did the right thing. I'm still wounded. I haven't found myself again yet. Besides, that man is dangerous. It's written all over him. Especially in those green eyes.

CHAPTER 4

NO CHANGE

Alicia

I FEEL TERRIBLE. I HAD NO IDEA ERIN KELLEY AND HER husband were victims in a horrible shooting. It all makes sense now. I wouldn't have known if Erin and I didn't go to the same hot yoga studio.

Some of the other women were gossiping about it today before class. She's been in a coma for the last three weeks. When Quinn mentioned her being in the hospital, I thought maybe she was sick or something. Not gunned down.

I mean, her home is in Commack. Homes in Erin's neighborhood are pushing into the million-dollar mark. It's not far from the house my parents left me. I know her neighborhood to be quiet and cozy.

My head is still spinning as I think of what was said at the studio. I was distracted my entire workout. I wish there were something I could do. I truly do consider Erin a friend.

We usually go for smoothies and energy shots after class and have a little chat. It's how I ended up as Mckenna's instructor. My business came up in conversation one afternoon, and Erin asked me to teach her daughter.

According to Erin, Mckenna's a bit shy outside of the family. Erin thought my soft-spoken manners would be good for her daughter. Apparently, she has a hot-headed father and four gruff and rough uncles. None of whom Erin thought were right to teach her daughter. She also didn't think she had the nerves to do it herself.

With the lessons, I've grown to like Erin more than I already had, and I adore Mckenna. She's a sweet young lady. My heart hurts for her and her siblings. Not one parent, but both their mother and father are holding onto life in hospital beds.

The loss of both of my parents devastated my world. I wouldn't wish that on anyone. I've been thinking about and praying for Erin's family since hearing the news. I don't know what they need, but I at least wanted to pay a visit to my friend.

The clicking of my heels halts when I get to the opened hospital room door. Light music floats into the hallway from the entryway, but that's not what freezes me. It's the large man sitting beside the bedside.

It's been a week since I hung up on Quinn. Yet, his eyes and voice have starred in my dreams. I even daydream about him.

The view I have of him now is breathtaking. He has his sister's hand clasped in his. His head is bent as if he's in prayer. Locks of red hair have tumbled onto his forehead. He is simply gorgeous in every way. To prove me right, his voice fills the small space.

"I remember telling Ma I didn't want ya when she was pregnant. There were too many of us already and ya were going to be a lass. Ach, we had no need for a girl." He gives a little chuckle. "Then ya were born. I stood sentinel over yer bassinet for weeks, not letting the others get too close."

He pauses to wipe away a tear. My breath catches. I know I should leave. I'm just frozen, unable to breathe or move. My lips tremble as I'm thrown back in time to watching my dad at my mother's bedside. Quinn's voice brings me to the present before I can get too lost in the past.

"I found out ya were the best part of the lot of us. Ya made us become men to protect ya. I failed ya, Erin, and I'm so sorry. Wake up for me. I'm going to fix this, but I need ya to wake up for me now." His words come out thick with emotion.

Swiping quickly at the tear that spills over, I force myself to take two steps back. My heels click. Two things happen simultaneously with my movement. The music breaks for a pause, and Quinn's head snaps up.

Those intense green eyes lock in on me. I freeze in place once again as his eyes sweep over me. I start to feel a little self-conscious. I already beat myself up on the drive over for going home to shower and change into this outfit.

Normally, I would have showered at the studio, throwing on my jeans and button-up. Today, I raced home to shower with the intent to come for this visit. I took time to put on a little makeup and recurled my bob. Hot yoga is rough on my hair, even with a head wrap on.

I took time picking the black pencil skirt and blue silk button-down blouse. The black patent leather heels were a last minute decision I nearly talked myself out of. Now, I wish I had.

Not just because they are so noisy and gave me away. The way Quinn's eyes travel back down my body, lingering on my breasts, my hips, and finally my legs, feels so dirty and totally out of place. I'll admit, somewhere in the back of my mind, I dressed up with the hope of running into him.

At the moment, I feel silly. I remember how hard it was for my dad to remember to put on shoes that matched when Mom was in the hospital. I couldn't focus on homework or anything else during those times. I don't know why I thought showing up like this was a good idea.

It was foolish, and I've already told myself that the last thing I need is to get involved with this man as I work to get my life together. Yup, totally inappropriate. That word seems to come up a lot with him involved. Spinning on my heels, I get ready to take flight.

"Alicia." His voice seeps into my veins.

"I-I should come back another time," I stammer over my shoulder.

Why did I look back? Why on earth did I look back?

He is standing this time, causing me to have to tilt my head up. The vulnerability from moments ago is still written on his face. I don't want to feel anything for this man. Yet, I'm drawn to him, which is why I do the best thing for us both.

I toss a wave and hightail it out of here.

Quinn

That lass does my head in. I don't know how she can annoy the fuck out of me and turn me on so much I forget my own name at the same time. My body wants to go after her, but my mind is telling me to stay put.

My brothers and I have been on rotation to watch over Erin. Ma and Da left a while ago so Ma could shower in her own home and spend time with the babes. Kasey and Molly need their grandma. All of this is a big adjustment for the family. I think we're all exhausted.

I can't say the last time my mum didn't stay overnight here at the hospital, with my da right by her side. I was happy to sit in while they take some time away. However, now my jaw ticks as I watch the swaying hips of the woman who's been on my mind for a week.

I need to talk to her. That call went all wrong the other night. I'll be the first to admit that I'm nothing but awkward when it comes to dating. Still, that woman made it a hell of a lot harder to try to ask her out.

I twist my lips into a frown as I watch her walk away. Trenton walks past her in the hallway, turning his head to watch her go by. I release a growl, feeling possessive and irritated.

"Now, that's a looker." He whistles when he enters the room.

"Stay here," I snap at him.

"Wait, what?" he calls after me, but I'm already in motion.

My long legs eat up the floor as I head in the direction Alicia retreated in. I have her in sight as the elevator arrives. She steps in and the doors go to shut. I get there just in time to stick my foot in the way of them closing.

The lift makes a dinging sound as it opens wide. Alicia looks up from her phone as I step on. Our eyes lock and I close the distance between us. She drops her head down shyly to break the connection. She has to feel the same thing I feel. This energy that's charging the tight space between us has a pulse.

The elevator chimes and others begin to crowd on, causing us to move closer together. Alicia tries to take a step back, but my hand shoots out. It lands protectively on her waist, drawing her into me to shield her.

I trap a groan between my lips when her soft curves press against me. She still won't look up at me, but she doesn't wiggle out of my hold either. She feels so right this close.

I dip my head to whisper in her ear, "We need to talk."

She lifts her head to look at me, her lush lips are parted, begging me to kiss them. I'm this close to listening. The lift stops again, allowing more passengers onto the car.

Alicia places her hands on my chest as we're squished more closely. The look in her eyes tells me I'm not alone in this. She indeed feels it too.

When we reach the lobby, the crowd starts to exit. I maneuver her body in front of mine to cover her as I lead her out. She relaxes into my hold on her waist, causing me to have hope that this won't be a fight.

As soon as we get off the car, my newfound confidence implodes. A stony-faced Kevin is standing outside the elevator. When he turns his eyes to me, I know my talk with Alicia is going to have to wait.

"We need to talk," Kevin says gruffly.

"I should be going anyway," Alicia rushes out.

She tries to take off, but I wrap my fingers around her forearm to stop her forward motion. She turns to look back at me. I grind my teeth against the electric current that zaps straight up my arm.

"This isn't over. We'll be having that talk," I say before releasing her.

"Not such a good idea, but it was nice seeing you again. I'll keep Erin in my prayers," she replies softly.

Before I can get another word out, she darts off in those sexy-as-fuck heels. I force myself to look away from her to give my brother my full attention. He's watching me closely when my eyes meet his. Kevin is only about half an inch taller than me, so we meet each other eye to eye.

I gesture with my head for us to take a few steps into privacy. Kevin nods and follows me. We both look around before he leans in to tell me what's going on.

"Cal did have something else outside of his assigned cases. That fuckup had another laptop stashed at the house. It's encrypted so Shane is working on getting into it," Kevin says in a hushed tone.

"Any idea what he was working on?"

"Debbie says he asked her to run a few plates and trace a few numbers, but he also told her not to log them. Other than that, I'm still shooting blanks. I feel like we are missing something right under our noses," Kevin says.

"I know what ya mean. I still need to go talk to Dugan. I'm not liking the slack on this investigation. They should have turned up something by now. It's seems like they're purposely dragging their feet on this one," I say.

"Yeah, I was thinking the same thing. I know Cal has made a lot of enemies on the force, but this is bullshit," Kevin replies.

"Aye, it is. Ya keep pulling those strings. We'll find the right one soon enough. For now, I'm calling in some favors. Cal is stable enough. I want him airlifted out of here. I get the feeling he's not safe sitting out in the open."

"I hear ya. We've been chancing it keeping him here this long."

I take a moment to run some things through my mind. Stepping in closer to my brother, I lower my voice. He leans in to listen.

"I'm not ready to make the move yet, but be prepared to make him vanish if need be. It will need to be neat," I say.

"Yer thinking they'll show their hand if the job is complete?"

"Aye, maybe, maybe not. We don't know whose hand to look for yet. I want the option."

"Got it," he says.

I pat him on the shoulder and nod. We'll figure this out. It's what we do.

"Was that the instructor?" Kevin changes the subject, a small smile turning up the sides of his lips.

"Not today," I warn.

"I see why she has ya twisted in knots. Can't say I blame ya at all." His smile grows.

"Fuck off," I mutter, turning to head back upstairs.

"Is that any way to talk to yer own flesh and blood?" he continues to taunt.

"Shut yer bake or I'll do it for ya."

"I guess she's special, all right. Threatening bodily harm. She may be the one," he says.

We step onto the lift, and I slap him in the back of the head. He chuckles as he rubs the spot, while shaking his head at me. I fold my arms over my chest and glare at him.

"She looks feisty, bro. Good luck." He gets in the last word, as always.

Aye, feisty she is, but there's something else. *Shy?* Maybe.

I'm always up for a challenge. I've never been one to give up easily once a task makes my list. Good luck indeed.

I'll need it.

CHAPTER 5

FULL HOUSE

Quinn

"UNCLE QUINN, ARE YOU SURE YOU KNOW WHAT YOU'RE doing?" Molly asks as I drop the pasta into the boiling water.

I look down at her little eyes staring back at me skeptically. The nerve. She's seven, why is she questioning me about whether or not I can make spaghetti?

"I've been feeding myself just fine for years," I reply.

"I don't know," she says, tilting her head while looking at the pot warily. "Mommy said you used to burn things a lot when you were little."

"Mckenna, come get yer sister," I call out.

"Molly, come on. We're waiting for you to play your turn," Mckenna hollers back.

Molly leans into me, rolling her eyes. She lowers her voice. "I hate playing Monopoly with them. Conroy and Mckenna don't think me and Kasey can count, so they always cheat us and steal our money," she whispers.

I give a hearty laugh. These kids are something else. I need to kiss my mum and sister for all they do.

"Aye, they've been playing ya for a muppet, have they? I'll finish dinner and come play with ya. Time to show them, yer no one's fool. We'll see them try to steal from ya with me sitting there." I wink down at her.

Her little eyes light up, and she clasps her hands together. In the next motion she's wrapped around my leg to hug me. Reaching down, I run a hand through her ringlets. The four of them are little terrors, but I wouldn't trade in a single one.

"I love you, Uncle Quinn," she chirps before releasing me and taking off.

"Hey, Uncle Quinn," Mckenna says as she enters the kitchen. "I finished washing the little kids' clothes. Did you want me to put your things in?"

"Ach, thanks, lass. Ya don't have to do that. I'm going to get their clothes ready for school after dinner," I reply.

"No biggie. I can totally help out with the laundry and cooking. Besides, I already have our clothes ironed and hung for the morning," she says brightly.

"Thank ya. There is something ya can do for me," I say, a hint of a smile on my lips.

"Sure, what's up?" She beams, bouncing farther into the kitchen.

"Stop cheating the wee ones. Ya and Con know better."

She blushes all the way to her roots and drops her head. I try not to laugh at her. Kevin and I did the same thing to Trenton and Shane until Ma got after us.

"I don't cheat them," she whispers.

"Ya don't stop it either, now, do ya?"

She shrugs in reply. I chuckle, turning my attention back to the pot with the meat sauce. I've had them at my place since Friday. We've had takeout every night since. I don't normally eat that much junk myself, so I figured I'd cook tonight for everyone.

"Do me a favor, grab the garlic knots out of the oven?"

"You know how to make garlic knots?" Mckenna's head snaps up.

She's giving me the same wary look as her little sister. I twist my lips, crossing my arms over my chest. I'm going to get after Erin for telling them those stories. I only used to burn shit because she was always pestering me. Yet, I think fondly on the memories. I don't mind her teasing if it means we can someday make more.

"I can cook just fine. Get them out before they burn," I grunt.

"You got it. It does smell good in here," she says, retrieving an oven mitt.

I shake my head as I drain the pasta. I cook better than their mum, I'll have them know. Little brats. I should send them all to bed without dinner and see what they think then.

"Oh, Uncle Quinn, I have a lesson tomorrow after school. I texted Ms. Rhodes to let her know to pick me up from here," Mckenna says as she walks up beside me.

My ears perk up at the mention of the woman who stars in my fantasies. It's been three days since our run-in at the hospital, and I can still smell her perfume when I think of her. She smells of vanilla and pineapples. A scent I've come to crave.

"What time?"

"I'm her last lesson at four. Uncle Trent is going to pick up Molly and Kasey tomorrow. I'm going to ride home with Jamie's mom."

"Jamie is the lass with the glasses and the braces?" I ask to make sure I know who she's riding with.

"Yeah."

"What about Con?"

She waves a hand. "He'll find a way home. I think he said he has something after school."

"I'll be ready for your lesson by four," I say, draining the corn on the cob.

"Oh, you don't have to come. I only wanted you to know where I'd be," she says nervously.

"Yer mum always tags along. I'm going to follow her traditions."

"It's not a tradition. I told you, Mom and Ms. Rhodes are sort of friends," she replies.

"It smells good in here," Shane says as he enters the kitchen.

"Right on time to set the table," I say.

"Never been afraid to work for my meal," he responds with a rub of his belly.

"Seriously, Uncle Quinn. You don't have to come with me," Mckenna says as she hands over plates and utensils to Shane.

"I'm going," I say firmly.

"Food," Trenton says as he walks into the kitchen next.

"Did I send out an APB? Where'd ya all come from?" I mutter.

"I've been at the office. Kevin mentioned ya having the brats. I came to check in," Shane says.

"Same here. I was with Ma at the hospital, though. Kevin is in the car, he'll be in in a second," Trenton replies.

"Oh, my God, he *can* cook," I hear a little voice gasp.

I turn to find Molly, Kasey, and Mckenna sharing a garlic knot that looks, from the stain around Kasey's mouth, as if they dipped it in the sauce. It was her little voice that made the comment. I roll my eyes at the three.

"Wee heathens," I mumble under my breath.

Alicia

A NASCAR race plays on the television, but I'm hardly paying it any mind, which is totally out of the norm for me. I live, eat, and breathe this stuff. Growing up with a mechanic dad obsessed with the sport, I got it honestly.

However, I can't manage to pull my attention from my own thoughts. The roar of the engines coming through the surround-sound system only serves as background noise to the rambling in my head. I sink farther into the couch and stare blindly at the screen.

"You've spent all weekend sulking. What's up with you?" Aidan asks as he plops down on the couch next to me.

"It's nothing. Just a lot on my mind," I mumble around a spoon of ice cream.

Karamel Sutra, my favorite. It makes all things in the world better. I need this weekend to be over.

"I call bull poopie," he says.

I lift my shoulders and go in for some more ice cream. Aidan snatches the carton, drawing a death glare from me. I shift the spoon in my hand to hold it like a knife.

"You don't want to do that. I know you value your life. Give it back," I warn.

"Yup, something is going on. You only threaten death when you're in a bad mood. I'm quite sure you were waiting to see this race for weeks now. You're not even talking and cheering at the TV. What's going on? You looked like you were doing good for a few days."

I sigh, sticking the spoon in the carton and slipping my

hands underneath me. I train my eyes on my wiggling toes, while crossing my legs before me on the couch. I curl my fingers into the backs of my thighs and rock from side to side.

"Giovanni called me Friday," I say in a rush.

A deep growl leaves Aidan's chest. He trains his angry blue gaze on me as his jaw flexes. Aidan never liked my ex. I understand that look. I know it well.

"Why haven't you blocked him? You said it's over. What doesn't he get? Do I need to step in?"

"Wait, let me finish. I didn't answer. I…I sort of met someone. I'd just left him when the call came in. I wasn't even tempted to answer," I say.

"You met someone? You heifer. Why am I only finding this out now, and why do you look like a mopey slug if you have a new beau?"

"It's not the right timing. I'm still a mess. He drives me crazy. He's bossy and too handsome and—"

"Wait, wait, wait. How on earth is it possible to be too handsome?" Aidan side-eyes me.

"Aargh, you haven't seen this man or his brothers. It's possible," I groan.

"Brothers? Any I might have mutual interests with?" he purrs.

Palming my forehead, I shake my head. Only Aidan. It's not like he has a shortage of guys calling his phone. I've watched my friend go through several stages before finding himself.

I wish I had half the confidence he has now. If I did, I wouldn't be so frustrated with my life. Which is one of the reasons I've been in deep thought about myself and my old relationships this weekend.

"I don't know. I haven't officially met the brothers. I've seen at least one."

"Okay, forget that. Let's get back to you. I know Giovanni took a big chunk out of your self-esteem. But, honey, you're going to have to let that go. The-one-who-shall-not-be-named paid a lot of money for that body and face she has, and you're still more gorgeous than she'll ever be, even on a bad day."

"Aidan—"

"No, listen to me. Her opinions and mean-spirited misguidance should never have been a factor. She was always jealous. You were too much of a friend to her to ever see it. Why do you think she'd wait to get you alone to plant those hurtful seeds?

"I wish you would stop measuring yourself against her. She was never your friend and you've never been beneath her," he says his last words more softly.

I look down into my lap. One of my biggest problems is that while I mentally checked out, I allowed myself to be verbally and emotionally abused. I was told so many times that I'm too this or too that. I could change this or I could change that.

I trusted both of the voices that were feeding me that harsh criticism more than I should have. In the end, it chipped at a big chunk of me.

"I know. It's just...I spent so much time listening to those two tell me what I could improve on and how I should try this or that. It's easier to say 'get over it' than it is to do," I reply.

"I get that. Trust me, I do, but you really should take a good look in the mirror. You're a stunning woman. You deserve a stunning man beside you."

"Why couldn't you be straight?" I grin at him.

"Oh, sweets. You're not ready for me. Although, we would make an exquisite couple. Can you imagine the babies?" he coos, causing me to giggle.

I open my mouth as he holds the spoon up to my lips. Waggling my brows at him, I give him a seductive look that sends him into laughter. It feels good to laugh.

"So tell me the real issue," Aidan says after a few beats.

"I'm afraid of him. He's huge, but that's not what scares me. I've never felt what I feel when I'm next to him. It's like my skin starts to buzz. You would think I was already his, the way he wraps himself around me protectively. No, no, it's possessively," I muse.

"Oh, that sounds so hot," Aidan says around a spoonful of ice cream.

I snatch a pillow and hit him with it. He looks down at the ice cream as if in shock, then back up at me with wide eyes. He pleads my forgiveness, gazing up through his lashes with a gorgeous pout.

"You owe me a pint," I mumble.

"You and Tari are so picky about people drinking and eating from your stuff. I don't get it," he comments.

"We're not going to go there again. My mom told you about that a million times when we were little, and Tari and I have told you over and over since. You know we weren't raised that way. You don't go eating off people's stuff," I chide.

"I know, I know. I was lost in all the hotness. You can't blame me. Please tell me again why this is an issue? I'm talking about this guy. He's hot, there's chemistry, sounds like he's into you. I'm lost."

"I'm not ready. God, you know how shy I was before Gio, and you just pointed out the problem. I haven't gotten over everything that was done to me. I'm not ready to get to know anyone else," I say pointedly. "Not to mention, he sort of took it upon himself to get my number. I'll admit. That sort of didn't help with my trust issues."

"What does that mean?" Aidan asks, sitting up straighter.

I love that my friend is always ready to protect me. Don't let Aidan's pretty-boy looks fool you. He's a fourth-degree black belt. Not to mention the times he had to defend himself when we went to the old neighborhood to visit with Tari.

"He's a PI," I state, leaving the statement hanging.

"So you're saying he looked you up? *Well*," he sings. "You know me. I think shit like that is hot. Or at least until it's not. Because if he turns out to be a psycho, I'll kick his ass."

"Calm down, killer." I chuckle.

"Just letting you know. I have your back."

Aidan has always been quick to fight for me. I used to tease and call him more hood than I'll ever be. He'll lay hands faster than Jesus if someone messes with me.

"I know and I love you for it."

Shifting over, I curl up under the arm he holds out for me. I snuggle into his side and settle in. Sometimes having roommates isn't so bad.

"Take it one step at a time," Aidan says in the most serious voice I've ever heard him use.

"Yeah. I could be blowing this out of proportion. Right?"

"How so?"

I take a moment to think. I could be in a funk for nothing. So like me to get all discombobulated over nothing.

"He may not be that interested."

"Shut up," Aidan grumbles.

"What?"

"Just shut up."

"Fine," I mutter.

CHAPTER 6

AGAIN

Quinn

"Come again," I say into the phone line as I turn onto my block.

"After all that mouthing off this morning, he got himself lifted," Kevin bites out.

He's clearly pissed. His accent is heavy as his voice fills the car. I stare straight ahead. Conroy is a cocky little fucker, but I never thought he'd get himself arrested. When he and Kevin got into it this morning, I wrote it off as Con being a teenager.

"Can it be fixed? Do I need to make some calls?"

"I'm on it. I thought it would be an in-and-out process, but the detective who pinched him isn't making it so easy," Kevin replies.

"What's his name? I'll see if Dugan can pull his collar."

"Her name. Her name is Detective Danita Moralez," Kevin mutters. "Saw Dugan haul ass out of here twenty minutes ago. I'll deal with this. His little ass will think twice about cutting school and landing in a pair of cuffs."

"Aye, if ya need me, ya let me know."

"Right," he says, ending the call.

Right as the line cuts off, Alicia pulls up in the driving

school Corolla. Mckenna bounces out of the house, rushing for the car. I unfold my body from my truck and saunter over to the silver vehicle with the two who are trying to dodge me.

It's good to have long limbs. I cross the distance before Alicia can get around to the passenger door. Her little legs don't carry her half as fast as she clearly tries to make them.

My lips turn up as I watch the look of frustration cross her face. I open the car door for her, but I don't give her much space to pass me. Reaching out, I clasp her fingertips before she makes it around the door. That hum is there again, coursing through our connection.

"Dinner, tonight?" I lean to breathe in her ear.

She turns to look up at me. Her lips pinch and her nose turned up.

"We're wasting time. I don't want to go over Mckenna's hour. I know you have things to do," she says, tugging her fingers free.

"Alicia," I growl.

I see the shiver that rolls through her. She closes her eyes slowly before opening them again. I crowd her space, inhaling that scent I've come to love. She lifts her hand to my chest, like in the elevator. Covering her small hand with mine, I caress the back of it with my thumb.

"Know this about me, lass. When I get something in my head, I pursue it until I'm satisfied. I want to know ya. I want to find out what makes ya tick." I pause, dropping my eyes to her lips. "I want my name to be the one that purrs from yer lips."

Her mouth drops open in shock. It takes everything in me not to dip my head to nip her bottom lip. Instead, I place my fingers under her chin to close her mouth.

"We're going to dinner," I say.

She shakes her head. "No," she replies, her voice husky.

"Aye, we are."

"No. No, we are not," she says, pushing at my chest.

I back away to permit her space. She climbs into the car quickly, and I close the door as I chuckle. I go to make my way to get into the back seat, but my cell rings.

I look down to see it's Dugan. I've been waiting for his call. My jaw ticks as I lift the phone to my ear.

"Blackhart," I bark in greeting.

"We need to meet. Somewhere secure. Just you and me," Dugan says in a hushed tone.

"When, where?"

"Fuck, I'll call you back," he says in a rush, cutting the call.

I look between my phone and the car. When Dugan calls with a location, I need to be ready to roll. Muttering to myself, I round the vehicle to the driver's side.

Tapping the top of the car, I bend to lean into the window. Mckenna looks up at me with exasperation. Pulling a face, I put her out of her misery.

"I need to handle some work. Ya drive safely and listen to Ms. Rhodes. If I'm not here when ya get back, go inside and lock the door," I instruct.

My eyes shift to Alicia. She's staring at me, biting her lip. I can see the desire and uncertainty in her eyes.

"I'll call ya, love. We can finish our conversation then," I say to her.

Alicia

"You can make a three-point turn here," I drone.

Quinn's words have me completely scattered. I haven't been focused this entire lesson. Mckenna has drawn me out of my thoughts several times. Thank goodness she's one of my best students. Anyone else and I would have ended the session by now.

She makes the turn perfectly. I can feel the excited energy coming off her as she breezes through the lesson. Maybe we can cancel the last few in her package. She already has her hours. She has gotten 100 percent better than when she started.

"Ms. Rhodes, are you okay?" Mckenna's voice breaks into my thoughts once again.

I know my focus is total crap. I brought her out here to this location for that very reason. Here, we are less likely to run into much traffic or busy streets. I've had her practicing turns to the point we're both dizzy.

"Yes, I'm fine," I say.

"Should I head back now?"

I look at the clock. We're actually over her hour by thirty minutes. I can't believe I've been that lost in my head. I fuss at myself. I can be scattered at times, but I'm usually on point once I get into this car with a student. I'm very serious about my job.

"Yes, yes, please head back," I respond.

"You shouldn't let Uncle Quinn frazzle you. He can be a bit of a bear, but he's a teddy bear at best. Well, that's if you don't get on his bad side or disturb his lists," Mckenna chirps.

"His lists?" My curiosity is piqued.

Mckenna frowns, she glances over at me quickly. I think she may have said too much. Her fingers begin to drum against the steering wheel. I'm definitely intrigued now.

"It's nothing," she says.

I can tell from her posture I'm not getting anything else out of her on the topic. I won't push. I don't want to prove a distraction from her driving. Besides, I don't need to know anything about Quinn.

"I think Uncle Quinn is Mom's favorite," Mckenna says out of the blue.

"Oh, really," I say softly. "What makes you say that?"

"In my mom's eyes, Uncle Quinn can do no wrong. She calls him every day for their morning chats. Her face lights up while she cooks breakfast. They have a way with each other. He looks after her, she's looks after him," she explains.

"They do sound close."

"I love that about them. Being a twin, I know what it's like to feel like you have to watch over your big brother," Mckenna states in the most grown-up way. "Conroy can be an entire mess. I think he ditched school today. My uncles are going to kick his ass."

"I bet," I say, trying not to laugh.

"I think my uncle likes you a lot. You should totally let him take you on a date."

"Oh, no. I don't think so. Your uncle and I should absolutely not go on a date," I retort, waving my hands in front of me.

"Oh, wait. Are you like…against dating white guys or something? I didn't think about that," Mckenna says.

"No, that's not it. I have no problem dating white guys.

I have in the past," I mutter, keeping to myself that I was engaged to one.

Italian in fact. Giovanni wasn't the first guy outside of my race that I've dated. I'd like to say my dating past was eclectic throughout high school and college.

"Is it the accent? Uncle Quinn can be the hardest out of all my uncles to understand at times. Don't let him get excited or angry. Even I get lost." She giggles.

"No, that accent is sort of hot," I let slip out before clamping my mouth shut.

"So you do like him," she squeals.

"Pull over here." I point in front of the house.

We arrived just in time. I'm not about to gush with a sixteen-year-old about her sexy-ass uncle who has me all types of twisted. Nope, not going to happen. I need her out of this car, and I need to get home to a bottle of wine and a cold shower.

She pulls into the spot and shuts the car off, turning to me with expectant bright eyes and a huge smile. I reach for my tablet as a distraction.

"It's cool. I won't say anything. Honestly, I think you're really sweet. It would be awesome if you started dating my uncle," she gushes once she sees I'm not going to say anything.

"I don't know about that. You have a couple more lessons in your package, but I think you're doing great. You can call and schedule your next time if you like," I offer.

"Sure. I don't know where we'll be staying, but I'll let you know," she says, disappointment coloring her words a bit.

I reach over to cover her hand. Looking into those big green eyes, I connect instantly with the despair I see.

When my world came crashing down around me, no one had the right words. I was thrown into a world of strangers that tried their best to make it better, but no one truly knew how. This must be twice as hard for Mckenna and her siblings.

A part of me wonders if her enthusiasm for her uncle and me to date is a distraction from the things going on in her world. My heart tugs for her. This I can understand.

"How are you doing?" I ask.

"I'm okay," she whispers. "I know Mom's going to pull through. I'm more worried about my dad. Nobody will tell the little kids what's really going on, but the fact that they don't tell me and Con much about my dad scares me."

"I'm sure that's not it. Maybe there's less to share at the moment. Think positive, sweetie," I encourage.

I remember being scared when my dad and mom wouldn't tell me what was going on with Mom. I know now they were trying to protect me. However, I felt confused and alone back then.

"Thanks for asking, Ms. Rhodes. Teachers at school just look at us with pity. It's... Thanks," she says.

"Anytime, honey. I'm here if you need," I reply.

I take out one of my cards and jot down my personal number for her to have. She's been texting the school's number. Those texts shut off at a certain hour, like the calls. I want to truly be there for her anytime she needs.

Her eyes light up as I hand her the card. "Cool. Thanks."

"No problem at all. Great job today. I'll see you next time," I say and start to get out.

Mckenna exits the car and waits for me to round it. When I get to the driver's side, she pulls me into a hug. My heart melts. She truly is a sweet girl. I still can't believe what happened to her parents.

She releases me and looks me in the eyes. This is one determined kid. I think it's cute that she's trying to help her uncle. I can see how much she cares for him.

"Think about it, okay? He's a nice guy," she pleads.

"I'll wait here for you to get into the house safely. Lock the door when you get inside like your uncle told you," I say.

She slumps her shoulders a little, but she nods and starts for the house. I wait until she's through the front door before I get into the driver's seat. Mckenna turns to wave before shutting the door behind her.

Climbing into the car, I take a cleansing breath. I won't let a silly infatuation keep me from doing my job. I can do this while avoiding him and his sexy words.

I sure can… Maybe… I hope.

"Suck it up, Ali," I say.

CHAPTER 7

COLD TRAIL

Quinn

IT'S BEEN A FEW DAYS SINCE DUGAN'S CALL. I'D BEEN waiting for him to get back to me for a meet. A quick visit to the station let me know that our old family friend is still breathing.

I dropped off some evidence to one of the detectives for a case unrelated to my sister's. Dugan gave me a nod, but we kept our distance. I got the distinct feeling he'd been using caution.

When I received his call today to meet up in Queens, I rearranged everything. I'd say I've been patient enough. However, I wasn't expecting anything that happened during the meet.

"You're not going to like this," Dugan warned as I opened the envelope.

He was right. I opened the barely there file to find pictures of Cal talking to some bad news dodgy wankers. I grunted at the photos as I flipped through them.

They didn't reveal much, but I still didn't like them. There's a lot I didn't like. The photos were only a portion of the list of things I added up during our little meeting. Dugan seemed jumpy and nervous.

"Watch your back on this one, Blackhart," he warned. "Those photos and this file are all I can do for now."

I got the sense this was the most Dugan was willing to give, but that he knows a whole lot more than he's saying. It's no matter, I plan to sniff out what my brother-in-law has gotten himself into. I've known Cal to get into some dumb situations but this…drugs, it's not like him.

Now, I'm sitting in my truck, reeling over the details I do have. I put my head back against the headrest and rub my tired eyes. My mind goes to Alicia. Mckenna had another lesson this afternoon. I had planned to join them before the call from Dugan.

I still owe the lass a call. It's not that I haven't wanted to or haven't thought about calling her. I haven't had the time.

Each day that passes and Erin doesn't wake, places more stress on everyone. The doctors seem hopeful and are telling us to be patient, but I don't think patience is a trait the Blackharts have much of. My father and my brothers are starting to show their tension on the surface.

A date may be just what I need to help me with my endurance. Looking at that pretty face over dinner could be the soothing balm that will pull me through. I lift my phone from the dash and call her number.

I look at the clock as the line rings out. I pucker my lips into a frown when it rolls to her voicemail. It's nine o'clock in the evening. Her driving school is closed by now.

With my mind made up, I start my truck and pull off. I can be there in forty minutes. I'll be satisfied with at least a drive past her house to ensure she's tucked in her home safely, ignoring my call.

"Ignore me if ya want. It won't last forever," I mutter to myself.

Alicia

I groan as lightning flashes outside of the car again. It's the third time it's seemed too close for comfort. Tonight is not my night. First, there was the five-hour class from hell. There was this one guy who kept asking questions in the middle of the videos. His nonsense prolonged the class even as I asked him continuously to hold his questions until after.

"Why me?" I groan in frustration.

Class ran over on the one night I needed to get some office work done. I couldn't leave for the night without getting it all completed. Tari and Aidan both had plans, so they took off as soon as I dismissed the session.

I was on my way out the door when that number I refuse to save to my phone appeared on the screen. I have too much on my plate to deal with Quinn Blackhart today. I know for a fact dipping a single toe into that water is going to get me bitten.

Now, I'm sitting in my broken-down car. The irony: I just had the school's vehicles serviced. I've been meaning to take my personal vehicle in, but I haven't found the time.

I've been sitting on the side of the road, waiting on roadside assistance for over an hour. Because I'm Alicia Rhodes and the world is plotting against me, my phone died almost instantly after I made the call for help. Of course, I didn't purchase the BMW Assist after it expired. For all I know, they could have tried to reach me several times by now.

My dad would've had a field day with this one. "I told you about those foreign cars. Anything you can't pop the head on and fix yourself needs to stay right on the lot," he probably would've said.

Boy, I can see him shaking his head right now. My first car was a Mustang after having that very argument for weeks. Although, in this weather, I'm not getting under that hood either way.

"Just my luck."

For a summer night, the temperature has dropped. I'm sure that has everything to do with the pounding rain outside the car. I'm actually only a few miles from home. I would have walked it if not for the rain.

I only wish I had broken down on a more populated road. I look at the locks on the doors for the millionth time. The lightning and rain are not helping my nerves. Closing my eyes, I rub my temples.

"I just wanted a glass of wine and a good night's sleep."

I think I need a vacation. I'm going to look for a two-week getaway. Yes, that's what I need. A knock sounds on the window, scaring me damn near out of my skin.

"Shit," I scream.

I squint to look out. The person has a flashlight shining into my window. Hope blooms that roadside has finally decided to show up. It seems like the rain has slowed a bit.

I roll the window down a crack to see outside better, but not enough for a hand to fit inside. The first thing that grabs me are the intense green eyes staring back at me. The second thing is the pissed-off expression on his face.

"Ya would rather sit stranded on the side of the road than answer my calls," he snaps.

"My phone died," I reply while rolling the window down more.

"Ach, Alicia. Yer out here in the rain, in the middle of the night, with a dead cell phone," he grunts. "Yer no muppet, lass. Ya must be knackered. I refuse to believe ya would walk around without a charger or a charged phone."

"Why do I feel like you've insulted me multiple times just now?"

"Ya look tired, love. It's the only explanation for the situation yer sitting in," he replies.

"What's a muppet?"

"It's cold, and I'm getting wet. Pop the hood," he says.

"What's a muppet?" I demand.

"I said you are no fool. I did not mean to insult you. Please pop the hood so I can see what's wrong with the car," he says tightly.

"Oh, fine," I mutter, reaching for the lever.

I step out of the car to follow after him. He's grumbling to himself as he flashes his light under the hood. I hunch over, rubbing my arms as I stand beside him.

He curses under his breath and slams the hood back down. I look up at him expectantly. My heart sinks with the look he gives in return. I was hoping he wouldn't tell me what I already know.

"I'll take ya home," he mutters.

"What about my car? Roadside should be on the way."

"Ya won't be driving her home tonight. She's peeled," he says. "They'll be giving ya a tow."

"I should wait here," I say, turning to get back into the car.

"Over me dead body," he says, his accent thickening. "Ya have no phone, and this isn't the best place to be stranded. In the rain, no less."

"I can't leave my car."

"I'll take care of the car. Let me get you home to safety," he reassures me.

The rain starts to pick up again. Reluctantly, I race to get my things from inside the car and lock up. Quinn places a warm, protective hand on my back. It feels like he sears right through my shirt with his heat.

I ignore it as best I can as he leads me around to the passenger side of his truck. He opens the door as my gaze scans the vehicle, trying to figure out how my little butt is going to get up into it. Before I can find my answer, hands cup my waist, plucking me off my feet.

I yelp as he lifts me, placing me inside the truck. My belly drops and my heart races; he has lifted me so effortlessly.

"Thank you," I say quietly after I'm safely in the seat.

"Aye, no problem, love."

After closing the door, Quinn runs around to hop into the driver's side, rushing out of the storm. I look over at him. His hair is wet, plastered to his face, turning a darker shade of red. His white T-shirt is soaked through.

"Sorry, let me get this out of yer way," he murmurs as he turns to move some things into the back seat.

Every muscle is on full display through the now-sheer, clinging fabric. My gaze goes to his nipples showing through. I have to fight to keep my mouth from dropping open when I spot the imprint of piercings clear as day, penetrating not one but both nipples. I can't stop myself from making a surprised face.

This man is full of surprises. I was absolutely not expecting that one. It seems so…I don't know. Quinn comes off rough and gruff. I can't imagine him walking into a tattoo shop asking to have his nipples pierced. I think of a totally different type of guy when I think of piercings in general.

I shift my eyes to his face. His eyes search mine the moment we lock gazes. I don't know why I feel like he's assessing and making notes inside his mind. It's as if he's checking off some imaginary boxes.

His eyes drop to my mouth and he licks his lips. It's the sexiest thing I've ever seen. It's slow, almost deliberately so, as if he's demanding my eyes to follow the path.

His gaze returns to mine with heat right on the surface. If looks could set a blaze, I'd be engulfed in flames. He reaches toward me, causing me to bite my lip to keep from saying a word.

Disappointment rushes in when I realize he's only reaching for the seat belt. He pulls it across my body, clicking it into place. I start to breathe again when his hands return to the steering wheel.

Get a grip, girl.

"Hold tight," he says, before starting the car and pulling off.

I force myself to look away from him. The things running through my mind would shame the least innocent. This man intrigues me on levels that simply shouldn't be. I squeeze my thighs together as I begin to imagine dragging my tongue over those piercings and tight muscles.

I'm so lost in my fantasies, I don't realize he hasn't asked for my address until we turn onto my block. My head whips in his direction as he pulls into my driveway. My lust is forgotten as I wonder how the hell he knew my car. He has only seen me in one of the school's vehicles.

"What don't you know about me?"

"Don't worry, there is still plenty for me to learn about ya on our date," he says matter-of-factly.

"There's not going to be any date. Wait a minute! How did you just happen to be on the road I was stranded on?" I narrow my eyes at him.

He gives me a wicked smile, leaning in toward me. I hold my breath and freeze, kicking myself when once again disappointment blooms as his lips do nothing more than caress my cheek. His cologne makes my mouth water. It was already circulating in the truck's cabin. Now it's fanning in my direction, taking over my head.

He pulls back, still smiling. I want to snatch that sexy smile from his face. He makes me feel like a trapped rat that knows the cheese will end me, but goes for it anyway.

"Once ya charge yer phone, we can talk about when yer free. I have the kids once or twice this week, and I'm covering at the pub a few days next week, but I'll give ya a list of my free days. Ya pick one and we'll have our first date," he says, as if I've not turned him down repeatedly.

He moves from the truck before I can retort. I mumble to myself as he comes around to help me out. This time, he makes sure to allow my body to slide down the front of his. I ignore the way my curves mold to his firm planes.

Avoiding his gaze, I look around, disoriented. I know I'm supposed to have something in my hands. I can't for the life of me think of what. Quinn chuckles above me, reaching over my shoulder into the truck. I want to palm my forehead when he hands me my purse and work bag.

"Thank you," I whisper.

"I'll be needing the key to yer car," he says.

"Oh, yeah," I reply, digging my key out.

"I'll call a friend and have him take care of it."

"The dealership can take care of it," I say.

"Do ya want me to drop ya to work in the morning?" he says, brushing off my comment.

"No, I can ride with Tari," I answer.

"Aye. Good night, Alicia," he breathes against my cheek, before placing another soft kiss on my skin.

He backs up with a smile on his lips and his eyes dancing over me. I must look like a mess. My hair is ruined from the rain, no doubt. The storm has finally stopped, but I'm already soaked through.

"Good night," I say.

Lifting a hand to my wet bob, I groan. Great, I look like a drowned cat. Boy, what a night.

CHAPTER 8

RECOVERY

Quinn

I'M COILED TIGHTER THAN A SPRING. I'VE BEEN DIGGING into Cal's little friends. I haven't a clue what made him get involved with a drug cartel. I've been trying not to think the worst. I've known Cal most of my life.

He can be a hothead, but this is over the top even for him. It's not adding up. If this turns out to be what it looks like, I'm going to kill him myself. I promise I am.

"This doesn't make sense," Shane says from his desk.

"Yeah, I know," Trent chimes in. "I mean, come on. Cal was pushed off the force because he wouldn't join the good old dirty boys' club. So, what? He's not making enough as a PI and decides to get his hands dirty."

"I call bullshit," Kevin says. "No one's strapped for cash around here. He's been trying to talk Erin into cutting her hours. How could he need the money?"

"He doesn't," Shane replies. "I've looked through their financials. They're not hurting for a dime. Erin's been poor-mouthing if you ask me. She's been more than modest."

"That's our sister. She's never been flashy or a show-off," I say. "So what's really going on?"

"I don't know what Cal has to hide, but he sure as fuck

went through a lot to hide it. I'm still trying to get into this laptop," Shane groans.

"Why go through all that? What did he think he needed to keep from us?" Kevin asks.

"I'll bet the farm it has something to do with the force. He's never gotten over being pushed out. He has dreamed of being a detective since we were kids," Shane muses.

I narrow my eyes in thought. Shane's right. Cal has been bitter for a long time. He felt Dugan could have done more to help him, but Cal had stepped on all the wrong toes. There was nothing anyone could do by the time things got out of control. If he had stayed on the force, he would have been miserable or worse—dead.

"Ya keep working on that laptop. I know answers are on there. Trent—"

My phone rings, cutting off my words. I look down to see my mum's number, and my palms start to sweat. I place the phone on speaker since we're all here together in the office.

"Hello, Ma," I answer.

"Thank Christ, she's awake," my ma sobs through the line. "She opened her eyes about an hour ago. She's a bit confused and having a rough start of it, but she's awake."

"Thank fuck," the four of us say in unison.

The relief in the room is palpable. You can nearly taste the shift that happens. Like a smooth brandy that eases the tension away at the end of a long day. The first sip always brings the sweetest release.

I think we're all savoring the moment, finally hearing the words we've been waiting for.

We're all out of our seats, grabbing keys and closing up

shop. I can't wait to see my sister with her eyes open. I start to make a mental list of things I need to stop for to take to Erin. Flowers, chocolates, a few novels to read, and notebooks and pens—all things she loves.

"We'll be there in a few," I say to Ma.

"Aye, they took her for testing, but she should be back by the time youse get here," she replies, sounding the happiest I've heard her in weeks.

"Do ya need anything?"

"Just me boys," she says.

"Aye, we'll be there," I say as a promise.

"See ya soon," she replies and hangs up.

Maybe we'll all be able to focus better now that Erin is awake. I can't help feeling like something is staring right at us. Each of our minds have been preoccupied; being able to see things objectively has been a strain. At least, I know for a fact that's the way things have been for me.

"I'll ride with ya," Shane says, tossing his computer bag over his shoulder.

I'm sure he wants to be able to work on the way to the hospital. From the look in his eyes, I can see the same determination that has been renewed within me. It's time to organize both what we know and the resources we have at our disposal.

Two lists I'll be writing out as soon as I get a chance. If there's one thing I'm great at, it's solving problems and finding answers. My mind is already moving more clearly.

"Should we tell her about Cal?" Shane asks, pulling me from my thoughts as we climb into my truck.

"I think we should hold off as long as we can," I reply.

"I guess yer right. One hurdle at a time," he says.

"Exactly."

There's one thing I'm certain of: Cal was up to something and whatever it was blew back to his door. Now it's time we turn the winds on those who made this critical mistake.

CHAPTER 9

SPARKS AND PROMISES

Alicia

IT'S BEEN A LONG DAY, MADE LONGER BY THAT RED-haired giant who I can't get out of my head. He had my car fixed and paid for it. His friend dropped it off this afternoon. I was flabbergasted when he told me all the work that was done and that Quinn had covered the cost entirely.

I tried to call him, wanting to return the money and thank him for his help. I've been getting his voicemail all day. Funny, when I want to talk to him, I can't get in touch with him. I have a suspicion he's avoiding my calls.

Walking to my car, I mutter into my bag while rummaging around for my key. Honestly, I'm happy to have my car back. I'm not a fan of driving the school's cars for personal errands and things unrelated to the business. It's always been a rule of mine.

"Do ya always walk around with ya head down? Yer not aware of yer surroundings at all, love." That rumbling voice startles me off my feet.

He scares me so bad, I jump, dropping my bag. Quinn catches my purse in one hand before it hits the ground. My hand goes over my racing heart.

He plucks the key right from my bag, handing it over.

Warmth fills my cheeks as I reach for my things. I'm both embarrassed and annoyed.

Quinn, on the other hand, looks unfazed. He folds his arms over his chest, looking as if it's his job to stand sentinel at my car. One breathtaking sentinel, I might add.

I roll my eyes over him as I try to catch my breath. Black construction boots on his feet. His long legs are wrapped lovingly by a pair of well-worn blue jeans. I raise my brow as I read the logo on his black T-shirt: WU-TANG.

What does he know about Wu-Tang?

He is full of surprises. I'm starting to get the feeling that Quinn Blackhart is nothing like I've led myself to believe. Nipple piercings and Wu-Tang T-shirts, I can't imagine what else he might be hiding. Not that I plan to find out anything else.

Aw, hell, but I have to ask.

"The Wu?" I say, nodding my head toward his T-shirt.

He looks down at it, lifting his head with a grin on his lips. "Aye, ya think yer the only one with eclectic taste in music?"

I frown. There is no way he found out my taste in music from his little investigation on me. I mean, there's no way he can get little details like that, right?

"Ya were blasting Alanis Morissette and the Wu that first day we met. I'm making an assumption ya like a variety of artists," he replies to the confused look on my face.

I frown at his memory of those songs playing that day. I'd prefer to forget that day and the reasons for choosing those particular songs.

I mimic his stance, folding my arms over my chest, with my key clutched in my palm. I glare at him.

"Do you always sneak up on women in dark parking lots?"

His steady gaze is prying as usual. I slam the shutters down before I reveal anything. I don't need him digging into my life anymore.

"Not in the habit of it. Actually, I didn't sneak up on ya. I'm a big lad. Don't know how ya missed me," he replies, humor clear in his voice.

"Whatever," I mutter, unlocking my car.

"Ya called, love. I'm here. What can I do ya for?" he says, reaching to pull me forward by my waist.

I look up at him. Those eyes could fry my brain cells. I look away, trying to step back out of his hold. His response is to turn us until my back is against the car door, his body caging me in. He plants his palms on the roof of the car on either side of my head.

"What are you doing?" I say shyly.

"I've been thinking of ya, Alicia. Ya owe me a date," he replies.

My mouth pops open. I didn't think he'd use the car to push for a date. I get irritated with the realization.

"Oh, no. Nope, you paying for my car to be fixed does *not* entitle you to a date. As a matter of fact, I was calling to ask you how much I owe you. I'll send it right to your account. Email and amount, please," I say.

He dips his head, placing his forehead to mine. Butterflies take off in my stomach, my body is super aware of every part of him. The leg he has wedged between my thighs, his arms caging me in, his breath tickling my lips—I'm conscious of every single thing down to the heat coming off him.

"When I do something for ya, it's never to receive

anything from ya in return. I fixed the car because it was something ya needed fixed. Ya owe me a date because ya feel this as much as I do," he says.

"Feel what?" I ask, feigning ignorance.

He releases a growl of frustration seconds before his lips capture mine. I feel sucker-punched by the searing kiss. His beard has a delicious stroke and burn that brings a heightened sensation to the enticing lip lock. I lift my arms around his neck.

"Ouch," Quinn grunts as my purse knocks him in the back of the head.

I try not to laugh. I didn't mean to hit him, but the look on his face is pretty hilarious. He eyes me accusingly. I bite my lip, looking up at him through my lashes.

"Sorry." I giggle.

"Aye, that amused ya?"

He pulls the bag from my hand and tosses it onto the hood of the car. His palms are on my hips again, drawing me into him. He glides them to my backside, melding our bodies together. This time, he lifts me into the kiss, pressing me into the car.

When I open to him, his groan vibrates through me. He wastes no time as his tongue swipes into my mouth, claiming and taming at the same time. He has a rhythm he demands for the kiss, and he shows me exactly how to follow.

I've never been devoured like this. I feel him everywhere. My toes curl and my core pulses with anticipation of what more he can offer if this is what he gives in a kiss.

I place my arms back around his neck, allowing my fingers to find his hair. He groans again, deeper and louder, cupping my jaw and tilting my head back to give him full access. I'm being consumed. That's the only way to put it.

His mint-flavored mouth welcomes me in for more. I take gulps of him as he draws sips of his own. I'm on the edge of sanity until he goes to coax my legs around his waist.

Snapping out of my trance, I start to push at his heaving chest. Quinn looks down at me as if he's just remembering himself. He pulls a hand down his face and mutters something I can't make out.

"Yer going to drive me insane," he says. "Fuck. Get in the car, lass. Before I lose any more of my noodle. I'll pick you up at six tomorrow night for dinner."

I shake my head at him, clearing it in the process. If the man kisses like that, I surely don't need to go on a date with him. My lips still feel like they're on fire. Not only from the kiss, but the soft burn of his facial hair.

"That's not going to happen. Thank you for taking care of my car. I'll be paying you back. Have a good night," I reply, grabbing my purse.

He opens the door, allowing me to scoot past him. I climb inside, still frazzled from that kiss. Pushing a hand into my bangs, I tug. If I pull hard enough, maybe my good sense will return. I can't believe I allowed that to happen.

"Alicia."

His voice is too close, causing me to turn. I'm greeted by those eyes as we come face-to-face. He pecks my lips.

"Give me a reason why we shouldn't go on this date," he says.

I blink at him slowly. I want to spill all my secrets to him. Let him into all my pain, but that's even more reason for me to say no.

My eyes close when I think of tomorrow's date. It's another day I wish to blow past without a thought. Which is probably why I should go on this date.

"It's complicated and you don't have that kind of time," I breathe without opening my eyes.

"I have time for ya, love. All the time in the world."

I open my eyes, and his green gaze sends reality slamming into me. I don't trust myself. Not with him.

"Quinn—"

"I'll see ya tomorrow at six. Ya can tell me all I need to know then. Be ready," he says, before backing away and closing the door.

I stare out the window as he stands on the other side, waiting for me to pull away. Inhaling a much-needed breath, I start the car and pull out of the spot. Distance is a very good thing.

"Nope, I'm not ready for that mess right there," I mutter to myself.

It was just a kiss. Not enough to make me lose my mind and throw myself to the wolves. I'll figure this out with some distance. Yup, I sure will.

Guys like Quinn are trouble for me. I'm not putting myself through that type of torture ever again. Sure, they say and do all the right things in the beginning. Then, five years later, I'm the one left with my heart bleeding out and my self-esteem in the toilet.

Nope, not going to do it. No distractions. I need to find myself.

Quinn

I had an entire list of things I needed to get done before I came here tonight, but I wanted to come in person. A call wasn't going to do. I had a feeling Alicia was going to object to me paying for the repairs.

Now, I stand here watching her drive away. That kiss wasn't what I expected. I knew there was something between us. I've felt it every time she's been near me.

However, that kiss. It was like sticking my finger in an electrical socket. My body is still humming from having her so near and tasting her on my tongue.

"Fuck me," I mutter, pulling a hand down my beard.

I almost mauled her right against her car. I forgot where we were. I had only meant to have a little taste. Show her she can't deny us, and put an end to the draw I always feel from her mouth. Instead, I got the shock of my life when my lips touched hers, and I couldn't stop taking more.

My cell rings, bringing me back to reality. I tug it from my pocket to answer. I smile when I see it's Ma. She's been in much better spirits since Erin woke.

"Hello, Ma."

"Quinn, ya sound like yer smiling," she says in greeting.

"Ya say that as if I never smile."

"Ya don't. Not unless ya have a steak and a beer before ya," she replies.

"Aye, we'll agree to disagree." I chuckle.

"Christ, the lad must have a lass. He just chuckled. Oh, the Lord heard me prayers. I'll be getting wee ones from me firstborn, I will," she says with glee.

I groan. I don't know why it's so important to my mum

that I have children. She's been after me since I turned thirty. Now that I'm thirty-five, she's been laying it on a bit thick about finding someone to settle down with.

My thoughts go to Alicia. Images of her swollen with my wee un come to mind. I frown at my thoughts.

For some reason, the lass is trying to push me away. She says it's complicated, but I'm determined to help uncomplicate it. I sigh. This may take some time.

It'll be a while before I get as far as settling down and having a family. Not that I intend to give up after that kiss. The connection I felt isn't something I plan to walk away from.

"What do ya need, Ma?"

"Ach, I can't call me own son to check in?" she asks.

"Aye, ya know ya can. I'll yarn to ya anytime ya want, but I know ya too well. Ya didn't call for a wee chat. What's up?"

"Lad's too big for his breeches, he is. I'll still take ya over a knee, Quinn," she snaps.

I try not to laugh. I know she would, right before my da takes a turn for pissing her off. My ma is as fiery as ever and my da is her perfect match. It's why he loves her so. She keeps him on his toes.

"I don't doubt it."

"It's time to tell the chisellers what's going on. Erin will be released in a few days. Yer da is arranging for her to have therapy at home. We'll keep her with us for now. The babes need to understand she's not going to be herself for a while," she says more softly.

"Aye, I was thinking it was time to sit them down."

"There's still no change with Cal?"

"No," I say. "But he's still fighting. Kevin says he's hanging in there, but the doctors don't sound as hopeful."

"We have to wait and see, I guess," she says on a sigh.

My jaw works. I nod as if she can see me. As mad as I am at Cal, I don't want my sister to lose her husband or the kids to lose their da. Cal is with the best doctors, better off where we sent him. Yet, there hasn't been much of a change.

"Aye, we will," I reply, blowing out a heavy breath. "What do ya need me to do? Whatever you need, I'm there."

"They're going to need more attention and love. I'll chat with yer brothers. I want each of ya to take them for a day of something special. I know ya would want to plan ahead," she says. "Especially now that ya have a lass."

"I don't have a lass," I mumble.

"Aye, sure ya don't," she scoffs back. "And I don't keep a baseball bat under me side of the bed."

I snort at my mum. She indeed has a Louisville Slugger under her bed. I grew up with my father spending his nights working at the pub. Ma would keep that bat under the bed in case she had to protect the family while Da was at work. I also know about the .38 she has in the bedside table.

"I'll plan something," I say with a small laugh.

"He laughs again! I want to meet her," she replies.

"I'll call ya later, Ma. I love ya."

"I love ya too. Still want to meet her," she says back and cuts the call.

My thoughts go to the family beach house. Erin takes the kids there all the time. Maybe I'll take them out for a weekend. There's no way I'm taking the little monsters to my cabin. Molly has broken enough things in my home; I can't imagine what she'd do to my private getaway.

"The beach house it is," I mutter to myself and start to make a list for a weekend away with the brats.

CHAPTER 10

DATE

Alicia

THE TRUTH IS… I'M NOT ENTIRELY SURE HOW TO FIX ME. However, today I believe I found the start. This would have been my first wedding anniversary. I woke to a call from Giovanni. It's his second call in the last few days, confirming I need to do a lot of things in my life differently.

I took the day off to try to figure some things out. I keep saying it's time for me to move on and get my life together, yet I've been holding onto the past so tightly. It's not just the wedding and drama from a year ago. In all honesty, whether I could see it before or not, I've been grieving the loss of my parents all this time.

Give me a reason why we shouldn't go on this date.

Quinn's words have caused me to be truthful with myself. I'm still stuck at eighteen. While I've been lost there, longing for my parents, life has been one big shitstorm I have failed to lift an umbrella to.

After some thought, I realized I have all the resources to get my life in order. It's time I do just that. Making some much-needed decisions, I determined it's finally time I got rid of all the wedding things I've been holding onto in my attic. I started with the wedding gown.

I was going to burn it, but figured I'd get some money for it instead. It sold almost as soon as I posted it. That was the charge I needed. Sort of like the universe has given me confirmation.

I look around at the mess I've made and blow out a breath. I'm surrounded by the boxes I brought down from the attic.

I've spent hours in my pajamas, either tossing or selling off gifts and other things from the wedding that never happened. I have no clue why I held onto all of this as long as I have. Still, I do know one thing. With each item, I feel like I'm setting myself free.

"Girl, you've been keeping secrets." Tari's voice carries over the crooning of Al Green, as her head pops into my room.

I look up from my seat on the floor. I knit my brows as I take in the mischievous smile on her lips. Picking up my phone, I pause the music to find out what she's going on about.

"Huh?"

"He. Is. Fine," she says, drawing out each word.

I look at her with further confusion. Seeing my reaction, she moves into the room, dodging boxes. This place is a mess, garbage bags and boxes everywhere.

"Why aren't you getting ready?" she whispers. "Your date is downstairs looking like a straight snack and you look like a mess. What the heck?"

I've been focused solely on the task before me. I check the clock and close my eyes as I let out a groan. It's five minutes after six. I haven't thought about the time or Quinn, and certainly not the date because I've been consumed with relieving myself of my past.

Maybe this is a sign. I shouldn't go. This purge feels right. I should be here to finish this.

"Tell him I'm not feeling well," I whisper.

"What?" she replies, looking at me like I've lost my mind.

"Tell him I'm sick or something. Just get rid of him."

She moves a little closer, placing a hand on my forehead. I purse my lips and scrunch up my face. I already know she's not going to be any help.

"Nope, no fever, but you must have bumped your head. I'm not telling that man no such thing. You want to bail on him, you do it yourself. I'm not going along with this one," she says.

"Ugh, fine," I mutter, pushing up from the floor.

I start to stomp out of the room to get rid of my date. Tari grabs my arm to stop me, spinning me to face her. She looks me up and down with a pointed look.

"Where do you think you're going looking like that? At least take the scarf off," she says.

I look down at my clothes and start to chew on my lip. I shouldn't want to impress him. I only need to go downstairs and tell him tonight is not a good night.

"Damn, I can't with you," she groans, snatching my scarf from my head.

"What?"

"If I didn't know you all my life…" she says, shaking her head at me.

She finger combs my wrap out, then tugs at the hem of my tank top to straighten it. She looks down at my Smurf-covered pajama pants, throwing her hands in the air in exasperation. I wiggle my toes and fidget with my fingers.

"I'm going to tell him I can't go."

"We're going to have a long talk about this," she says before turning me and shoving me out the bedroom door.

I need to call this date off, but knowing Quinn has the ability to pull me in, I'm dragging my feet. I walk downstairs in no rush at all.

My point is proven the moment I stumble to a halt when I enter the foyer where he is waiting. I thought the man was lethal in jeans and a T-shirt. The things he is doing to this navy-blue tailor-made suit are obscene. The crisp white shirt and green tie are just him showing off, because he nailed it with the suit alone.

Every long, defined limb is displayed to perfection. For such a big man, his tailor got it right. Not too snug and not too loose, the fabric molds to his frame perfectly. I have to keep from fanning my face.

The tie stands out as it makes his green eyes pop. They look more intense and vibrant. His thick red locks are tamed into a combed style with some type of product. In my head, his hair has gone from Sam Winchester on the show *Supernatural* to Kit Harington from *Game of Thrones*, walking the runway. Whatever he has put in his hair is not only holding it in place, it's defining his natural red curls more.

Having his hair combed away from his face has opened it up to show off his masculine beauty. The man is gorgeous beyond belief. Even his flaws make him pure perfection. The tiny scar above his right brow only enhances his good looks.

"Exactly the look on my face when he walked in," Aidan says, bringing my attention to the fact that he's standing in the foyer as well.

Quinn ignores him as he takes in my attire before he flicks his wrist out to look at his watch. A frown takes over his features. Yet, none of this diminishes the sight before me. Every gesture increases his attractiveness.

"I did say six o'clock?" he says when his eyes lift back up to me.

"I was distracted today. Maybe it's best we cancel," I reply.

He moves closer, closing the gap and crowding my space. I feel the pull that always seems to appear when he's near. It's like an invisible hand drawing me to him.

"Ach, I don't think that's an option, love. It's my turn to be yer distraction," he says, while gently stroking my cheek.

Distraction.

Why does the word sound so enticing coming from his lips? Isn't that exactly what I want to avoid? Yet, here I am, leaning into his touch and his words.

"Well, damn," Aidan breathes, fanning his face.

"You can say that again," Tari adds.

I roll my eyes at them both, trying not to show how affected I am by Quinn's simple touch. The twinkle in Quinn's eyes tells me that I've done a piss-poor job of doing so. There's something else that I catch in his green depths.

Something that tugs me closer still, causing me to reconsider this date. Quinn intrigues me way more than he should. While confident on the outside, I sometimes get the feeling he's not so much on the inside.

Somehow, knowing he could have one simple flaw makes it easier to consider getting to know him. Not that my ex didn't have flaws. Giovanni had a hell of a lot, he simply liked to turn them around to make them seem like my own.

Quinn is nothing like that. I don't know how I know this or what makes me think it, but I war with the thought. I think of the mess upstairs. Maybe I could use a break from that disarray.

"If I agree to go on this one date with you, will you stop showing up where you're unwanted?" I ask, a hint of teasing in my voice.

"Ach, I don't believe I've shown up anywhere I've not been wanted as it is. But if that promise will get ya dressed and out the door, then, aye, I will not show up anywhere I'm unwanted," he says with a sexy smile.

"Okay, you stay here. I need time to get ready."

"Our reservations are for seven," he says with a hint of frustration, running a hand over his beard.

"I'm sorry. I truly got lost in… I'll need at least a half hour to an hour. If you can't change the reservations, we can go ahead and cancel," I say, biting my lip.

Now that I've decided to go, I hope he can get us a later reservation. It would be a shame for his efforts to go to waste. He looks and smells amazing.

He starts to murmur to himself. I can see an internal battle begin within his eyes. I wait for him to cancel the date or, in his take-charge manner, bark out a night to reschedule.

"Well, go, will ya? Get ready," he says like an impatient kid.

I roll my lips, trying not laugh at him. I think it's the little moments like this that pique my interest most. The moments I see a small crack in his gruff and brooding exterior.

"Why don't I help you get ready?" Aidan says as he goes to follow me upstairs.

"I was thinking ya could stay right here to keep me company," Quinn says.

I can't hold my smile in. Quinn either doesn't see that Aidan has no interest in me, or he just doesn't care. The look on his face says there's no way Aidan's following me upstairs to get dressed.

Tari and I fall into a fit of laughter as we turn and retreat to my room. I move a little faster to go back upstairs. When I enter my room, the full force of the mess I've made hits me. Maybe I shouldn't be going out. This is much more than I realized and I still need to get through it.

I climb my way through the maze to sit on my bed and breathe for a moment. When my backside hits the mattress, something stabs me in the butt. I lift up, rubbing my cheek with one hand while reaching for the item with the other.

Tears fill my eyes when I see what the culprit is. It's a picture frame, holding a photo from my engagement party. I look so happy and oblivious. I can't believe how naive I had been.

"Maybe I'm not ready," I say to Tari as she sits beside me on the bed.

"Aidan has been much harder on you than me…until now," Tari replies, snatching the frame from me. "You're one of the best people I know. You have a big heart, and you will give the shirt off of your back to anyone.

"I think that's why people are so damn comfortable shitting on you. Enough! You can't go through your life scared to live. You've finally woken up. Now, screw your past. Learn from it and move forward. You're too strong to let it hold you back.

"Go on this date. Get to know him. If you feel like this

guy is taking advantage…cut him loose, but at least try," she pleads.

"Trying is what scares me," I whisper.

"What do you always tell me and Aidan? Do it afraid. You started your own business afraid. You bought that other house afraid. Those were some of the best moments in your life. Besides, you didn't see the way that guy looked at you. He's no Giovanni," she says, with a sharp look.

"I don't know. Maybe we should talk on the phone for a bit."

"Girl, if you don't get your ass up and get dressed, I'm going to drag you into the shower and dress you my damn self. Take your own advice, boo. *If it doesn't scare you, it's not worth it*," we say the last words in unison.

Tari throwing my own words back at me sinks in. She's right. I can't avoid dating forever. This fear I have of Quinn is both disturbing and exciting at the same time. I don't know how to explain it, but my gut is telling me to explore it.

"All right, I'm going to jump in the shower. Can you help with my hair and makeup?" I relent.

"I got you. I'll pick something out for you too," she says excitedly.

"Oh, hell no. I've got this," I say, giving her side-eye.

"Fine," Tari says, folding her arms over her chest.

———————————

Quinn

I look at my watch again. I'm frustrated I had to change everything for the night. I couldn't simply move our dinner reservations back. I had special plans; there was no way I could hold the room or a private table at the place I'd planned for.

Some quick reorganizing and I was able to arrange something a little different. Not what I wanted for our first date. This was actually on my list for our next one.

"I didn't think it was possible, but she wasn't lying," Alicia's roommate says from the accent chair across from me.

"Excuse me?" I respond.

I've felt him staring at me for the last twenty minutes. There was no way in hell he was going upstairs to help Alicia get ready. I've investigated one too many cases where the "gay" best friend was shagging the wife. Guys that were "gay" until the female needed a shoulder to cry on. Next thing you know, she's doing more than crying on that shoulder.

Not my woman, not while I'm around. I've been curious about her choice of roommates since the two introduced themselves. I haven't dug into Alicia's life as much as she thinks I have. Now, I sort of wish I had. This has blindsided me a bit.

"Your accent is pure delicious," he says.

"Thanks, I guess."

"Alicia said you were too handsome. I didn't think that was a thing. But damn if she wasn't right," he continues.

I lift a brow at him, not saying a word. His eyes roll over me in appreciation. Something else flashes in his gaze. I know it's coming. I've been a PI too long not to anticipate what comes next. I'm actually amused.

"It would be a shame if I have to mess up that gorgeous face. I love Alicia like a sister. Her ex almost had me behind bars. As you can see, I'm too pretty for that shit, but I'll do my time with a smile if anyone hurts those two girls up there," he says with a straight face.

"Aye, good to know she has had someone to look out for her. But let me be clear about a few things. If ya ever feel froggy, then ya leap this way, I'll teach ya how many bones ya can break when I put ya on yer ass.

"Next thing I want ya to listen to real close. I'm not her past, but I am her present and future. Alicia's days of playing with boys has come to an end. She has a man now. I'll protect her—heart, mind, body, and soul—with my life. Ya don't have to worry yerself."

I say my words with as straight a face as he gave me. I'm not fazed one bit. He breaks into a smile, his eyes sparkling.

"Yeah, you'll do. I like you." He nods.

"Isn't that grand?"

"The brooding thing is hot, by the way."

"Aidan, cut it out." Alicia enters the room.

I turn toward her and nearly swallow my tongue. She looks stunning. The strapless black dress hugs her breasts and her waist, flaring out around her hips. Her short legs are on display in a pair of blue heels that make her limbs seem longer.

Her face is made up to perfection. However, I've seen her with no makeup and think she's as breathtaking without it. Something is a bit different about her hair. It's feathered back away from her face, opening up her features.

I'm so drawn to her, I don't realize I've stood and moved my feet to cross the room until I'm standing before her. She tips her face back as I hover above her. She peers back at me with those pretty eyes. It's a true test of my will not to dip my head to take her lips.

"You're gorgeous, love," pours from my mouth as my brain somewhat kicks in.

"Thank you," she says, shyly ducking her head.

"We should go. I had to rearrange some things, but I got us squared away."

"Okay."

My hand goes to the small of her back, leading her out the front door. It's impossible to miss the spark between us. I flex my fingers and draw her closer to my side.

Alicia's friends walk to the door behind us like parents seeing off their daughter on her first date. I'm amused by their protectiveness. I have questions about why they're this way. I caught Aidan's words about her ex. I plan to find out more about him soon enough.

I smile as I watch her look around for my truck. Pressing the button on the key fob, I unlock the Jag I drove tonight. She looks up at me with her head tilted to the side.

"I thought it would be easier for ya to get in and out of, shorty," I tease.

"Oh, really," she says with that gorgeous, shy smile. "I may have an easier time, but I can't wait to see you curl your giant self in it. I'm sure it's as hilarious as when you scrunched up in the back of the Corolla."

I lean down next to her ear. "I'll fit just fine," I say.

When I pull away, the desired effect is written on her face. Her parted lips and the dilation of her pupils are everything I was looking for. She lowers her lashes, trying to hide her reaction. Again, I refrain from kissing her. That's last on my list for tonight.

This is going to be a long night.

Alicia

I'm very impressed by his choice of restaurant. Quinn definitely has taste. That has shown throughout the night. His
choice in music during the drive here, his selection in wine,
the restaurant itself—they all earned an A.

This place is both romantic and elegant. All seem a contrast to the man sitting before me. I'm finding that to be a
common theme. With each moment I spend with him, I
learn something new that challenges my first impressions.

"Looks delicious," I say, pointing my fork at his plate.

"Aye, it is," he replies.

He cuts a piece of steak, placing mashed potatoes and
green beans on the fork along with it. Reaching across the
table with his long arm, he places the fork to my lips. I lift
a brow. I'm so not in the habit of eating off of other's forks.
It's a pet peeve.

However, this man has had his tongue down my throat,
so I'll make an exception this time. I open my mouth and I
wrap my lips around the offered fork. I can't help the moan
that leaves me. The food is like buttery heaven, melting in
my mouth instantly.

Quinn's eyes drop to my lips. He reaches his other arm
across the table and wipes the corner of my mouth. I watch
as he sticks his thumb in between his lips and sucks. His
eyes remain fixed on me the entire time.

Lowering my eyes, I turn my attention to the plate before
me. My throat has gone completely dry watching him make
a simple gesture look like a thorough seduction. Needing

to find a distraction, I reach for my glass of wine to take a much-needed sip.

"Oh, that's divine," I say as I cover my mouth.

At this point in my mind, I don't know if I'm talking about the food and wine or watching him. It's been this way throughout dinner. He makes a comment that sounds one way, but has my mind thinking another. Harmless actions have sent my pulse racing a time or two.

Even now, the way he cuts and places a forkful of steak into his own mouth seems like an act of sin. I didn't know a man could make chewing look so sexy. Quinn has it down to a science.

"I want to know more about ya," he says as he places his fork and knife down.

Oddly enough, I'd rather continue watching him savor the steak in front of him. Quinn appears to be a man who takes his time to appreciate the things he enjoys. That's something else I've noticed about him. It's like he's been methodically working his way around his plate as he enjoys his food.

Interesting.

"What exactly do you want to know?" I force myself to reply.

I'm relieved when my voice comes out evenly. Lord knows my pulse is doing the total opposite on the inside. I've tried to remain even-keeled throughout dinner. Although I'm not too sure I've been successful.

"What makes ya tick? What ya like and don't like? Why ya have a male roommate?" he replies.

I roll my lips as laughter fills me, my shoulders shaking with it. I had a feeling Aidan was going to come up. Feeling the pull between us, I can't seem to stop the words from pouring from my mouth. I give him the honest truth.

"I hadn't planned to have roommates at all. Male or female," I say.

He tilts his head at me. I can see him assessing me. I watch as the wheels turn, fidgeting a bit in my seat under his scrutiny.

"Aye, there's more to it than that. I can see it in yer eyes and hear it in yer words. When it's my turn to tell ya about me, I'll be straight with ya. Ya can do the same with me," he says in a tone that practically pries the words from my lips.

I drop my eyes to the plate before me. The half-eaten chicken and vegetables start to blur a little. Inhaling deeply, I fight the tears back.

"Today would have been my first wedding anniversary. A few weeks before the wedding…" I snort. "Actually, a year to the date we met, I woke to the U.S. Marshal at my door. They were there to evict me from my home.

"For a year and half…my so-called best friend had insisted I let her manage my personal life and business while I focused on my wedding. I wrote the checks every month. She…she had statements and printouts for the bills she supposedly paid. Because she intercepted and sorted the mail, I never knew anything was amiss until that day.

"I was homeless. Aidan and Tari were already living in the house my parents gave me. I had to move in with my friends until I got that colossal mess under control," I explain.

"So yer impatient," he says.

I lift my head to look at him, blinking a few times as his statement settles in. Thinking over my words, I try to figure out where he pulled that assumption from. Nothing I said would lead anyone to think of me as impatient. People always tell me I'm one of the most patient people they know.

"What? I'm not impatient."

"Yes, ya are. Ya were about to marry some eejit, instead of waiting for me," he says with a sexy grin.

I purse my lips, but can't help laughing. Quinn winks at me, reaching to take a sip of his wine. This time, I watch him, trying to feel him out.

"What makes you think he was an idiot?"

"Ya got away, lass. He's an eejit," he replies. "I'm old enough to know if ya find a treasure, ya hold onto it tightly."

My cheeks heat. I pray all my blushing doesn't show through my brown skin. I love the musical note of his words and how he puts them.

"How old are you?" I ask, hoping to keep him from asking about my ex.

"Thirty-five. Not much older than ya," he replies.

I narrow my eyes at him. Again, I search my feelings to see how I feel about him investigating me.

"Okay, enough of this. How much do you actually already know about me?"

"Not as much as ya think. I only wanted yer phone number at first. I plucked yer address and work address out later," he responds.

"Plucked...plucked from where?"

"The background check," he says as if it's so simple.

Sitting back in my seat, I fold my arm over my chest. Quinn follows the gesture with his eyes. They linger for a moment, before rising to meet my gaze.

"You did a background check on me?"

"Aye." He nods.

"And you don't see anything wrong with this?"

"No, I don't," he says completely unfazed.

"Let me put this another way," I say, leaning forward. "You wouldn't find it creepy if a boy did a background check on Mckenna to get her number and called her to ask her out? Then, showed up at her house or her job."

The deep frown that takes over his face is priceless. I've clearly made my point. He folds his arm across his chest, mirroring mine.

"I'm not a boy, and any lad sniffing around my niece will be sure to turn in the other direction if he does his research properly," he responds.

Groaning, I roll my eyes at him. Perhaps my point was lost after all. He pulls his phone from his pocket and taps away at the screen. My phone pings in my clutch beside me. Retrieving the device, I look at the screen to find an email from Blackhart Securities and Investigations.

Curiosity burns through me. Opening the email, I find a secure attachment. A second email comes in providing a passcode. When I get the file open, it's a background check on Quinn. Scrolling through, I'm astonished by the details within the file.

"Nice credit score," I tease.

"Now, we're on an even playing field. Ya have everything I have at yer fingertips, but as I said, I didn't dig into yer life. Only took the information I needed," he says.

"Okay." I nod, closing the email. "It's still creepy, but I guess this makes it a little better."

"My intentions were never to creep ya out," he says, his demeanor changing slightly.

That vulnerability is showing through again. I watch the play of his thoughts run across his face. There's something endearing about it.

"Do you do this with all your dates?"

"Ach, I don't date much. I'm particular about a lot of things. I don't have patience for many, and they don't have patience for me," he answers.

"You're telling me a man as fine as you doesn't date," I scoff out before I can think about my words.

"Ach, so ya admit ya find me sexy," he says in that teasing tone.

My cheeks burn and my ears get hot. I want the floor to open up and suck me in. However, I'm not as embarrassed as I'd be with anyone else. Quinn's presence offers a comfort I haven't been able to explain and have never felt before.

"Oh, my gosh. I didn't say that."

"Aye, ya definitely did. It's okay, love. Being attracted to me is good for our relationship."

"I think you're forgetting this is only one date," I retort.

"Hm," he grunts, returning to his steak.

I start on my food again, forcing myself to stop watching him as I do. I try to pace myself through the meal. It's delicious and if I weren't on a date, I would have devoured the entire thing by now.

The lemon and spices in the chicken have my mouth watering. The wine has only enhanced every bite. I can't remember the last time I came to a restaurant and enjoyed myself this much.

"Do ya mind if I ask why the wedding didn't happen?" he says, breaking into my thoughts.

I don't lift my eyes from my plate. I've been honest with

him up to this point. Yet, this is a bit too much honesty for me. My stomach knots and churns.

"I don't think I'm ready for that," I murmur.

"Alicia?" he calls, causing me to look up.

"Yes."

"I will listen when yer ready," he says, his eyes showing the sincerity of the offer.

It's a welcome offer. It feels like a lifeline I didn't know I needed. Of all things, Quinn strikes me as a good listener. Throughout the night, I've noticed he listens intently to everything I say.

It's reassuring. It's also new to me. I place that on the pro side of tonight. The scale is heavy with those. I'm wary to say that I haven't found any cons.

Wary only because I haven't found a reason not to go on another date with him. That's not good for my plan to stay single as I get my life in order. Although, I won't get my hopes up. This date seems almost too good to be true.

"What made ya want to be a driving instructor?" he asks, changing the topic.

I give a secret smile. The answer to this usually sends guys running. No one wants to date a woman who can kick their ass on a racetrack. I'll be keeping that to myself as well this evening. Instead, I go with a partial response.

"I wanted to start a business. My ex wanted me to eventually be a stay-at-home mom and housewife. The school was something I could manage remotely."

"Hm."

"What does that mean?"

"What does what mean?" he replies.

"*Hm.* You make that noise as if you don't approve."

"I didn't say I don't approve. I think yer a very intelligent woman. I will support whatever ya want to do with yer life. My brother-in-law has been trying to talk my sister into staying home full-time." He makes a disgusted sound in the back of his throat. "Ya don't cage a bird with spread wings. Ya remind me a little of Erin."

My eyes soften as I remember him talking to his sister in the hospital that day. Another moment where I got to see a softer side of him. I guess it's true that you can't judge a book by its cover.

"How is she?"

"She's awake. I'm taking her kids to our family beach house while they move her in to stay with my parents. She'll be able to start therapy there," he says.

"That's great!"

"Aye, it is. Ya never did return for a visit," he says, looking me in the eyes.

"How would you know?"

"If ya had, my family would have mentioned it. Ya don't forget to mention a lass like ya," he answers.

"So someone is always there with her. That's nice," I say, ignoring his words.

"Ya don't take compliments too well," he muses.

I shrug. It's a correct observation. It's become hard to over the years. Hearing my flaws somehow became more acceptable than being able to hear praise. I frown as that realization surfaces.

"Maybe," I mutter.

"We'll have to fix that. I intend to shower ya with praises, love." His voice drops as he says the words silkily. "I have a long list of them for ya."

"It's only one date," I remind him.

"Hm."

If he makes that sound one more time…

I grin at my thoughts and the interesting man sitting across from me. Reaching for my glass of wine, I down the rest. I get the feeling I should've avoided this date after all. With Quinn, I've opened a box I don't think I'll be closing so easily.

Quinn

We've both been silent on the drive back to Alicia's house. I've been thinking about all of the things unsaid. Alicia's expressions speak for themselves. There is so much beyond the shyness I've read. I've learned a lot by watching and listening to her.

She has an internal battle going on when it comes to me. I don't plan to allow that to keep me from pursuing her. I know now more than ever that I want Alicia Rhodes. The lass is smart, ambitious, and she has a sense of humor. I may have joked that she's impatient, but she's a very patient woman in all she does.

"I had a nice time. Thank you," she says when I pull up outside her house.

The driveway is full, so I park at the curb. I reach for her arm when she tries to sprint her way out of the car. Giving her a stern look of warning, I cut off the car and get out.

When I open her door and help her out, she won't look up at me. Chuckling to myself, I place a hand on her back to lead her up to the front door. I hope she doesn't think it will be so easy to get rid of me.

When we stop at the front door, I turn her to face me. Wrapping my arms around her waist, I tug her closer to me. She lifts her hands to my chest, her palm and her purse pressing against me.

Placing my fingers beneath her chin, I tilt her head back so she makes eye contact with me. We search each other's gazes. Her uncertainty is showing through. I want to clear away her doubts.

"I did enjoy myself," I say. "But the night wouldn't be complete without this."

Dipping my head, I capture her lips. It's even better than I remember. The taste of wine and the chocolate dessert she had still flavor her tongue. You wouldn't think I had an entire meal the way I'm starving for her.

When I feel her completely melt into the kiss, yielding herself over to me, I groan in satisfaction. The heat and chemistry between us charges to a new level. Our tongues dance together as if they've known each other for eternity.

I've clearly underestimated her power over me. Everything else has gone silent. For the first time in my life, I'm focused on one thing in a single moment. I don't need a list to sort out this woman before me.

I would remain in this moment forever if I could. I try to draw it out as long as I can. Cupping the back of her neck, I slip my fingers into the shorter hairs at her nape. Guiding her head, I deepen the kiss.

A growl rips from my lips when my phone begins to ring. It's been silent all night. Of course, this would be the very moment someone needs me.

Breaking the kiss, I peck the tip of her nose. "I'll be calling ya," I say, placing one last kiss on her lips.

I pull my phone out as I watch her stumble into her home. I smile. I feel as drunk as she looks after our heated exchange.

"Blackhart," I clip into the phone.

"I have something you might want to look at," Shane's voice comes through the line.

"On my way," I reply, ending the call and heading for my car.

CHAPTER 11

UNCLE DUTY

Quinn

"UNCLE QUINN, I HAVE TO GO POTTY," MOLLY CALLS from the back seat.

"We're almost there," I tell her for the millionth time.

It's the third time she's informed me of this in the last two minutes. Never mind the fact that I told her repeatedly to use the bathroom before we left the Golden Clover. Shane needed to follow up on the lead he stumbled upon last night. It was his weekend to watch the kids.

I took on the task for him. Since Da has returned to the pub, I only needed to check in to the restaurant for a wee bit before I had the rest of the day free. I dropped the twins off at their school for their functions, which left me with Molly and Kasey.

I'll be needing a stiff drink after a day with these two. I think I've had enough of being bossed around by a five- and seven-year-old. They have more demands than a terrorist.

"Can we have ice cream? Will that be okay to add to the list?" Kasey asks.

"After we go see a friend," I reply.

"Are they going to come with us for ice cream?"

"Ach, I don't know."

"Right, not on the list," she murmurs to herself.

I roll my eyes. This visit to Alicia wasn't on my list until about an hour ago. She hasn't been answering my calls today. She's back to avoiding me.

Our date went well. That kiss kept me up all night. I haven't figured out what her objection to dating me is yet. I know she's attracted to me. She feels this thing between us as much as I do. At first, I thought it might be because she's still attached to her ex, but something in her body language last night made me cross that off the list.

I want to see her face when I ask her why she's dodging me like a fugitive. If I can talk her into taking a break with me and the girls, I'll count it a miracle. I already know she's not instructing today. Tari was kind enough to give me her schedule for the next week.

I think I like her friends already. I don't take Aidan's warning personally. There's something about Alicia that makes you want to protect her.

"Uncle Quinn, I don't know if I'm going to make it," Molly warns as I pull into the parking lot of Alicia's driving school.

"Ach, we're here. Unfasten your seat belt," I say, rushing to get out of the truck.

I open her door and scoop her out of the booster seat in the back of my pickup. Kasey runs across the seat, so I can help her out as well. I make a mad dash for the institute with a girl in each arm.

"Aidan, where's yer restroom?" I bark once through the door.

His eyes grow wide at the sight of me holding the two girls. Grabbing a key from the desk, he waves me to follow him. I'm grateful for the short distance. Molly's cheeks are red and her face is screwed up.

"Stay here," I say to Kasey as I place her down on the floor.

"I've got her," Aidan says.

Nodding, I rush into the bathroom with Molly. We get her knickers down and hold her over the toilet just in time. The look of relief on her little face almost makes me laugh.

"Don't laugh at me, Uncle Quinn. That was almost a serious situation," Molly chides as she looks up at me.

I roll my lip and nod. I don't know how my sister does it, bless her heart. There have been a few close calls today—everything from near fights to almost running into things for lack of paying attention.

"Hey, Uncle Quinn." A tap comes from the door. "You guys need to hurry. I have to go next."

I look up at the ceiling. I should have known. I make quick work of finishing up with Molly and grab Kasey before she wets her pants.

I nearly have a heart attack when we step back out of the restroom and Molly is gone. Aidan isn't standing guard any longer either. I rush back to the front to find Molly sitting on top of a desk in front of Alicia.

So much for making a surprise entrance. These two have blown my cover. Molly has a sucker in her mouth, with her legs swinging. Her eyes are alight as she listens intently to Alicia's words. They look like two old friends, which is interesting. Molly tends to be on the shy side.

"Uncle Quinn, you know Mommy's friend?" Kasey looks up at me to question.

"Aye, it seems I do," I reply.

Alicia turns her head to look up at me. At first, I see the

wary look in her eyes, but that quickly fades into a look of appreciation. I watch as her eyes devour me from head to toe. I'm only wearing a plain black Metallica T-shirt and a pair of blue jeans with rips in the thighs.

Not my favorite pair of pants. I cringe every time I think about the tatters in them, but Mckenna bought them for me as a birthday gift. I wear them enough to make her happy.

Yet, the way Alicia's eyes pass over my body, you'd think I was in a suit again. My own gaze falls to her exposed calves. She's wearing a skirt and heels today. I mentally coax her to get up so I can see the full effect.

On cue, she stands, giving me my heart's desire. A white T-shirt with her blue business logo on it, and a gray pencil skirt that hugs her hips completes the sexy look. I'm ready to put in a job application to work here if this is what casual days consist of.

She moves toward me, and I can't take my eyes off her swaying hips. Well, I thought she was coming to me. She stops in front of Kasey and squats, offering my niece the sucker in her hand.

"Thank you," Kasey sings. "Oh, these are the ones Mommy gives us."

"Yup," Alicia says back, tapping Kasey on the nose. "A little birdie once told me these are your favorites."

"Smart birdie," Kasey says around a mouthful of lollipop.

"Yes, that she is." Alicia chuckles.

She stands and turns those wary eyes back on me. Reaching for her fingertips, I draw her closer. She looks nervously between the girls, bringing a smile to my face.

"Don't worry. Our secret is safe with my entourage," I tease.

"What are you doing here? Are you just going to show up whenever I ignore your calls?"

"Aye, so ya admit yer ignoring me."

She clamps her mouth shut and twists her lips to the side. My thumb dances back and forth over her knuckles. I'm dying to tug her in for a kiss. Her lips are painted a medium brown that looks both natural and inviting. The slight shine to them is the only thing giving away that she has on even an ounce of makeup.

"I've been working," she says in that soft voice. "I couldn't answer when you called."

I lean into her ear, pausing to let my breath fan against her skin. When I hear the slight hitch in her breathing, I know I have her right where I want her.

"Lies," I say in her ear. "I can see the pulse in your neck jump when ya lie to me. Yer avoiding me. Now, I give ya 'til the count of ten to tell me why."

Alicia

His cologne alone has my brain misfiring. Add to that his nearness and the sound of his voice rumbling over me, I can't find a thought, let alone complete one.

Why am I avoiding him?

It may have something to do with him trying to suck my soul out through my face. Two times in a row Quinn has kissed me senseless. I'm having a hard time figuring out how I feel about that.

I don't want to repeat the past. Having stars in my eyes

didn't help me one bit. I'm trying to slow this train down to make sure I see the scenery for what it is.

Tilting my head up, my gaze follows after him as he backs away from my ear. I suppress the shiver that tries to rock my body as best I can. Quinn already knows too well the effect he has on me. I'm not going to give him any more proof.

"You promised no more unwanted visits," I say.

"That's not an answer to my question," he tosses back.

I sigh, tugging my hand free from his hold and placing it on my hip. My fingers feel like a lighter has been waved back and forth over them. His touch has done all types of things to my insides.

I rub at my forehead with my free hand. I can't help but wonder if I have any more brain cells left in there. I was gone the moment I watched him storm into the front door with a niece on each hip. He hadn't noticed me in his rush, but I sure as heck noticed him.

I swear those jeans alone are going to have me committing myself this afternoon. That's the problem. I need to reclaim my sanity. I need distance to evaluate my disheveled and disorganized thoughts.

Maybe an actual list of pros and cons would help me because I'm failing at pulling it together. There is a difference between what I want and what I think I can have. Until I figure out that disconnect, I need to stay away from Quinn. When he's around, I only see what I want.

"I need space to think," I blurt out.

He watches me silently for a moment. That vulnerable window opens for a split second.

I don't know a better way to put this. It's what I think is best for now. Quinn nods. The shutters closing on all his emotions. I want to reach out and stop the retreat I see happening, but I'm not ready for that.

"I've waited this long to find ya—"

He cuts his own words off, nodding at his thoughts. His jaw works beneath his beard. My fingers inch to reach up and cup it.

My head is a mess. I don't think Quinn knows what he's trying to get himself into. It's not fair to him for me to start something new, knowing I'm carrying the baggage I have. I'm not a teenager, ready to jump from relationship to relationship without addressing the real issues.

I don't think it's right to lead him into my broken world. I'm only beginning to slowly unpack my issues. If I'm honest, I like him, but I need to do this for me first.

"I have a lot to figure out about me before I can step into a relationship," I try to explain.

"I hear ya giving me excuses. I don't hear ya giving me a chance. The best relationships happen when both parties are willing to grow together. But I'll respect what yer saying. Ya have a good day, love," he says, leaning in to kiss my cheek.

The spot his lips brush warms, sending a tingle across the side of my face. It's a fight not to reach up to cradle my cheek. Instead, I lace my fingers together in front of me.

Disappointment slams into me when he pulls back. I allow my shoulders to slump, and I frown. I try to school my expression quickly, dropping my head in hopes that Quinn doesn't catch the expression.

"Girls, let's go get yer poke," he calls out to his nieces who've taken over my desk.

"Yay, ice cream!" they squeal in unison.

Looking up, I see them making their way out. The girls are so tiny next to Quinn. His big hands swallow theirs.

"Can I have sparkles?" Molly asks.

"I want caramel and gummy bears," Kasey sings, looking up at her uncle like he's the greatest in the world.

"Aye, we'll get the whole shebang."

"Bye, Ms. Rhodes." Kasey turns to wave.

"See you later," Molly calls shyly over her shoulder as her little legs try to keep up with Quinn.

"See you later."

Waving back, I earn two huge grins. Bouncing at Quinn's sides with excitement, they return to talk of their ice cream. As his steps carry him over the threshold, something tugs inside me. Shoving the feeling down, I turn away as they disappear outside.

Tari stands with her arms folded across her chest, and Aidan is beside her with his hands on his hips. Both of them are glaring at me. I consider turning to leave out the front door as well.

"I'm not saying nothing," Tari says, shaking her head.

"I am. We all know you never come to work all cute and sassy like that," Aidan bites out, waving a hand at my outfit. "If you ask me, you were avoiding his calls knowing he'd show up."

"Glad I'm not the only one seeing the truth around here," Tari says.

"Nope, I'm seeing it loud and clear. I don't understand you, sweets. You cling to the trash but push away the good one. I mean, come on. Look at all that." He waves his arms wildly in the direction Quinn just left in.

"Yeah, my ovaries are waving. He ran in here with them

babies to handle business like a G. That's plain sexy." Tari fans her face.

"Mind you, he's their uncle not their daddy. I'm just saying," Aidan adds, giving me a pointed look.

"Don't you two have work to do?"

"Yeah, we do. On you," Aidan replies. "Come sit in my office and tell me again what the problem is."

"You don't have an office," I mutter.

"You know what I'm talking about. Come sit your ass down."

I blow out a breath and stomp my way to my desk. This is going to be a long hour. I can't wait for the next defensive driving class to start.

CHAPTER 12

UNCLE TIME

Quinn

"Uncle Quinn, Uncle Quinn," Molly calls as she comes running down the stairs.

I groan. I just sat on the couch to put my feet up. Why did I think that would last?

"For the love of God," I mutter under my breath.

"Uncle Quinn," she continues to holler as she stomps to a stop in front of me.

I'm fond of this beach house for its peace and tranquility. These wee ones have done nothing but argue since we got into the car to make our way here. The four of them are out to drive me insane.

"What is it now?"

"I wasn't finished my bath. Mckenna emptied my water," she says as she stands before me, shivering in a towel.

"She emptied the water while ya were still in the bath?" I ask, rubbing my chin.

That doesn't sound like her older sister. Maybe Con, but not Mckenna. I don't know what's gotten into them tonight.

After a day on the beach, you would think they would all be too knackered to terrorize each other. I thought the sun and water would make this evening smooth sailing. Again, I deem Erin a saint.

"No," she whispers and turns red. "I had to poop. I got out to use the toilet."

I purse my lips, trying not to laugh. I drew her bath in the master bathroom, the only tub in the house. The toilet has its own door. Mckenna probably didn't realize she was still in the bathroom.

"Come, love. We'll get you into a shower and your PJs," I say.

"Fine," she mumbles.

An hour later, I'm still on the verge of tearing my hair out as Molly and Kasey argue about which bedtime story they want me to download to my phone. I have to bark at Conroy to turn his music down in his room, and I can't stop rolling my eyes at Mckenna. She has her nose buried in her phone as she sends text messages while squealing and giggling.

"Night, Uncle Quinn." Kasey yawns sleepily as I kiss her forehead.

Molly is already snoring. The two fight like cats and dogs, but refused to sleep apart. Kasey is a brave one, she is. Molly sounds like a baby buzz saw.

"Night, love," I murmur.

My phone rings as soon as I walk out of the room. I reach into my pocket to pull it out quickly. My anticipation dies when I see it's Ma and not Alicia. I haven't heard from Alicia since walking out of her office, but a man can hope.

"Hey, Ma. What about ye?"

"Hey, love. I'm hanging in there, I am. How are ya holding up?"

"I'm breathing. They haven't killed me in my sleep," I say.

"Ach, they're not that bad. They adore ya, they do."

"Aye and I them. How is she? Has she settled in okay?" I say softly. I wish I could be there with my sister.

We all thought it best to allow Erin to settle in before the kids overwhelmed her. It's understandable that the wee ones miss her and will want to cling to her more. Hopefully, Erin will be adjusted some by the time I take her clan back.

"She's been crying a bit. She misses the chisellers and her husband. It's a lot for her to deal with, but she's strong. I think she'll be fine when the babes are here," Ma says.

"Is there anything I can do?"

"Yer doing it," she says. "Ya make me proud, Quinn. How's your lass?"

I roll my eyes. I should've know that was coming. I've been trying to keep my mind off Alicia. Not that I'm having much success.

"I don't have a lass," I say.

"Aye, so we're back to this. Ya never used to lie to yer mum. I'll leave ya be for now. Kiss the grands for me."

"I will. Love ya."

"Love ya too, Quinn."

Alicia

"You're missing him?" Tari says as she sits on the side of my bed.

I look down at my *Guns Digest* and *Guns and Ammo* magazines and smile. Yeah, she's right. I'm missing my dad.

Cars and guns, that was our thing. I know my way around a range as well as I know my way around a racetrack and under the hood of a car.

I nod. "Yeah, I guess I am. Is it weird that I still cling to this type of stuff? You know, the car races, these magazines, and everything."

"Not at all. You love all of it as much as he did. I used to think you were so badass. I used to be so jealous. I wanted to be a part of that, but I got that it was your thing. Just because your dad is gone doesn't mean you shouldn't still enjoy whatever you want," she replies.

I gather the magazines, so used to having to hide them because Gio thought it was stupid and unladylike. I hold them to my chest as if they were my dad, embracing both the memories and my interests.

"I wish I could talk to him. You know?"

"I get it. You guys used to bond over this stuff. Maybe we can go to a range some time. I know it's not the same, but if you want…"

"I'll think about it."

"Cool, don't sweat it. It's an offer. How about we talk about what's really on your mind?" she says.

I should've known she wouldn't leave without prying. However, I'm tapped out on the war happening in my head. I would like my dad's advice on so much, but that doesn't mean I want to talk about it with anyone else.

"Let's not and say we did," I reply. "I'm thinking about going for a walk. You want to come?"

"Ugh," she groans. "Why can't we chill on the couch with wine or some tequila like normal people? I'm just saying."

I laugh and toss a pillow at her. Although, wine and

vegging out doesn't sound so bad. I look at my phone, wondering what Quinn is up to.

Aidan and Tari tore into me until I had to start teaching a class that afternoon Quinn dropped by the office. A lot of the things they said made sense, but that hasn't changed the fact that I think I need to finish addressing some of my internal battles first.

I sigh at myself. I need to leave that bad idea right where it came from. Wine and the couch it is.

Great idea to keep me from doing something stupid.

"I get to pick what we watch," I say as I put my magazines away and stand.

"I'm with that as long as it's not racing or horses. *Project Runway*, I can rock with you, but I only want to see the end of a race when they're in those suits looking cute and grimy with sweaty hair."

"Seriously?" I laugh.

She shrugs. "What? Facts. I'm not about that race life. I thought it was cool when you did it because you were a girl and shit. Oh, and you got me close to cute boys who could drive." She giggles.

I have so many fond memories from those days. Sometimes I wonder what my life would have been like if my mom hadn't gotten sick. I had big dreams of driving my own car on the NASCAR circuit.

Another time another life, Ali.

So true. It's not the same without my dad, but I still miss it. Something else to revisit. Maybe not professionally, but for fun.

"Let's go, you." I laugh. "There's a car auction on. I wanted to watch it."

"We need more wine," she groans.

"I just bought a case."

"I know," she says pointedly.

"Fine, we can watch *The Originals* and *Sabrina* on Netflix."

"Now, I truly believe you're my friend. I damn sure wasn't spending my Saturday night watching no freakin' auction."

"Whatever." I chuckle. "What happened to your date?"

"Oh, you mean dude who started sending dick pics before we even went out on a first date? I mean, he's one confident boy too," she says and rolls her eyes. "Yeah, I'll pass."

And just like that, I spend the rest of the night in tears of laughter.

CHAPTER 13

HEAT OVERLOAD

Quinn

A GROWL RUMBLES FROM MY CHEST AS MY HAND COMES down on my desk. It's never been this hard for me to put together the staff schedule. Squinting at the screen, I try to force myself to focus.

Get it together, Quinn.

Picking up the baoding balls on my desk, I work them in my right palm while muttering to myself. We have enough staff. I've been doing this for weeks now. It should be easy.

Clay is on vacation, and I need to cover for my brothers and myself again this week. Da has returned to the Golden Clover, but we've still been stepping in for Erin and Ma. Helping with the kids is a full-time job in itself. Not to mention, we are all still working feverishly to find out what the hell Cal got himself and our sister into.

Alicia's place was about ten miles out from the warehouse you checked out last night.

"Fuck me," I grumble, pulling a hand down my face.

I can't keep her off my mind. Every time I try to focus, her heart-shaped face pops in my head. Two weeks. I've given her two weeks.

That should be enough time, shouldn't it?

What I need is to list what I know about Alicia. That will help me get my thoughts in order. Then, I can figure out my next step. Placing the baoding balls back down, I pick up a pen and notepad and get my thoughts out.

"What's this?" Kevin asks, snatching the notepad from my desk and dancing out of my reach. "One. She says she needs space. Two. She was engaged a year ago. Three. Things went bad right before the wedding. Four. She's independent and self-aware. Five. Agreeing to give her space left her looking disappointed."

"Give me that," I growl.

"I've been waiting on the schedule all morning and this is what you've been up to?"

"This would be the time to mind yer own business."

"That's what I'm trying to do. I can't get out into the field until I finish up here. Which means, I need that schedule," he says. "Is this about the instructor?"

"Aye," I grumble, falling back in my seat and crossing my arms over my chest.

Moving back toward my desk, he tosses the pad down. I grab it, placing it in front of me. My focus is on my list and not him.

"This isn't like you. You're not getting things done, and everyone has been staying out of your way because you keep biting their heads off."

"Mm."

"Listen to you. You're like an angry bear. We have too much going on around here. You're the one who keeps this place together. You need to deal with this shit so you can focus."

I lift my eyes to look back at him, folding my arms again. He mirrors the gesture, standing over my desk. I frown when he doesn't look like he's going to leave me be.

"What do ya suggest I do, then?"

"Bridget," my brother calls, pulling a groan from my lips.

Bridget saunters over with a file in her hands. It's funny how my brothers call on her when they think I need reeling in. Grinding my teeth, I push a hand through my hair.

"What's up, boss?"

"Get Quinn out of here. He needs to deal with his shit so he can get back to work," Kevin grunts.

"And how is she supposed to help me?"

"I don't know. The same way she always does. I really don't give a fuck. Get focused, bro. I need you here and focused, so hurry the fuck up."

Bossy ass.

He storms off to his desk, leaving me glaring at his back. He's right that I need to get focused. I'm just annoyed by his unhelpful solution.

"Well, let's do this, big guy."

"Hm."

Alicia

"I'm ready to sweat some stress away," Cathy drawls beside me in her Southern accent.

She's one of the other ladies here at the yoga studio that I've become friends with. She's a Texas transplant. We clicked instantly. I love her larger-than-life personality.

"Tell me about it," I mumble.

I've been needing to destress more lately. With so much on my mind, I need to give myself a break. Time to just be, no thinking.

"Oh, honey. I'd kill to have a body like yours," she says.

"Well, at least one of us feels that way," I murmur.

One of my biggest battles has been accepting me for me. I don't think I'm unattractive, but I've taken some hard hits to my armor in the past. I promise if I hear the words—*pretty for a dark-skinned woman*—one more time, I'm going to lose it.

I also struggle with my body image. I've never been rail thin and I'm not Instagram thick either. I fall right down the middle, I guess. My breasts aren't small, but I wouldn't call them huge. My ass is what I call *just for me*. I can appreciate it. That's what counts.

However, my ex had a way of making me feel like I was beautiful one minute, while taking shots at me the next. I started to question myself, and then I started gaining weight, which only fueled his behavior more. I'm finally getting back to a point where I'm in love with every part of me.

Any parts I don't like, I'm working to get in line with my own vision for who I feel Alicia is. For the first time in a long time, I've learned to say screw everyone else's opinion. To *me*, my thighs and tummy need work. So I come to hot yoga three times a week to get the results *I* want.

"We're all our toughest critics. You've come a long way. I remember those chubby cheeks you had a year ago. You were adorable then and just as beautiful now," she says with a smile.

"Thanks, Cathy."

Her words are warming. For me, this is a part of the process I need to get myself together. I'm doing what feels right to me. The way I'm handling Quinn is the same, and it's starting to feel like I'm doing the right thing. I'm taking my time.

"Sweet baby Jesus. Holy cow. Who is that?" Cathy gasps.

I'm smiling from ear to ear when I turn to see who the newcomer is who has her drooling. My smile falls when I find Quinn and a tall woman at his side. She's all legs, with her perky breasts and big smile. Her brown skin is flawless.

I shouldn't feel the jealousy that rises from the pit of my stomach, but it's there. She leans into Quinn to say something, causing him to give a little grin. I've never wanted to hurt someone so much in my life. I didn't even fight my so-called best friend after the drama she caused, but I'm ready to fly across the room and beat the snot out of this woman for talking to my man.

What the hell? My man? I've lost it!

"I have never wanted to be a bead of sweat so badly in my life," Cathy says beside me.

I know what she means. I follow a single bead of sweat down the bridge of his nose. It hangs from the tip, clinging to his face as if even his sweat can't stand to let go of him. I think the temperature in the room rises even more when he turns his head in my direction.

His gaze locks on mine instantly. His stare feels like fingers beckoning me to him. When I don't budge, he starts across the room toward me.

"He's coming this way. Do you know him? He looks like he wants to eat you alive," Cathy whispers.

"I-I know him," I stammer out.

"Oh, honey. I officially bow down to you. I thought the barista that drools over you was a hottie. This one is a god," she says and whistles.

I don't have time to process what she's talking about. Quinn closes the distance, hovering over me while maintaining eye contact. I tilt my head back.

"Hello, love. It's good to see ya," he says smoothly.

"You sure did move on quickly," I say saltily.

He jerks his head back and those greens widen. I throw daggers at him with my eyes. His little friend walks up, pulling my icy glare in her direction.

His hand lands right above my backside, turning us both to face the smiling Amazon. She's prettier up close, her hair is pulled up into a neat naturally curly ponytail. I have a mind to punch her and step on Quinn's foot.

"Bridget, this is Alicia. Alicia, this is Bridget. Bridget works for the firm. She's one of our female security specialists," Quinn says.

"Nice to meet you. Girl, you've had the boss tied up in knots over you." She laughs.

"Shut yer gub," Quinn growls.

"That accent, phew," Cathy says. "Hi, I'm Alicia's friend Cathy. You can call me Cat."

"Nice to meet you," Bridget replies, taking the hand Cathy offers to Quinn. "You know, we should find a few spots. I think the boss wants to talk to your friend."

"Yer jealous," Quinn says next to my ear, making me jump.

"No," I say, twisting my lips.

"Aye, ya are," he says with humor in his voice. "Have ya been missing me?"

"What are you doing here?"

"I've been feeling a little stiff lately," he says, lifting his arms over his head to stretch. His T-shirt lifts, revealing his taut stomach, a tat, and a drool worthy *V*. Red hair trails from what seems to be the bottom of his tat down into his gym shorts. Thin shorts that have my eyes widening. "Thought I'd come get in a stretch. Work out the kinks."

"What?"

With the shake of my head, I tear my eyes from his lower body. His words reach my ears, but I'm not too sure I understood a single one. Quinn's body is the type women dream about or stare at in photos. I'd lick my phone if I had a pic of him on it.

Eat your heart out, Giovanni.

Quinn closes the space between us. I'm too dazed to take a step back. Lifting his big hand, he brushes my cheek.

"I haven't been able to stop thinking about ya. How have ya been, love?"

"Quinn—"

"It's a simple question. Tell me how ya been. A lot can happen in two weeks."

"I'm fine," I relent. "How have you been?"

"Ya may not want to admit that ya missed me, but I've been missing ya." His eyes search mine. "I'd like to take ya to dinner again…when yer ready."

"Okay."

The word slips out. His finger brushing back and forth on my cheek has me under his spell. My belly is filled with dancing butterflies. Those green eyes are only aiding his trance.

"Okay, yer ready, or okay, we can go when yer ready?"

"Welcome, everyone, we're going to get started," the yoga instructor calls out.

My wits come back to me, and I take a much-needed step back. Pushing a breath out, my eyes drop to the floor and remain glued there. It's for the best.

"Can I answer that after class?"

"Aye, take yer time."

His lips touch the top of my scarf-covered head, causing me to look up into his smiling face. His eyes seem to be searching for something again. A bead of sweat on his cheek catches my attention, making me groan.

I must look like a sweaty mess. I have to wonder if he was caressing my cheek or if he was trying to wipe the sweat from it. I turn and head for my mat that either Cathy or Bridget so conveniently placed beside the one waiting for Quinn.

Needing space to think and breathe, I grasp the edges of my yoga mat and towel, dragging them back. I only realize my mistake when Quinn steps onto his. He is now shirtless, back muscles on display. I have the perfect view of his tight ass and those thighs.

My concentration is as good as shot for the entire duration of class. It's hot as hell in here, always is. However, today it's like someone turned the temperature up to inferno.

I mean, come on. What man that big is this flexible? I don't know if those last few drops of moisture on my mat are sweat or drool.

Quinn shifts into downward dog and I collapse into child's pose. I tuck my face away, my head between my shoulder blades. That's it, I'm done. This isn't in the least fair to my sanity. I thought I'd at least get to giggle at him fumbling around.

"Damn it," I groan into my sweaty towel-covered mat.

The class continues as I have my pity party in my secure balled-up position. Thank God it will be over soon. I'll have to get in an extra class this week. This one doesn't count for much.

"Namaste," the yoga instructor calls, to my relief.

Others around me begin to leave the room, some stay to have a moment to themselves. I try to do the same, turning onto my back and stretching out my limbs.

Sensing his presence, I open my eyes. Quinn is standing over me, his eyes devouring me from head to toe. I'm a little disappointed he put his shirt back on. I wanted a full look at the piercings and the tat I noticed. I couldn't make it out without tripping over myself or getting caught staring.

I look down at my sweaty cleavage. My tank top is soaked. My nipples are pushing at the gray fabric.

I slide my eyes back closed. I don't even want to think about the sweat stains on my white-and-gray pants. I peek through one eye, but I don't catch him staring at said pants. Instead, I find him looking at my feet. I wiggle my toes and cross my thighs, causing his eyes to lift to mine.

He tilts his head to the side, gesturing for me to follow him out of the room. I nod, but I don't get up off the floor. I still need a moment. Quinn nods in understanding, turning to walk out with Bridget. A guy rushing out of the room nearly walks into the tall woman. Quinn places a protective hand on her back to move her out of the way.

It doesn't matter that she only works for him. The gesture has me popping up off my mat, rolling my things up, and rushing out of the room. I step out the sliding doors to find Quinn standing there with a towel in his hand, wiping sweat from his face and arms.

That body has made my brain mush. It's the exact reason I should hightail it out of here. Yet, when my eyes lift to his face, something within Quinn's stops me. It's that unexpected vulnerability I've seen there before.

Swallowing the lump in my throat, I lick my dry lips. My arms tighten around the mat and towel I have pressed to my chest. Shifting from one foot to the other, I push my words out before I chicken out and take off.

"I'm free this evening."

The smile that takes over his face is blinding. The beard framing his lips is that much more attractive as it highlights his gorgeous smile. His teeth aren't as perfect as they seem at first glance. Although, nice and white, his front right tooth sits a bit farther back than the left. It's endearing actually.

He reaches for my waist, pulling me closer to him. Cringing at my own funky, sweaty body, I try to escape. He only tightens his hold, keeping me close.

"When I have it my way, ya will know every sweaty part of me and I, *you*," he says. The way he says *you* without the accent drips over me like warm honey.

I stop wiggling in his hold, afraid I'll slip in the puddle of goo he has turned me into. The heat coming off of him is comforting, drawing me in. Not for the first time, it dawns on me that I'm like a moth to a flame with him.

Never before have I experienced this. Sure, Giovanni was attractive, but he never gave me this feeling of…pure electricity and not-so-restrained desire. Quinn also intrigues me; it's disturbing and alluring all at once.

Ignore how good his arms feel around you. Keep your wits, Alicia.

Quinn

She looks like a deer caught in headlights. I should let her be. She agreed to a date tonight, but I've been waiting for two weeks to feel her in my arms. I'm not ready to let her go so soon.

Kevin throwing me out of the office with Bridget trailing behind me like my damn babysitter was one of the best things he could have done. It was Bridget's idea for me to come here after I told her what has had me so unfocused. Being a childhood friend, Bridget has always had a way of talking me off the ledge.

"I'll pick ya up at seven."

"Uh, yeah, okay," Alicia says.

Something draws her attention. Turning to see what it is, I find Bridget and Alicia's friend Cathy standing off to the side engaged in an animated conversation. Leave it to Bridget to find a new friend.

Dipping my head, I kiss Alicia's soft, damp cheek. She turns her face back toward me, those big brown eyes dropping to my lips. I want to have my fill of that plump mouth of hers, but I resist.

I want to respect her need for space, but I'm also listening to my instincts. If not for that look in her eyes, I would have come here, set eyes on her, worked out, and left. Yet, that look was there the moment we locked gazes across the room. Her features revealed her desire for me, along with the clear jealousy.

"Ya did hear me say she's my employee?"

It's important to me that Alicia is secure in my feelings toward her. Shifting in my hold, she tugs the bundle in her arms closer. She drops her eyes to my chest as she bites the corner of her mouth. Reaching beneath her chin, I lift her gaze back to mine.

"Ya have been the only one on my mind since I met ya. I couldn't coordinate my staff today, because ya have done a number on me. Bridget has been a friend of the family since she was a wee lass. My brothers sic her on me when they can't reel me in. *Banphrionsa*, ya have nothing to worry about."

She narrows her eyes; a fire ignites in her glare. I like when her anger shows. She's stunning when those eyes become animated with emotion and her cute nostrils flare.

"Banph—what? What did you just call me?"

"Princess. *Mo banphrionsa.* My princess."

Her eyes soften, and her small body relaxes in my hold. A hint of a smile turns her lips up. No longer able to resist, I move my hand from her chin to the back of her neck. My lips are pressed to hers before she can protest.

She moans into my mouth, disrupting all my thoughts. I've been craving this for weeks. Yet, I force myself to break the connection.

"Seven o'clock."

"Oh, wait," she says breathlessly. "Can I meet you there?"

Pulling away, I stare at her in question. Her eyes are glazed over as she stares at my lips. She shakes her head as if to clear it.

"Tari…I promised to go with her to her poetry reading tonight. It totally slipped my mind. But it's only an hour," she says in explanation.

"I'll come with ya," I offer.

She releases a small laugh and smiles. "It's a woman's group. Ladies' night. I'll ride with her and she can drop me off after. We should be done in time."

"Aye, I'll text ya the address," I reply, kissing her forehead. "See ya then, love."

"See you then."

CHAPTER 14

RIGHT ON TIME

Alicia

"Okay, sexy. Off with you. Go have a great time." Tari pulls me in for a hug as we pull up to the restaurant.

She pries the wrap I wore over my dress to the poetry reading from my fingertips. I watch longingly as she tosses it into the back of the car. I'm nervous as it is. She just took my security blanket.

"Are you sure I should be here so early? Don't I look desperate?"

"No, you look punctual, which you are not and were not for your last date."

I laugh at the scowl she gives me, tugging her in for another hug. The hug is more to help me calm my nerves. Tari pulls away, grasping my shoulders.

"Go. Be great."

I look down at my dress then back up at her. She waves me off, kissing my cheek before I get out of the car. When I get out and she pulls off, I'm left staring at the entrance of the restaurant, wanting to turn and order an Uber.

"Be cool, Alicia," I mutter under my breath as I walk inside the restaurant.

My eyes swing around the waiting area. There's no

green-eyed giant waiting for me. He told me he'd be waiting here, probably thinking I'd be late.

This is another gorgeous restaurant. Quinn certainly knows how to pick them. Looking around again, I'm thoroughly impressed.

You can do this.

I can't stop fidgeting with the skintight, blue dress draping my body. I don't know why I let Aidan and Tari dress me for this date. It would be great if someone could please tell me if I've lost my mind. It's very likely that I have. Never in a million years would I have picked this bandage dress.

It was a gift from Tari for my birthday. She had such big hopes that I would wear it that night. Nope, wasn't happening, which is why I don't know how I'm standing here in it now.

I shift on my black, peep-toed, patent leather, four-inch heels. Looking down, I wiggle my toes. The silver nail polish on my hands and feet are the only thing I've picked out tonight.

A hand rests on the waist, causing me to jump. There's no hum or instant spark, so I immediately know it's not Quinn. However, the face I look into is the last one I expect to see. Giovanni stands before me with those dark eyes and that perfect smile. All the things that fooled me into thinking he was charming and flawless.

"You look amazing," he murmurs as he devours me with his eyes.

It's funny, I can honestly say that look makes my skin crawl. I once craved for him to look at me like that. Now, it would be amazing if he'd keep it moving and get his damn hand off of me while he's at it.

"Don't touch me," I snap, stepping away from him.

"Come on, babe. You can't avoid me forever," he says. "I've been calling. You won't answer."

"Uh, I would think that would give you a clue. Stop calling."

He chuckles, giving me a crooked smile. It's meant to be seductive, but it's falling way short. Kind of like Giovanni himself.

"We still have unfinished business. We need to sit down and have a chat."

"The hell we do," I seethe, folding my arms over my chest. "All we have ever had to say to each other has been said."

"I don't think we have. You called things off. I think I deserve more—"

"More what? Of my time to waste. We're not good together. At least, you're not good for me."

Hearing myself say the words out loud proves to be satisfying. I truly mean them and believe them. I can do better, and I damn sure deserve better. The realization is somewhat liberating. I mentally pat myself on the shoulder.

"Can we have a conversation about this?" he says tightly, reaching for my waist.

The hum I've grown to relish hits my back at that exact moment. Quinn's big hands land on my waist, tugging me into him protectively. I don't need to turn to know it's him. His cologne is my second clue to his presence.

"If ya want that hand, ya won't be placing it on her again," Quinn's voice rumbles through my back, raising goose bumps all over.

"Who are you?" Giovanni says through clenched teeth.

His face is contoured in anger as he watches the way I

sag into Quinn's warmth. Jealousy is radiating off him. The look is satisfying enough, but Quinn's next move takes it over the top.

"I can show ya better than I can tell ya."

I pinch my face in confusion a second before Quinn tips my head back and drops a toe-curling kiss onto my lips. I lift my hand and curl my fingers into the strands of hair at the back of his neck. He completely scrambles my thoughts.

Giovanni who?

"Hello, *mo banphrionsa*," he says against my lips.

"Hello."

The word comes out breathlessly. My cheeks are warm with embarrassment. Yet, those green eyes promise I have nothing to be embarrassed about as he looks back at me like the most desirable and precious woman on earth.

"Hey, Gio!"

Spearing my gaze back in Giovanni's direction, I find a curvy, video vixen-looking chick bouncing up to his side. He looks highly annoyed and pissed off. His eyes are narrowed on me as he ignores his date. She seems to be completely oblivious, linking her arms around his.

Gio plasters a fake smile on his face, turning his eyes to Quinn. He places an arm around the chick at his side. I scrunch my face up because I know he's going to say something nasty, in true Giovanni form.

"Didn't know my fiancée decided to move on. No wonder she's bursting out that dress. Trying to keep you interested, bro. Don't fall for it. It's not—"

"Ya might want to shut the fuck up now," Quinn seethes. "It's embarrassing enough ya lost yer fiancée. Be careful ya don't get battered in front of her too."

"Is that supposed to be a threat?"

"Ach, I don't make threats, lad. That would be a promise."

I cover my mouth as a laugh bubbles up. Giovanni stands there with his mouth open, flexing his jaw, a vein popping in his forehead. Truly, I don't know what I used to see in him.

"You two have a good night," I call over my shoulder as Quinn leads me away.

———————————

Quinn

"Thank you," Alicia says softly to the violist that I tipped to play for her.

I didn't know watching a woman listen to music could be so erotic. Alicia enjoys life with everything she is when she lets go. I've been mesmerized by her from the first note.

The glow on her cheeks, the way her lashes rest upon that glow. The soft shy smile playing on her gloss-covered lips. The serenity in her eyes when she lifts them to me. It's all a sensual seduction I don't think she intends, but she does it so well.

"Would you like her to play another?"

"No, thank you," she says through a bright smile.

Another enjoyable dinner with this woman. I appreciate her soft-spoken nature. It belies the fire I've caught a glimpse of every now and then.

We've managed to ignore the glares of her ex. In my book, he is irrelevant. Though I can't blame him for being jealous. Alicia has been turning heads all night.

She surely had my tongue hanging out of my mouth

the moment I laid eyes on her. The burning rage that ran through me when I saw her stepping out of that asshole's reach is the only thing that prolonged me devouring her lips on sight. I'd been running a little behind as I had to answer a call from one of my teams.

"How are your nieces? And Conroy, right?"

"Aye, Conroy." I frown internally at the mention of my nephew. He's testing his boundaries a bit too much. "They're all grand. Ya know the wee ones couldn't stop talking about ya. I didn't realize ya knew Erin so well."

She gives a wistful smile. Her fingertip glides around the rim of her glass. Her silver nail polish sparkles in the elegant lighting of the restaurant.

"We've been going to the same yoga classes for almost a year. The girls have come along a few times. The studio offers daycare," she replies.

"I'm in awe of how much she does in a day. It hasn't been as easy to step in for her as my brothers and I thought."

"I'm sure. How is she? I miss our walks to the smoothie shop."

"Getting there. She won't be running the house or joining ya at yoga anytime soon, but we're all hopeful."

"You're a very loving brother."

Sitting back in my seat, I shrug while I study her face. She looks good enough to eat this evening. That dress not only complements her gorgeous skin, it molds to her body the way I can't wait to. Her ex is an eejit. Only a fool would walk away from a woman so beautiful and intelligent.

"Ya don't speak much about yer family."

Her eyes soften, her head tilts to the side. Her face takes

on a sweetness and innocence. The expression tugs at my heart a wee bit.

"You really didn't read the background check."

"Ach, I'll never lie to ya, lass. I've told ya. I want to learn about ya from yer own lips. Not from a file," I reply.

She takes a deep breath. Her eyes take on a distant look. Her lips wobble a bit.

"My mother passed away from cancer when I was a teenager," she says. "I was seventeen. She and my father were so in love. It didn't take but a year before he had a heart attack on the very same day she passed away. They were both so young."

The pain on her face speaks volumes. Suddenly, I think I'm starting to understand Alicia a wee bit better. All the pieces are coming together. I'm able to place that pain I've seen in her eyes. My heart aches for her.

"Sorry for yer loss."

"Thank you."

"No siblings?"

"No, it's only me. I always wanted a big family, but they never had more children. My parents were too busy spoiling me." She chuckles. "Then there were my best friends. They were like my parents' other kids. They took Aidan, Tari, and…"

She trails off and frowns. The best friend that betrayed her. I read between the lines.

Her eyes turn hard, her full lips pinch, that fire rising again. This isn't a topic she likes. I remember the conversation from our first date and I get it. I'm just trying to figure out how the ex fits into all of that.

I study her for answers so I don't have to pry. As if

reading my mind, she speaks before I tick off my next question on my list.

"Go ahead and ask. It's killing you," she says on a sigh.

"I'd rather not. I have what he'll never get his hands on again."

"Is that right? Are you sure you have me?"

The seductive play of her words is new. The sassy hum in her voice has my cock twitching in my pants, proclaiming his approval. Leaning in, I reach to tuck a strand of hair behind her ear. She cuts her gaze away from me.

"Don't be shy now, love. Aye, ya belong to me. Yer welcome to tell the world I'm no longer available."

She takes a shuddered breath. Her breasts heave with the gesture. Her eyes penetrate mine when she turns them back on me.

"Did I ever have a chance to say no to you?"

"Of course, if ya truly wanted to. If that's what the universe wanted." Placing my hand over hers that's still tracing the rim of her wineglass, I lift it and lace our fingers together. "But I believe the universe is as keen on me making ya mine as I am. Ya feel that. Ya have to."

"Maybe," she says with a cheeky grin.

"*Maybe*," I parrot her word with a chuckle. "Aye, ya mean to take the piss out of me."

She gives a breathtaking laugh. Her head tipping back, lips parted. That soft voice filling the air is like music to my ears.

"I'm assuming that means I'm teasing you," she says through her laughter.

"Aye."

"It's funny. I've never picked up on so much of an accent from Erin."

"I'm the oldest. My parents weren't here long before I was born. I've taken to the Norn Iron speak more than the others," I reply.

"That makes sense."

"Alicia?"

I've been changing my plans for the night for the last twenty minutes. Alicia has a way of turning my lists on their heads. I've surprised myself with how willing and able I am to bend for her on the drop of a dime.

"Yes, Quinn."

"I want ya all to myself. Are ya ready to go?"

My thumb makes circles in the center of her palm. Her eyes fill with lust, surely mirroring my own. She lowers her eyes a bit as she peeks her tongue out to wet her plush lips.

Dinner was delicious, but I'm ready for a private dessert. We've been too far away from each other. The slight nod of her head is all I need. I signal our waiter.

"Yes, sir, what can I get you?"

"We'll take the chocolate cake to go," I reply. "Bring the check."

CHAPTER 15

A GOOD GUY

Alicia

WE PULL UP TO QUINN'S HOUSE AND AGAIN I'M impressed and intrigued. It stood out to me the first time I came to pick Mckenna up for a lesson from here. It's not like the other houses on the block. His home has more of a modern feel. It's different, but beautiful.

When thinking of Quinn, I would expect something simpler, maybe even smaller, being that he's single. It's the opposite of him, but not. Although the curb appeal is as organized as Quinn seems to be, the sleek design is a contrast to how I see him. For him I think of something more…rugged.

When he opens the door and guides me in before him, the inside of the house matches the exterior. Modern with clean lines and immaculate furnishings. The walls range from stark white to gray, while pops of cool and warm blues accent the room and complement the mahogany wood floors.

"You're so neat for a man," I say as I look around his open living room.

I don't normally go back to a guy's place, but Quinn makes me feel safe and protected. I've been having such a good time tonight. I want to drag it out as long as I can.

"I like to keep things organized in my life," he replies as he walks up behind me. "It helps."

Turning in his arms, I look up at him. He has removed his suit jacket and rolled the sleeves of his gray dress shirt up over his elbows. My hands rest on his bulging biceps all on their own.

It's a fight not to curl my fingers into the hard muscle. Not for the first time tonight, I find myself seized by those green eyes. I'm not able to stop myself from reaching up to brush a lock of hair off of his forehead. Quinn grasps my hand, turning his head to kiss the center of my palm.

"Helps with what?" I ask to distract myself from the tingle that starts in my hand and shoots to my belly.

Instead of answering the question, he crushes my lips with his. He brings my hand he kissed to the back of his neck before he wraps his arms securely around me. Inching my fingers up, I lock them into the silky strands at the back of his neck.

His tongue tastes of the bourbon sauce his steak was cooked in. The flavor explosion in my mouth has a moan bursting free from my lips. He groans, grasping my ass in his hands.

My belly flips. The feel of his large hands on me, the scent of his cologne filling my head, and the sounds of pleasure filling the air—has me lifting onto my toes as my free arm wraps around his neck. He deepens the kiss. I lock my fingers in the top of his hair tightly.

Maybe coming here wasn't such a good idea. I've become consumed by the warm feeling he continues to cause to bloom inside of me. Going on a date is one thing. Letting things go too far tonight is another.

I know what I need personally and mentally. However, when it comes to Quinn, I don't know how to follow through with Operation Revive Alicia. My thoughts have me withdrawing.

"Quinn," I pant against his lips, moving my arms to push at his chest.

"Aye, I know, I know. I've just been wanting to do that all night," he says.

Placing his forehead to mine, he exhales deeply. His hands return to rest on my waist. He gives us both a moment to compose ourselves.

Kissing my forehead, he grasps my hand, leading me over to the couch. The gray sofa looks plush and welcoming. In direct contrast to the leather one I had imagined he'd own. Again, I note that this is not the décor of a single man.

"Make yerself at home. I'll get silverware for the cake," he says, pecking my lips.

My eyes follow him as he moves for the kitchen. I tilt my head to the side as I admire his ass moving away from me. As if on cue, he looks over his shoulder, catching me in mid-ogle. I bite my lip as my cheeks heat. His eyes drop to his own backside, then lift to my face again. His lips kick up into a crooked grin.

I cover my face with my hands as I chuckle into my palms. Taking a seat, that feeling of security tightens around me, making my resolve thaw. Settling into the couch, I do my best to be in the moment.

He's proving to be a good guy. Relax and be you. You can trust him.

Trust. There's that word. As terrifying as it is for me, I feel I can use it with Quinn.

I take a cleansing breath. He reappears, placing bottles of water on the coffee table, next to the takeout bag of dessert. He holds out a fork and two spoons for me to choose. I take a spoon and his face lights up as if I've done the most wonderful thing in the world.

"What?"

"Yer all right by me, love. I never eat cake with a fork," he says, winking at me.

"Something we have in common."

"Aye, along with our love of chocolate."

It isn't lost on me that his eyes roll over me with his words. Shaking my head at him, I go to reach for the bag with the boxes of cake. He quickly blocks the way with his body, placing the rest of the silverware on the table.

"Allow me."

He takes the seat beside me, his hand swallows my ankle as he lifts it to remove my shoe. He places my leg in his lap as he reaches for the other to repeat the process. Shyly, I pull my legs out of his lap. Quinn gives me a small smile, but doesn't protest.

He takes my spoon and retrieves a box of cake from the bag. Curling my legs beneath me, I settle in as he opens the sweet treat. The aroma hits me as soon as the lid pops open. My mouth waters instantly.

"Thank you," I say before taking the spoonful of cake into my mouth.

My eyes close and a moan pours from my lips as the fresh taste of cocoa and caramel melt on my tongue. The cake is delicious. My eyes lift to find the heated look in Quinn's eyes.

Clearing my throat, I shift on my butt a little until my feet are completely beneath me. Without a word, he lifts the spoon to my mouth again. My lips wrap around the spoon, but this time I clean it slowly. Not breaking eye contact.

"Mm."

He grunts, but says nothing. Not that he has to. His eyes are doing a whole lot of talking for him. They've darkened a few shades to almost a hunter green. His eyes are hooded as those long lashes provide the smallest bit of a shade to his passionate gaze.

I lift my hand up to cover my mouth. "Who decorated for you?"

"What makes ya think someone did it for me?"

Stopping to think, my shoulders sag. That was a little assuming and stereotypical. He could very well have put this place together on his own.

"You did a very lovely job," I murmur.

"Aye, my mum and sister did grand. Didn't they?" He chuckles.

With a frown, I swat at his shoulder. I should've thought twice about that. My hand stings the moment it connects with his hard muscles. Tugging my hand back, I cradle it to my chest.

"You're not funny," I pout.

"Ach, I'm sorry, love. Let me see." He chuckles, taking my hand and bringing it to his lips.

I dig my toes into the soft cushion as the kiss tingles up my arm, making its way straight down to my belly. It's all I can do to keep from swooning. His alluring gaze isn't helping at all.

"I love how close you are with your family," I blurt out to distract myself.

"It's hard not to be. We own family businesses together.

We all live in about the same neighborhood. We're always together."

"Businesses?"

"Aye, the PI and security firm belongs to me and my brothers. Then there's the Golden Clover. My da opened a pub a few years after coming to America. After having the five of us, my parents expanded the place into a restaurant," he explains as he continues to feed me more cake.

I reach for one of the bottles of water and open it to wash down some of the addictive confection. Replacing the cap, I fidget with it as I watch him and absorb his words.

"How did you guys get into private investigating and security? I mean, that's a long way from the bar and grill industry," I muse aloud.

"The pub was like a second home. I think it reminded Da of Ireland. It's down the street from a police station. Cops were always around, they'd come to the place to kick back when they weren't on the job. My father became close with a few of the guys, which led us to moving in next door to his best friend's family home.

"As a wee lad, they were all heroes. I know for me, I wanted to be just like them. Protect and serve. Thomas, Da's best friend, and Dugan, my godfather, tried to warn us all off. I learned the hard way that the force isn't what I thought. I still love to protect and help people. For me, the firm is a better way to do it." He ends with a shrug.

"So, all your brothers were cops?" I ask around a mouthful of cake.

"No, I made detective before I left. As did Kevin. Trenton was a firefighter for a few years. Shane served as a marine.

Somehow we all found our way to the firm, using our skills to help others that way," he replies.

"That must be nice. Getting to work with your brothers all the time."

"Ya would think that. Ya haven't met them yet." He laughs.

Looking down into my lap, I don't comment. The thought of meeting his family isn't something I'm willing to ponder just yet. We fall into a comfortable silence as he feeds me the rest of the cake.

When it's all gone, he takes the empty carton to dispense of it. He returns to take the seat beside me, patting my thigh. I shift my butt off my legs, and he tugs them gently from beneath me into his lap.

Quinn starts to rub my feet and my head falls back. I melt right into the couch. My belly is full, I have a tiny buzz from the wine at the restaurant, and now this. The best foot rub I've ever had.

"Why are you single?" I groan.

"That good, aye."

"You have no idea," I moan.

"Do you still think ya need space?"

I release a lazy sigh. He has me cornered. At the moment, no I don't want space from him at all. I also think it's time I let him know this isn't about him. Not really. I open my eyes to see his face as I talk.

"Have you ever felt like you've taken a wrong turn somewhere?"

"Aye, I've been there."

"I've always excelled at things. My parents were so proud of me. After they both passed, I still made things happen,

but...I don't know. Not as...organized...planned out...
I...I lost direction."

"Ach, that's understandable, love. Ya lost two of the most
important people in your life," he says softly.

"I was only eighteen when Dad died. I guess after losing
them both, I just wanted someone to love and to be loved
by someone. I dated a few guys here and there. Then, I met
Gio. He was so nice to me in the beginning. We dated for a
while before he started to take digs at me.

"It started out subtle. 'Babe, you know you should try your
hair like this.' 'Alicia, you know I'm going to the gym. You
should come with.' Talking about it now, I don't know what
made me say yes when he proposed." I release a bitter laugh.

"Ya don't have to talk about this."

"No, it's the only way for me to explain. Anyway, I put up
with his shit because my best friend...the one who tried to
take everything from me. I mean...as little girls, we slept in
the same playpen while her mother watched me for my parents. My parents treated her like their own daughter. I...I
trusted her like a sister.

"She would side with Giovanni. They'd gang up on me
about my hair and weight and...I started to think something was truly wrong with me.

"I was so distracted with trying to be perfect in their
eyes, I didn't see what was going on right under my nose. I
was driving myself into the ground to plan the perfect wedding. Gio's mom loved me. They had such a big family. I did
everything I could to be accepted. To have a family..."

"Alicia—"

"Let me get this out," I whisper. "Please."

He inhales deeply. "Okay," he replies, still massaging my feet.

"I had Tari and Aidan, but they had their own mess. Tari's mother isn't the most maternal, and Aidan's parents sold their home and moved across the country as soon as he officially came out to them. We were all lost in some way at one point. They couldn't give me what I needed. I was so sure Gio and his huge family could."

I scoff. Some of the things I know were said behind my back, I can't believe I seriously thought of marrying into that family. I know I had to be living through a moment of insanity back then.

"At the time, that was what I wanted—a family, love, security. Until I watched my true security get snatched away from me. Having my home taken from me...it's like the lights came on. I realized I only had two people in my life I could trust—"

"Tari and Aidan," he says before I can.

"Yeah." I nod and swallow. "It dawned on me I couldn't trust my fiancé the way I needed to. I didn't want to marry a man who made me hate myself. I was never enough for him. Finding out my best friend tried to clean me out made me question everything and everyone.

"I spent days in shock. When I shook it off, I knew I didn't want Gio, and I didn't want the life I was allowing myself to live. That man swore up and down he loved me. For a split second he almost had me convinced not to break things off, but I kept hearing a voice in the back of my head screaming at me to run before he broke me completely."

I ball my fist against the tears. I will not shed another tear for the wedding and family that I never got to have. It's something I've promised myself. Not another single tear.

"Yer a strong woman, love," Quinn says.

"Ha! I blamed myself," I continue. "At first, I placed it all on me. I was so damaged from their verbal and mental abuse. I told myself that maybe I mistreated her somehow, for her to betray me. You know, I was a bad friend and didn't see she needed the money. I kept thinking that if I got the surgeries Gio wanted me to or worked out more... I...I'm still building myself back up."

I leave out that I had scheduled a few surgeries for after the wedding. The two had worn me down, and I was going to get my breasts done and a tummy tuck as some type of warped wedding gift to Giovanni. I still can't believe I was willing to go so far.

"How can I pick someone right for me if I don't know who I am? I don't want to go into something new if I'm not a whole woman. I need to fix who I am," I say.

"One, they were both pieces of shit. Two, yer stronger than ya know. Three, ya don't pick a man. He picks *you*. The right man always knows the one. When he finds her, he treats her like the precious treasure she is. He shows her that she's whole in every way.

"Some shitty people broke yer trust, love, but I'm here to earn it for myself. Give me a chance to show ya I'm a good man and that I'm worthy. Don't let them steal our future with their misuse of yer past," Quinn says.

I drop my eyes to my hands in my lap. I want to take the chance. I do. I'm just not able to say so. He moves to rub my other foot, and I close my eyes without a word. Actions speak louder than words, and Quinn's actions are doing a lot for him.

He pauses, causing me to open my eyes. He's leaning over for the remote on the table. I burst into laughter when he turns on the stereo and "Baby Shark" comes blaring through the speakers. I know the song from riding with Erin and the girls a couple of times.

Quinn grunts, rushing to turn the music down before he changes the song. I'm still laughing. This is the best feeling I've had in so long.

"Ride" by Twenty One Pilots comes on, and my tension melts away completely. It's the right song for the moment. I let my guard down a little more.

Quinn

"Yer gorgeous when ya laugh." The words spill free from my lips as I watch her.

"I love your taste in music," she teases.

"Aye, go on, take the piss out of me. Kasey figured out how to use this thing, and she's been driving us all nuts with that song. I had them last night. That song was stuck in my head until I passed out," I reply.

She erupts with more sweet laughter. Sliding closer, I cup her face. Then run my thumb across her bottom lip.

"Can I kiss ya, love?"

"Thanks for asking. Yes—" Her words cut off as I lean in to kiss her, but she places a finger to my lips before I can take hers. "You can kiss me if you promise to answer my questions."

"Aye, I intend to. I'm organizing how," I say before nipping her finger.

She pulls the digit back, giving me access to her mouth.

She tastes even better after eating that slice of cake. I place my hand on her waist and squeeze. I love that she has meat on her bones. The more cushion for her to handle a big lad like me.

I reluctantly break the kiss. I could spend the night lost in those lush lips, but she wants answers. I've dodged her questions twice. Not because I don't want to answer. I've been trying to list how best to unpack all that is me.

She has her own baggage. Now that I know what it is, not only do I wish I had put her ex on his ass, I understand her and I don't want to run her off.

"I don't date much because it's hard to find a woman willing to put up with me," I say.

"What does that mean?"

"I'm the oldest of five. We're all pretty close in age. My ma was always busy with us. I was a busybody. I got into everything. I couldn't sit my wee arse still.

"Da would tell me to be a big lad and help out. As an adult, I get that was his way of getting me to stay out of my mum's hair while she took care of the wee ones.

"It sort of backfired. I would make lists to help Ma keep things going smoothly around the house. She called me her little helper. That reinforced me making them. The older I got, the more the lists helped me focus and handle daily tasks. I kind of can't function without them. It drives my family insane," I explain.

I focus on her cute little toes as I wait for her to say something. I lift my head when she shifts. She climbs into my lap, cupping my jaw in her hands.

"So, you're sort of OCD?" she asks softly.

"Not sort of, love. I lose my ever-loving shit if things aren't organized and done in proper order. I have to make the lists. They keep me calm, focused, and…I don't know. I see things others don't. The last month has been full of adjustments for me. I'll admit that I've gotten better because I've been adapting to help my family through all this better than any of us thought I would."

"Well damn, a lot of things make sense now. I must drive you up a wall."

"A wee bit, but not as much as ya may think."

"I'm a hot mess. You sure you want to take me on?" she says, that shyness coming to the forefront.

She's worried about me wanting her. Hell, I was sure she'd run off as soon as she found out that I live my life by list after list. I cup the back of her neck and take her lips.

I don't hold back from devouring her completely this time. We both lock our fingers in each other's hair. My grasp is tight in the shorter strands as I hold her to me.

Nothing has gone as I planned tonight. I was late to the restaurant, I wanted to take her to a movie after, and this trip to my house was a complete deviation from my plan. Yet I couldn't care less. Alicia calms me in a way I've never felt. Changing my plans around her makes sense in my head.

"I want to taste ya, love."

"What?" she pants, her gaze glazed over.

I nip her chin and her head falls back. Her smooth neck is mine for the taking. Raining openmouthed kisses down her throat, I let my lips and tongue do the talking before I move back to her ear.

"I want to eat yer pussy."

"Quinn," she moans.

Gently, I tilt her body until her back meets the cushion of the couch. My eyes travel greedily over her as she lies beneath me. She's perfection. I wouldn't change a thing about her. I want to worship every inch of her gorgeous body.

Her breasts are heaving in the confines of her dress. She begins to squirm, drawing my attention back up to her eyes. So many emotions are playing there—nervousness, uncertainty, lust—are only a few I believe I pick up on.

Placing a hand on her belly to still her, I lean in for her lips again. Sensing her melting into the cushion, I start to trail kisses down her neck to her collarbone. I savor her, committing each point of contact to memory.

Moving lower, I dip my tongue between her full breasts. A deep groan vibrates from my chest. Turning my head, I suck her skin into my mouth. Her back bows and her fingers lace into my hair.

My hands glide to the hem of her dress, while I kiss my way down the center of her body. I push the dress up to her waist, revealing her lacy panties and sweet scent. I'm salivating for her. Bypassing the place I want most, I grasp her ankle as I raise to my knees. My lips explore her soft skin, moving toward her knee.

Our eyes lock, hers pleading for more. Her lips are slightly parted. She darts her tongue out to wet her lips, tightening my cock in the confines of my pants.

My tongue traces the crook of her knee, moving to glide down the back of her thigh. Nipping at her butt cheek, I kiss my way to her inner thigh. I'm punched in the gut by desire when I come face-to-face with her core.

Placing a kiss to the top of her mound, my lips open to cover her fabric-covered petals with my mouth. I growl when my phone rings before I can complete the task. This is enough to bring my grown arse to tears. In my line of work, we never ignore our phones.

Placing my forehead on the top of her mound, I reach for my phone in my pocket. Her scent is driving me mad as I bring the phone to my ear.

"What?" I snap, not having the patience to give a proper greeting.

"I think ya'll be wanting to talk to Moralez. She might know what Cal was up to. Yer going to want to hear this," Kevin replies.

"Fuck," I bite out. "Where are ya?"

Alicia runs her fingers through my hair, over my scalp, sending goose bumps rising. Reaching for her hand, I lock our fingers together. It's going to kill me to leave her tonight.

"My place," Kevin answers.

"I'll be there in thirty."

I hang up the phone, not moving. I need to lie here to compose myself. Another moment when her presence brings me calm.

"Work?"

"Aye, I'm sorry," I reply and lift my head. "I'll drop ya home."

"Okay, that might be best."

My jaw tightens. I want to address the comment, but I need to get to Kevin's to find out what Detective Moralez knows. I place Alicia's words and the look in her eyes on my list of things to tackle later.

We're not done, love. Ya won't be shutting that door on me again.

CHAPTER 16

REVEALING SECRETS

Quinn

I'M PISSED AS HELL. IT LOOKS LIKE CAL WAS WORKING a case to take down some dirty cops and drug lords. This is one big shitshow. Nothing is adding up.

"So, we now know what, but no one has a clue about who," I say to my brothers as we stand around Kevin's kitchen for breakfast.

I've been here all night. Detective Danita Moralez has an entire file on what Cal has been working on, but there are too many holes in the case. Cal was definitely holding things back from her.

"Exactly," Kevin bites out.

"He said he was about to have everything I needed to build the biggest case of my career. According to him, it was too dangerous for me to know all the details and players until he could put the final pieces together," Detective Moralez says. "He did say he would have them dead to rights when he did hand it all over."

The room is filled with tension. None of us are impressed with what we've learned. I, for one, want to wake Cal's ass up so I can put him back to sleep. We should have him transferred back to the hospital to see who comes for him.

"He can't let go of his hard-on for the force," Trent says through clenched teeth.

"It was his dream all his life to be a cop. I'm not saying this shit is smart but I understand his motives," Shane says.

"Cal was a good cop. What happened to him was wrong," Moralez says.

"So, is that why you agreed to help him? How do we know we can trust you?" Trent says with narrow eyes.

"Back off," Kevin warns.

"Which head are ya thinking with? She could be selling ya the eyes out of yer head. Ya won't bring the devil to our door for a pair of fucking kex." In his anger, Trenton speaks as quickly as our da and with as much of an accent.

Kevin stands from his stool, staring down our younger brother on the other side of the counter. I shake my head at the two. We need answers, not to turn against each other.

"Ya want to be in fucking tatters, ya talk to me like that again," Kevin growls. "I told ya that I trust her. That's enough. Stop acting a maggot."

Trenton narrows his gaze back at Kevin, but he doesn't say another word. He works his jaw as he stands with his arms folded over his chest. It's the same look he gets any time Kevin or I have to cut him down a notch or two.

However, I'll admit I was thinking the same thing as Trenton when I first arrived last night. It took a few hours of observing her to fully place my trust in her. That and a thorough check into her background.

"You're thinking that Con knows something?" I ask, changing the subject.

"I think he does," she replies. "Cal had the kid with him

once while he was working the case. I was pissed at him for taking him along and then bringing the kid to the meet with me. It was sloppy."

"What the fuck?" Trenton grunts.

"He said it was complicated and he had everything under control. I don't know…the kid seemed…I can't put my finger on it. I could only see him through the windshield."

"Was Cal's ass using?" Trent asks.

"No," Shane says. "You know him better than that. I think Con had been challenging him as much as he's been challenging us."

"Still doesn't explain why he would take the lad with him," I say, rubbing my temples.

Drawing a hand down my beard, I try to figure out our next step. We still need to get into Cal's computer. It's taking way too long to crack it. Shane is one of the best, which makes this more frustrating.

"We can't trust anyone," Kevin says.

"We should continue with our everyday lives as if nothing else is happening," Detective Moralez says.

"No one else knows you were working with Cal on this?" Trenton asks.

"Not that I know of. I'm sure I would have been on the other end of a bullet weeks ago if they did."

"Hmph," Trenton mutters.

"Let's see if Con will talk. Meanwhile, we'll take what we know from this file and see if we can track where Cal had been going," I say to my brothers.

"Got it," Shane replies.

"I don't like leaving her out there with no protection," Kevin says, drawing my attention.

"You don't have a choice. I'm a detective. I have a job to do. I can take care of myself," Moralez says.

"We can have one of the girls integrate herself into her life," Shane offers.

"Ach, no, we can't. Bridget and Q have left for the baseball player's detail. Willow and Jazz are both on cases they need to stay on," I reply. "That leaves Autumn, and I don't think she's ready for something like this."

"I thought we were sending that guy a male crew," Shane says in confusion.

"Aye, Knox's sister-slash-assistant was the original point of contact. I'd told her I was sending two of our guys. Knox reached out with the new request a few weeks ago," I reply.

Trent narrows his eyes. "What's that about?"

"Ach, long story, but his reasoning seemed solid. Only reason I agreed."

"Well, we can pull one of the guys, can't we?" Shane says.

"Hello, I'm still here. I said I'll be fine. I'm a big girl. I've been doing fine this long," Moralez insists.

"I'll do it."

We all turn to look at Kevin. I lift a brow. He shrugs it off, looking Detective Moralez in the eyes as he speaks again.

"We can make it look like we're dating. You said you've been steering clear of Cal's case. If no one knows you were working with Cal, it'll work," Kevin says.

"No," Moralez snaps.

"Are you sure that will work?" Shane asks. "You don't think that will draw suspicion?"

"No, I don't think it will at all. The good detective and I have history. We had an interesting reacquaintance at the precinct. I think it will work in our favor," Kevin says with a grin.

"I think it's a grand idea," Trenton says slyly.

I glare at Trenton. He's goading Kevin, not the best idea. I ignore my brothers as they glare at each other.

"It would make us feel better, lass. If this is as big as I think, it's not just going away. I like to dot my i's and cross my t's," I say.

"I don't need a babysitter," she snaps.

"Good, because I'll be your boyfriend," Kevin replies, moving closer to her.

"Argh, un-fucking-believable," Moralez says, placing her hands on her hips.

"Such a dirty mouth, love. You plan on kissing my brother with that?" Trenton teases.

"Shut yer bake," Kevin grunts. "Not going to say it again."

Trenton throws his hands up, with mirth dancing in his eyes. I'm glad he can hold onto his humor. I'm too pissed to be amused.

I don't feel nearly as close to closing this case as I want to be. We just have more questions. I don't like this sitting-duck feeling.

Needing a break from all this, I pull my phone from my pocket and try Alicia for the second time. Walking into the living room, I rub my temple. The call rolls to voicemail like last time, causing more tension in my shoulders.

She's avoiding me again. I have a list of things to handle before I can get to her, but I'll get to her. Now that I know what's going on in her head, it'll take a lot more than her ignoring my calls to get rid of me.

Alicia

"What in the ham sandwich is wrong with you?" Aidan asks as I drop another stack of driver's manuals.

I've been a mess all day. I can't stop thinking about last night. I've never had a man look at me the way Quinn does. Scratch that. I've never had a man touch me the way Quinn did.

"I think it's Quinn," Tari says like a know-it-all.

I've felt her gaze on me all day. I knew it was only a matter of time before she started in on me. Aidan has been busy all morning with lessons. I knew once he settled into the office, he'd zero in on my mood as well.

"Nothing is wrong with me," I say in exasperation.

"*Sure,*" Aidan drags out.

"I'm fine."

I bend to collect the manuals from the floor. Aidan comes over to help me. He looks in my eyes, narrowing his gaze on me. I try to lock my feelings down before he can get a read, but totally fail.

"Girl, please. Every time I've checked in, you've been dropping things all over the place and you jump out of your skin whenever your phone rings," he says.

"I thought it was just me," Tari says. "She has been jumpy."

Tari walks to get the other stack of books I still need to move into the front of the shop. It's funny, she wants to help now. I've asked her a hundred times to do this for me. Tari is great with lessons, organizing the schedule, and answering the phones. Yet, if I need something moved or set up around here, she suddenly becomes so busy. It's the one thing that drives me crazy about her. I purse my lips at Tari as Aidan and I continue picking up the books I dropped.

"Don't you guys have work to do? Why are you always watching me?"

"Don't go snapping at us because you're all disjointed and conflicted," Tari sasses, cutting her eyes at me as she walks by.

"I'm not disjointed. I have a lot on my mind."

"That is a lot of man," Aidan says.

"Sure is." Tari giggles.

"Whatever," I say to the both of them.

Getting to my feet, I carry the books to their final destination. A customer walks in needing a notary, which gets Tari out of my hair for a few minutes. Walking to the back classroom, my focus turns to getting the place set up for the next class. I have a defensive driving course this evening.

I let a groan drag from my lips when Aidan enters the room behind me. I should've known I wouldn't get rid of him so easily. Tari will be in here as soon as she's done, I'm sure.

"So, what happened last night? I wasn't expecting you back home so early," he prods.

"We went to dinner. It was nice."

Feeling his eyes burning into me, I turn to see Aidan with his arms folded over his chest as he glares at me. I shrug, mirroring his stance. He throws his head back and his hands in the air.

"I can't with you. I know that date wasn't that damn boring," he says in exasperation.

"Once we got to our table, it really wasn't that eventful."

"Huh? What happened before you got to your table?"

"Giovanni."

I watch as anger clouds Aidan's face. His hands go to his hips and his shoulders stiffen. He looks like an angry supermodel.

"What the hell?"

"I guess he was on a date. Never took me any place that nice when we were dating. Anywho, he was a complete ass and Quinn shut him down," I say with a little grin.

"Oh, my God. I would give my left kidney to have been a fly on the wall," Aidan replies, his eyes lighting up. "Please tell me he at least choked him up or something."

"Nope, he didn't touch him, but I know Giovanni felt his words. And I quote, 'Ya might want to shut the fuck up now.' 'Be careful ya don't get battered in front of her too.'" I snicker.

"Oh, you almost have that sexy accent down." Aidan chuckles. "I would have loved to see the look on Gio's trifling face."

I wave him off. I haven't told him the best part of that encounter—the look on Giovanni's face after Quinn kissed me was the most satisfying reaction of all. I smile just thinking about it.

"So, you guys had to go somewhere else after dinner or something. You were home early, but not that early," he continues to pry.

"We may have gone to his place for a little while."

"See, I knew it. Come on, spill, heifer. Is that why your hair looked a little tousled when you walked in the house? Tell me you let that man take you to the land of the gods that birthed him and back," he nearly croons.

I shake my head and laugh. I don't know what to do with this man. I love him dearly, but he's insane.

"You know you're a nut, don't you?"

"My mother may or may not have dropped me on my head a few times. Then again, she's not the brightest bulb in the shed so I never stood a chance," he says, shrugging it off.

"No, I did *not* sleep with him."

"Oh, hell no. That's a lie," he squeals, clapping his hands together. "You totally just blushed, which I love. The way your cute little brown cheeks glow. Ugh, he made you blush before your first date. I thought I was going to die, it was so adorable."

"Whatever." I roll my eyes.

"What did I miss?" Tari asks as she rushes into the room.

Turning away from them, I get back to setting up. Leave it to these two and I'll be here gossiping for the rest of the afternoon. I still have some work to do at my desk before this evening.

"I'm not sure. I don't think she slept with him, but he got somewhere near those panties," Aidan says.

"You let him hit it?" Tari gasps. "Damn, I totally had my money on you making him wait at least two months."

I whirl on them, pamphlets clenched tightly in my hands. My mouth is hanging open. These two are always betting on something.

"I know you two haven't started a bet on my damn sex life. I'm going to choke you both," I snap.

"Well, did you or didn't you?" Tari asks.

"None. Of. Your. Damn. Business."

They both laugh at me and high-five each other. I can't with them. My thoughts are too all over the place to deal with their antics today. They are pushing all my buttons.

"Something happened," they say in unison.

"Go. To. Work," I demand.

"Yes, boss," Aidan mocks.

My phone rings, causing me to jump. The two of them start to laugh more. I shoo them out of the room to go to work. Blowing out a long breath, I dig the phone from my pocket. I don't recognize the number but I take the call anyway.

"Hello," I answer.

"Hey there, beautiful."

I pull the phone from my ear. I have to be hearing things. I know Giovanni can't be on my line. Once Quinn threatened him last night, I was sure he'd go crawl back under a rock.

"I block you so you call me from another number? What don't you get? I'm done. It's over. Stop calling me," I snarl.

"Someone gives your fat ass a little attention and now you're all mouth," he says.

"Wow," I say as I jerk my head back. "I guess you're saying what you always really wanted to say. Why don't you kiss my fat ass?"

I hang up the phone and force myself not to throw it across the room. He's such an asshole. I don't know what I ever saw in him.

CHAPTER 17

WITH CERTAINTY

Alicia

MY FEET ARE KILLING ME. THIS TURNED INTO THE longest day ever. Aidan and Tari have already gone home. Class ended about thirty minutes ago, but I need to get some more work done before I can call it a night.

I also need some time to myself. Which is why "I Can't Make You Love Me" by Tank is playing in the background. It's the perfect tune for the way I feel right now. Giovanni's call is still burning in my mind. I can't believe I was so wrong about him.

My mother taught me better. As a young girl she warned me about guys like Gio. The ones who sing you songs of pretty things and forever, pretending to be a king when in fact he's nothing more than a court jester.

Dropping the cash I've been counting on the counter, I place my palms on the cool wood and dip my head between my shoulders. It stings that I once thought I was in love with that man. In all honesty, I think I was more in love with love than Giovanni.

"Oh, Mommy. What was I thinking?" I murmur out loud.

Pushing off the counter, I turn to walk over to the large

mirror Aidan insisted we put up by the front desk. He said it's for us to be able to have a view of the front when we're at our desks or in the back. I think it's more for him to check his golden cuff when a hot customer comes in.

In this moment, I use it to take a look at myself. Something most people take for granted in the mornings. At least, I do. I never truly look at myself beyond making sure I've done the basics. I never take the time to *look* at the woman in the mirror.

Not like I am now. Now, the sadness in my own eyes is clear. I can see the gaping hole in my own soul. The one left behind by loss and hurtful words.

I take stock of the entire woman I'm looking at. To me, the woman in the mirror isn't fat at all. My blue button-down blouse complements my figure and my complexion. Giovanni never implied I should bleach my skin, but that other monster had a number of times. She always tried to make me feel bad about my darker skin.

"Remember who you are," I say to my reflection.

I love the brown face looking back at me. Blowing out a breath, I push my hand through the front of my bob, remembering the long waves I used to wear because it pleased *my man*. I chopped it all off the week after I left him.

As if divinely chosen, "Beautiful" by Christina Aguilera comes on. My head tilts to the side. Reaching out, I trace my face in the mirror with my fingertips.

Overcome with emotion, I wrap my middle and hug myself tightly. I take the words to heart. I am beautiful. On the inside and out.

"You're beautiful, Alicia," I whisper to myself.

It's been hard, but I've worked to build the life I have. I

own this place, I own my car, and by grace, I still own at least one of my homes. I give back to my community. My heart shines through who I am, but that's just a part of me.

My brown eyes, glowing brown skin, and the natural curves that belong to me are all a part of who I am. I own them. They're mine. They're what I was given and I love them. I love me.

"I love me. I am beautiful," I yell this time, throwing my arms out at my sides. "I love me!"

I rock from side to side, closing my eyes. For the first time in a long time, the truth of the words sinks in. They resonate in my heart.

"I am beautiful. I love me," I nearly sob.

"Aye, love. Ya are and ya should," comes from behind me.

I jump, turning to find Quinn on the other side of the counter near the door, watching me cautiously.

"Hey," I say softly, swiping at my tears.

"Hey, love."

Which leads me to him.

He's called a few times today. I wasn't ready to talk to him. I'll be honest. The man has me hooked. I want to think he accepts me for me, but what if he can't. Like, really can't.

I wasn't joking when I said I'm a mess. If he truly needs everything in his life to be in order, we'll never work. It's like we're doomed before we've even gotten started.

And that's a reality I'm not ready to face.

I want to hold onto the hope he has given me. I should've known I wouldn't be able to avoid him for long before he'd show up. However, as I look into those eyes, I feel like he's exactly the person I need here with me.

"Ya shouldn't be in here by yerself with the door open this time of night," he says as he rounds the counter to me.

I look to the door. I meant to pull the outer gate and lock the front door after everyone left, but I got distracted. I can see Quinn has pulled the gate down and the lock is turned.

I truly was in my own world. The music is up pretty loud as well. That's so unlike me. I frown at myself, turning back to Quinn.

"How do you know I'm here by myself?"

"I watched Tari and Aidan leave twenty minutes ago."

"So you're stalking me?"

"Ach, ya don't know much about being in a relationship, do ya? Coming to see ya home is not stalking. I would have been in sooner, but I was finishing a call."

"I didn't know I was in a relationship."

"Ya seem to be a wee bit slow when it comes to that," he replies, dipping to lift me off my feet and onto his waist.

"Quinn," I yelp.

"Aye, Alicia. That is my name," he teases, walking over to the countertop. "I happen to love hearing it on yer lips, by the way."

Depositing me gently onto the counter, he wedges himself between my thighs. I tilt my head back to look up at him. I close my eyes when his hand traces from my temple to my jawline.

"Don't know how ya could ever question this beauty. Ya took my breath away the first time I saw ya. Ya radiate light, love. It's what draws me to ya," he says.

"When you have people drilling into your head how you're not so perfect, you can start to question yourself," I whisper back.

"Name a part of ya that's not perfect."

I open my eyes to look at him. I'm not sure I want him to see me bare. It's one thing to have doubts about myself in my head. To reveal those out loud is another. I don't think I can.

"I don't know," I say. Still not ready to answer with my true feelings.

"Aye, ya do. Tell me yer lies, so I can trade ya for truth," he replies.

"I could stand to lose my belly and thighs," I say hesitantly.

"Ach, I wouldn't have it," he says, placing his hands on my thighs and giving a gentle squeeze. "I love watching the sway of yer hips and the way yer thighs kiss each other. It makes me want to have them cradling me in their warmth. And I don't know what belly yer talking about."

"You'll tell me anything. You want to get in my pants."

"I've told ya before, and I'll tell ya again. I'll never tell ya lies. I want more than to get into ya kex. I want in here." He points to my heart then my head. "And in here."

I search his face before turning within.

What if Quinn is for me? The chemistry is there. Don't I owe it to myself to explore that? Loving myself means knowing what's the right thing to do for me.

"Tell me something," he says to my silence. I nod for him to continue. "Now that ya know ya love yerself, will ya let me show ya how a man is supposed to worship ya?"

"Are you sure you want to do this with me? I'll only complicate your world," I reply.

"Love, ya complicate my head enough already. I can't breathe without thinking about ya. What I know with certainty is that I want ya. I want everything about ya. I belong to ya. If ya'll have me, I'm offering all of me. In return, I want ya, all of ya," he says with a sincerity I feel in my bones.

I throw caution to the wind, ignoring all the excuses that try to pop into my head. *Trust*. That's what I need to learn to have again. I think Quinn is a safe place to start that recovery.

I swear this playlist is possessed, it's cranking the songs out in perfect sync. Beyoncé's "1+1" starts to fill the air. My teeth sink into my top lip, my eyes water as I roll them half-closed. When I look up at him, I nod, relinquishing myself to his pursuit.

He plants his palms on the countertop on either side of me, dipping to peck my lips tenderly. It's almost as if I'm a wounded bird he's trying to be cautious with. I melt when he kisses the tip of my nose, before returning to my lips.

My eyelids are next, then he brushes my lips again. I appreciate him taking his time with me. I allow myself a cleansing breath.

When he kisses my forehead, he places his hand into the back of my hair before he captures my lips and consumes my mouth. Reaching my arms around his neck, I hold him tightly, needing to feel his warmth and that sense of protection.

He deepens the kiss, engulfing me in his big arms. I open up to him, silencing the voice in the back of my head that tries to tell me I'll never be whole enough to love. Quinn's kisses say otherwise, and I get the feeling he aims for them to.

I whimper when he breaks the kiss. He makes enough room between us to take his T-shirt off, placing it on the counter beside us. My mouth falls open. I couldn't get a clear view in yoga class with all the sweat and distance.

Now, it's all right before my eyes. He has a crest tatted across his chest, with a dragon coiled around the outside of it. It's so realistic and intricate. In the center of the crest, in a smaller crest, are the initials Q.B.

The piercings I noticed that night in the rain, actually pierce through the faces of two lions. The balls of the piercings are positioned to look like the lions' eyes. The artwork is almost as impressive as the body it's on.

Reaching out to touch the detailed ink, I think better of it and pull my hand back. Quinn grasps my wrist, placing my palm on his warm skin. I look up at him, but he's watching my fingers on his torso as I touch him tentatively. Lifting my other hand, I push his hair from his face, bringing his attention to mine.

That intense gaze pins me to the spot. He lifts his hands to the buttons of my shirt, pausing as if to ask for permission. I give a slight nod, and he begins to release the tiny fastenings one by one. My heart is pounding in my ears.

When my shirt is open and the blue lacy bra is revealed, I have to fight not to shrink into myself. Quinn's large palm reaches into the fabric, gliding up my side. He stops beneath my breast, running his thumb back and forth over the underside of my mound.

He repeats the motion back and forth, inching higher with each pass. I don't realize I'm holding my breath until his thumb runs across my tightened nipple. Air whooshes through my parted lips. This is slow torture. His hand on me, the look on his face—anticipation is building within my core, threatening to split me in two.

He shifts to push the fabric from my shoulders, his fingertips floating across my skin. I help him to get the shirt off before he tosses it on top of his. With shaking hands, I cup his face, drawing him closer. His beard feels so soft under my touch.

Our lips meet and he takes full control of the kiss. He unclasps my bra, allowing my breasts to bounce free. Carefully, he peels the straps down until I release his face so he can remove and discard the garment.

"Yer gorgeous," he says, testing the weight of my breasts in his hands.

"Thank you," I say, lowering my eyes to his chest.

"Alicia."

I lift my gaze again. He repeats his words with his green eyes this time. I give a weak smile, but that's not good enough for him. Taking my lips, he shows me his words with the most passionate kiss of my life.

He pops the button on my jeans and releases the zipper. Slowly he slides his hands into the back of my pants, caressing and kneading my backside. His lips travel to my neck, nipping and sucking as he goes. My moans fill the air and my toes curl in my shoes.

"Lift," he commands.

Placing my hands on his shoulders, I rise. Pushing the pants and panties over my hips, he guides them down my legs. I wiggle the flats from my feet as he tugs the bunched-up clothing the rest of the way off.

His eyes devour me as if he's mapping out his plan in his head. Which he probably is. A smile covers my lips as that thought crosses my mind. It's so clear to me now. I've watched him organize things in his head since the day we met.

I suck my lip into my mouth as he runs the back of his hand from my collarbone down over my breast. Leaning in, he starts a trail of kisses from my earlobe. Moving down to follow the path his knuckles took, his tongue flicks out to taste and tease along the way.

The scent of his shampoo and cologne fill my head as he makes the slow tortuous trip to my breast. I close my eyes as he takes my right nipple into his mouth. My back arches and my cry floats through the room.

He tugs my body closer to the edge as he so lovingly laps at my hardened peak. His hands caress my thighs, warming me from the outside in. My want for him only increases.

"So beautiful," he murmurs against my skin.

When he reaches between my legs, he groans as his fingers are met with my soaked folds. My peak pops free from his mouth, the sound echoing through the space. He looks at me in awe. I watch as he lifts the same hand he touched me with to his lips. He sucks his fingers into his mouth.

He's killing me. The way his eyes close—like he's savoring one of those steaks he seems to enjoy so much—it sends a shiver through me. When his eyes lift again, I don't know whether to run or hold on for dear life.

I go with the latter as he drops before me, tossing my legs over his shoulders. Clinging to the edge of the counter with one hand, grasping his hair with the other, I try to stay inside my skin. From the first lick of his tongue, he commands my body's attention.

It's sensory overload—the sound of his enjoyment, the feel of his wet, warm mouth, his beard brushing against my inner thighs. He's taking me on a journey with him. I don't feel left behind or as if pleasing me is a chore.

"Mmm," he hums in pleasure. I would think he were on the receiving end.

"Yes."

My head falls back as my hips rock against his greedy mouth. Quinn does nothing half-assed, not even eating pussy. The louder I get, the deeper he pushes in. He's deliberate about each action—every stroke, lick, slurp, suckle.

One palm has wrapped my thigh to keep me still while the other reaches between my legs to part me open for his assault. This man aims to savor, worship, and own.

My clit, my lips, every inch of my essence is well loved by his mouth. The sight of his red head bobbing catches my attention in the mirror. It's so hot to watch. His pale skin between my brown thighs, not nearly as tanned as I'm used to seeing, but still sexy as hell.

The way his back muscles flex with his efforts, I gush simply at the sight. He moans his approval, drinking up every drop. It's not good enough for him, though. He's going for the grand prize.

"Oh shit, Quinn. I can't breathe," I pant.

"Then come," he says into my center.

He pushes his fingers into me and I do just that. My thighs clap around his head as they quiver. I squeeze my eyes shut, trying hard to suck in some much-needed air. It takes a minute for my racing heart to calm a fraction.

I hear more than see him stand and begin to shift in front of me. When I lift my heavy, lazy eyes, his pants are gone, revealing thick thighs and a thick dick that's pointing straight at me. His big hand eats up the base and yet there is still plenty more length.

I expected him to be large, but...wow. He's definitely

overachieving in this department. Yup, I needed all that prep to take that on. I grasp the edge of the countertop as he rolls on a condom.

When he's done, his lips crush against mine, distracting me from staring. I can taste me all over his face. Sticking my tongue out, I trace my essence around his mouth and beard. His lips turn up into a smile as his breath fans mine.

"Easy, love," he says softly when I rock back away from him as he starts to penetrate me. His crown is so thick. "I'll be gentle."

"Quinn," I whimper.

"Fuck, yer tight," he says through clenched teeth. "Open for me."

I pull my legs up, wrapping them high around his back. My ankles lock and I relax, allowing him to rock his way in. My nails dig into his shoulder blades as I slip my arms beneath his.

After a few passes, I start to take him easily. Curses rip from his lips. His fingers dig into the flesh of my ass, bringing me closer to the edge of the counter.

"Alicia," he grinds out.

His pace starts to increase, alternating between long, deep strokes and shorter ones. My eyes find the mirror again, and this time I note the pretty woman in the arms of the strong body standing over her. Her lips are parted in ecstasy. Her thick, strong thighs are cradling his body.

She's gorgeous and she's me.

Quinn throws his head back at that exact moment. From the angle of the mirror, I can see the bliss on his handsome face. The sound coming from his chest intensifies the look of complete elation covering his features.

It shouldn't be possible, but he's even more gorgeous in the throes of passion. His hair has darkened with sweat. The vein in his neck has popped, showing that despite the beat-down he's placing on my pussy, he's showing some restraint.

My insides coil and my heart slams almost as hard as he's pounding into me. I find his shoulder with my lips and latch on. It's the best I can do to keep from screaming my head off.

"Don't hold back," he says into my ear, his voice husky and low. "Give me what I'm craving. I want it all."

"Oh, my God," I cry. "Quinn, Quinn, Quinn, shit."

"Fuck," he rasps through his teeth. "Aye, love. Just like that."

Tilting my body back with his palm in the center of my breasts, he latches onto my left peak. I go from the beginning of an orgasm to a fireball growing so intense and explosive, I see stars when I close my eyes. I scream so loud, it bounces off the walls.

What in the hell have I gotten myself into?

Quinn

I don't know what I've done in my life before this woman. I've had sex before, but this…this is not sex. This isn't even fucking. I've never felt connected to someone in this way.

From the moment I entered her, I knew I'd be changed forever. Like a man lost for years—finally able to walk into his home again—I've come to life. I've returned to the home I never knew was looking for me.

"That's it. Come all ya like," I say against her sweaty forehead.

I'm still hard, moving through her orgasms. She has me soaked, but I wouldn't have it any other way. Although, I wish I had the restraint to wait until I got her to a proper bed or at least my home.

It's just…walking in on her and hearing her words almost brought me to my knees. I wanted her to see and feel how beautiful she is to me. Now, I have her in my arms, and I don't know who I've done this for more—her or the selfish man inside of me.

"Quinn, please," she whimpers.

"Please what, love?"

"I can't. I can't stop coming," she says with a plea in her voice.

"Aye, but I can't stop taking ya. Ya feel so good," I groan.

I tap her thigh with my palm. She releases me from her tight hold with a look of relief on her face. I don't pull out of her body. Instead, I still and lift her right leg to my shoulder. She's limber from yoga. Her leg stretches just the way I want.

Turning my head, I lick her ankle and nibble on the skin. My head is scrambled. I had planned to take my time with her. I'd mapped out exactly how I wanted to take her. That was before I got a taste of her and before her tight, wet pussy got a hold of me.

She flutters around me as I kiss and lick up her calf. Clasping her leg to my shoulder, I start to move into her once again, slowly. Our eyes meet and something tugs inside of me. I bring her toes to my lips and suck them into my mouth.

She parts her lips and widens her eyes. Amused, I smile around her cute big toe. I don't stop moving into her tight walls. I want to stay lost inside of her for as long as I can.

"Fuck, yer going to finish me doing that," I groan out, releasing her foot from my mouth as she squeezes her pussy around me repeatedly.

She curls her sexy lips into a smile. I lift a brow at her, silently asking if she's sure she's ready for that challenge. She sucks her lip into her mouth, the dare clear in her eyes.

"Ya asked for it," I warn.

Drawing her yet closer, I pick up the pace. Shifting her leg on my shoulder, I open her to me farther. I drop my eyes to watch our connection. I'm fixated on the image before me. Her bare brown mound taking me in over and over.

"Quinn," she cries out. "Yes, yes, yes. Oh, God, yes."

I lift my eyes to see hers fixed on something beyond me. Turning my head, I find the mirror she's watching our reflection in. I noted the fixture my first time here. It's a great security measure. However, at the moment, it's a perfect picture of the two of us.

My eyes find hers in the mirror. I don't stop rocking into her tight body. Instead, I watch the pleasure I'm giving her. It's a turn on and much too hard to ignore.

Wanting to watch us more, I pull from her body. Turning back to face Alicia in the flesh, I take her mouth in a deep kiss as I lift her from the countertop. Placing her on her feet, I guide her over to the counter beneath the mirror without breaking the kiss. Her legs are shaky, but I support her.

I nip at her bottom lip before I pull away from her mouth. Turning her back to my front, I place her palms on the countertop. Lowering behind her, I go for a second taste. I lick her from front to back, humming my pleasure.

I could stay like this all night, but I'm torturing us both. I drive her right to the edge before I stand. My legs bend as I enter her from behind.

"Quinn," she calls out breathlessly.

It's the sweetest sound I've ever heard. The sound of her ass clapping against my skin only adds to the music we're creating. I groan and moan my own pleasure. The sight of her breasts bouncing in the mirror has me growing harder inside her.

Our eyes lock in the image before us. The look of lust in her eyes is like a sucker-punch. I want to put that look on her face as often as I can. I cup her full breasts, pinching and rolling her nipples between my fingers, causing her expression to intensify.

"So wet," I groan when she gushes against me. "Ya wanted to watch. Do ya see us? Do ya see how perfect ya look in my arms? Do ya see how beautiful ya are, love?"

"Yes," she whimpers.

I move my lips to her ear. "Yes, what?"

Her body quakes. Releasing her left breast, I lock my fingers into her hair and tug her head to the side. My lips find her neck, caressing the soft skin. I take my fill of her sweet scent and flavor. My greens meet her hooded browns in the mirror as I lick a path up to her ear.

"Yes, what?" I repeat.

"Yes, I see," she pants.

"Yer perfect," I say, licking the shell of her ear.

"*Quinn.*"

"Aye, love. What do ya need?"

"I...I...I don't know. Please."

"As ya wish." I chuckle darkly.

Her hand goes to the mirror, the other lacing with my hand I still have covering hers. I nudge her legs farther apart with mine. Shifting, I take straight aim for her G-spot. I know when I have it exactly right from the singing that comes from her lips as a waterfall takes place over my cock.

I can't hold on any longer. Splaying my palms over her belly, I hold her back to my chest. I give a couple of final thrusts and spill into the barrier between us, calling her name.

We collapse against the countertop, our chests heaving as they drip with sweat. I kiss her shoulder, relishing the feel of her small body beneath mine. Carefully, I slip from her warmth, having one thought run through my head.

I'm taking her home with me.

"I want to make ya pancakes for breakfast," I say sheepishly.

I love the laugh that bubbles up from deep within her. Giving her enough room to turn and face me, I lock her inside of my embrace. My heart is pounding as I wait for her reply. Not from our lovemaking, but because I fear she's going to try to run.

She looks up through her lashes, with a sweet smile on her lips. "I like strawberry pancakes. Can I have strawberry ones?"

"Ach, all ya have to do is ask. I'll give ya anything ya want."

CHAPTER 18

OOPS

Quinn

I'VE BEEN WATCHING ALICIA SLEEP FOR THE LAST HALF hour. She's gorgeous in her sleep. It's like watching a precious doll resting in my bed.

Everything about her is perfection. Her chin, her ears, even the arch of her brows. She looks like she was molded and painted by a master artist.

After helping her to clean up the money we scattered on the counter during our lovemaking in the school, we locked up and headed for my house. I was pleased when she agreed to leave her car behind to ride with me in my truck. I wanted her with me, as near as I could get her.

Reaching to brush a lock of hair out of her face, my mind goes back to last night. Each session only became more passionate and intense. I watched her come to life last night beneath me, over me, beside me. There isn't a way that I didn't take her. I covered every position I had on my list.

Looking down at her body beneath the sheets, I'm tempted to have her again. She opened up, but I know I didn't reach that place she's keeping locked away. The temptation to find the right thread to pull is too great.

I reach for her hip in hopes to coax her inner vixen out.

However, my phone buzzes on the nightstand. Tearing my eyes away from her cute nose and lush lips, I grab my phone to read the text.

"Fuck," I mutter under my breath.

I totally forgot Shane said he'd be bringing the kids over for breakfast this morning. It's his day with the kids, but somehow I got roped into breakfast and a sleepover tonight. I turn back to look at Alicia, debating whether to wake her.

She hasn't been asleep for that long. I decide to allow her to rest a little longer. A smile turns up my lips when I remember her request for strawberry pancakes. I'll be making those this morning along with the usual for the brats and my brothers.

I won't fool myself into thinking Kevin and Trent aren't going to show up for breakfast. This place will be a full house soon enough. Alicia will be getting to meet most of my family. I groan. That may send her running again.

With that thought, I sigh and toss my legs over the side of the bed. Running a hand through my hair, I start to make a list to start my day. I didn't go for my run this morning because I was in the middle of a much different type of workout.

Shower, dress, and make breakfast.

I'll get to planning the rest of my day after Alicia wakes. I want to spend more time with her. While having her in my arms all night was phenomenal, I want more. Shane will be taking his turn with the kids back.

I want to spend the day listening to that sweet, soft voice and watching that smile on her pretty face. I need to take her back to get her car, but I hope to make that a trip for much later in the day. Hopefully, long after I've made her pancakes, drawn her a nice bath, and spent the day holding her in my arms while we do nothing but breathe each other in.

A quick shower and I'm dressed in a pair of jeans as I make my way to the kitchen. A look at the clock tells me I don't have much time before the clan arrives. Pulling out all the ingredients I need, I get started with the omelets and sausage.

"Smells good in here," Trent says as he enters the kitchen.

I can't remember the last time one of my brothers actually rang the doorbell instead of using their key to get in. Things may need to change now. I want Alicia to spend more time here with me. My brothers walking in all times of the day and night isn't going to work.

"Did ya close that case I gave to ya?" I ask my brother as he takes a seat at the kitchen island.

"Come on," he groans. "One morning without talking about work and cases."

"Fine."

"Wait, what? You never give up that easily," Trent says suspiciously.

"It can wait," I say, shrugging.

"Who are you and what have you done with my brother?"

"What did I miss?" Shane asks as he and the kids walk in.

Molly and Kasey claim seats at the kitchen nook, while looking to see what I'm up to in the kitchen. Again with the wary looks, as if I haven't fed them just fine a few times already. They've had no problem filling their bellies and running off to tear through my house any other day.

Wee bandits they are, the crumb snatchers.

"Uncle Quinn, you got bacon?" Con calls from the living room.

"Aye, a good morning to ya too," I reply.

"Sorry," he mumbles. "Good morning."

"Morning, Uncle Quinn," Mckenna sings.

"Suck-up," Con says, reaching for the remote to turn on the television.

I purse my lips, looking toward the master bedroom. Not for the first time, I wonder what made me place the room on the first floor. It made sense before I had so many people in my home constantly.

"What's up with you?" Trenton asks.

I turn back to my brother with a frown. I didn't think about how I'd tell everyone that my girlfriend is here. If I had my way, this wouldn't be how I'd do things.

"I need coffee," Kevin calls as he enters the house, giving me a second to think.

I shift on my bare feet. I can't think of a lass I've introduced my family to. Sure, Alicia knows the girls, but I don't think she knows Con, and she's never met my brothers.

The four of us can come off intimidating when all in a room at once. I don't want them showing their arses in front of her. My lips part to tell them exactly that, but my words are cut off before I can get them out.

"Quinn, do you have a brush? My hair will snap this little comb in ha—" Her words stop short when she steps through to the kitchen. "Oops."

She looks sexy as fuck. Dressed in one of my dress shirts. It's falling off one of her shoulders as it swallows her body. Her hair is wild, stands every which way. The wide-eyed look on her face is adorable.

She's frozen in place. Moving over to her, I shield her body with mine. I draw her into me, and she automatically lift her hands to my chest. She's too gorgeous for me not to steal a quick kiss.

"I knew it. I knew something was up," Trenton hoots.

"Well, who do we have here?" Shane says.

I groan, pressing my forehead to Alicia's. I still have her covered from the view of the others, holding her tightly in my arms.

"That's the instructor he's been batshit over," Kevin says slyly.

"Oh, my God, Ms. Rhodes," Mckenna squeals.

"All right, Uncle Quinn!" Con says.

Why me? She stiffens in my arms. The pounding of tiny feet greets my ears before the two wee lasses wrap around Alicia's legs.

"Hi, Ms. Rhodes," they sing in unison.

"Hey girls."

"Ach, do any of ya have manners?" I call over my shoulder.

"I…I'm sorry. I didn't know you had company," Alicia says softly, fidgeting in my hold.

"Sorry. I forgot they were coming for breakfast this morning. Give me a minute. I'll come get ya settled in the room," I say.

"Okay." She nods.

"Come on, girls. Let's get the pancakes started. Ms. Rhodes will be back," I say to Molly and Kasey.

"Pancakes," they sing, rushing back to the kitchen area.

Alicia turns to rush off, but I catch her wrist. Tugging her back to me, I curl a hand into her messy hair and devour her mouth. She must have found the toothbrush I left for her. She tastes of my toothpaste.

Whistles erupt around us, causing me to release her reluctantly. Alicia's eyes are dazed as she gives a shy smile. It takes everything in me not to follow her back to the room as she turns and walks away from me.

"I never thought I'd see the day," Trenton says. "He's a goner. She's in his home, wearing his shirt, using his shit, and he hasn't lost his noodle."

"Aye, I was thinking the same thing." Kevin chuckles.

"It looks good on him," Shane says.

"Why don't youse make yerselves useful? I could use help with the food," I reply.

"And we're here to help…eat it," Trenton says.

"Ach, why didn't Ma stop with me?"

"Because she didn't reach perfection until I came along," Trent says. "The last two were her attempts at duplicating me."

"And ya believe that shit too, don't ya?" Kevin says shaking his head. "Go see to ya girl. I'll start breakfast."

"Don't touch the strawberries," I warn.

"I knew you were a kinky fu—"

"Swear jar, Uncle Trent," Molly calls out. "That's three dollars. I heard the other two. You too, Uncle Kevin. You owe a dollar."

"Fine," Trent says, clearly regretting his own rule.

"I'll be broke around the lot of ya," Kevin mumbles.

"Better that than Erin wringing our necks when she finds out what Molly picked up from us," Trenton says.

"Aye, I'll agree with that. She's been threatening us since the twins started talking. Molly is going to get us all battered," Shane says.

"Trent, yer a stook. There was a better way to handle it. I

coughed up twenty dollars in one day alone," I say, frowning at the eejit.

"All of you can stop your complaining. Molly hasn't said a bad word since the swear jar started," Trent boasted, puffing out his chest.

"Eejit," Kevin, Shane, and I say in unison.

"Don't touch the strawberries," I repeat.

I could stand here arguing with these three for hours. Instead, I turn and head for the master bedroom. I want to catch Alicia before she comes out of my shirt.

Alicia

I rush back to the bedroom as fast as my legs will take me. My face is burning with embarrassment. I heard the TV playing and thought Quinn was watching it while making my pancakes. I had no idea I'd find Erin's kids and three fine-ass versions of Quinn, including a dark-haired one.

When I woke, he was gone. I brushed my teeth and planned to take a quick shower. When I went to get my hair under control, I only found a comb. There was no way that tiny thing was going to tame this mess that's been tugged at, sweated out, and ruined. I didn't want to go through his things, so I grabbed the first shirt I could get my hands on and went to find him.

"Nice going, Ali," I mumble to myself as I pull off Quinn's shirt and start to put on my own things from yesterday.

I'm wiggling into my jeans when Quinn enters the room. He's shirtless, mind you. With those thighs putting a hurting on those light blue jeans. The man knows how to wear a pair of pants. That *V* is on display and his tattooed chest has images of last night flashing in my brain.

Phew. Did all of that really happen? Damn.

Nope, it couldn't have. Yet, the soreness between my legs says otherwise. Wow, I don't know what I thought I was doing before Quinn. It wasn't sex, that's for damn sure.

"Why do ya look like yer trying to run?" he asks as he wraps his arms around me.

"I can take an Uber to my car," I reply.

"Alicia," he groans, bending to tuck his face into my neck. "Don't make me chase ya, love. I already crossed that off my list."

"I was on one of your lists?" I frown, not sure how I feel about that.

"Aye, my list of priorities."

"Wait, so since you've slept with me, I'm no longer a priority?" I ask as my hackles go up.

"Ach, that's not what I said. At least, it's not how I meant it," he replies, moving to look me in my face. His cheeks are red. "I had making ya mine on my list. I've done that. Now, I have ya listed under something else. Still a priority, just a different one."

I narrow my eyes at him. He keeps a straight face. He's serious.

"What am I listed as now?"

"Oh no, my ma didn't raise a fool. I'll tell ya once I've crossed it off."

"Why can't you tell me now?"

"Yer already planning to run from me. I won't be giving ya any more reasons to," he says.

"I don't think I like that answer."

"Trust me." He cups my face. "That's all I ask. Trust me. I'm not out to hurt ya."

"You sure are asking a lot of me," I half tease.

"I know, but I've offered ya as much. Stop fighting it. I want to introduce ya to my brothers. I'll be introducing ya as my girlfriend."

Butterflies lift off in my belly. After last night, hearing him call me his girlfriend this morning does something to me. Remembering the way he cherished me makes me want to have that on a regular basis.

He made sure to be attentive and patient all night long. Not once did I feel like it was all about him. His words matched his actions, and boy, were his actions noteworthy. Quinn deserves an award for his skills.

"So, I'm your girlfriend?"

He gives me a look before his lips crush mine, instead of giving a reply. His kisses are like a drug, addictive and seductive. Lord knows he has seduced me into his clutches.

I place my arms around his neck, and my body melts into him. He lifts me up to his waist, pulling a laugh from me. I break the kiss to look him in his eyes. He nips my chin and pecks my nose.

"Ya rushed out of my shirt. I wanted to take it off of ya," he says.

"You can't possibly be thinking what I think you're thinking."

He places his forehead to my chin and exhales. He rubs my back, while he moves toward the drawer on the other side of the room. Retrieving a T-shirt, he allows me to slide down his front. Sure enough, I feel him through his jeans.

I bite my lip as I look up at him. He gives me a wicked smile and wink. My eyes follow his muscles as he pulls the T-shirt over his head. Once he has it on, he catches me still staring. His lips turn up, and he crowds me until my back is to the dresser.

"Yer eyes say yer thinking the same thing, love. I can get us both there before they start to miss us," he says low.

"What about my pancakes? You promised. Besides, I'm starving."

"Can't have ya starving on me, and I'll never break a promise to ya."

He takes one last sip from my lips. Before I understand what he's about to do, I'm over his shoulder, yelping. He ignores my protest as he starts out of the bedroom. He plants his lips on my backside, followed by a slap.

"Quinn," I growl. "If you don't put me down."

"Benefits of a man who cherishes ya, love. He'll carry ya wherever ya need to be." He chuckles. "Get used to it."

"My feet work," I bite out as I bounce on his shoulder. I lower my voice as we get closer to the kitchen. "Quinn, don't embarrass me like this."

His steps halt. He lets me slide down his body. His eyes sparkle with mirth as he looks down at me. He lifts his hand to cup my face.

"Do ya know yer so pretty when yer angry?" he says.

"Do you know I'll kick your ass if you embarrass me in front of your family?"

My fists are balled at my sides. I mean business. I've embarrassed myself enough already. Quinn rolls his lips as if he's trying not to laugh at me.

"Swear jar, that's one dollar." Molly's voice pulls my

attention. I look down to see she's made her way into the hallway.

Quinn bursts into laughter. His entire face lights up with it. It makes it hard to stay mad at him.

"It's her first offence, Molly. We'll give her a break," Quinn says as he lifts his niece onto his hip.

"Well, all right," Molly says warily.

"Thank you," I say.

Quinn tucks me under his arm, kissing the top of my head. We start for the kitchen again. Everyone is scattered around the kitchen with a plate in front of them. All except for the brother who was waiting for Quinn that day we got off the elevator. He's at the stove flipping pancakes.

Quinn places Molly on her feet, and she runs over to a waiting plate. She's shoveling food into her mouth in no time. I start to fidget as all the other eyes in the kitchen turn on us.

"This is my girlfriend, Alicia," Quinn says proudly. "Ya know the girls. That's their brother, Conroy."

"Hey." Conroy nods, trying to be cool.

I smile. He looks sort of like his uncles, same as Mckenna. Cute kid.

"Hello," I reply.

"I've seen you somewhere before," the dark-haired brother says, his head tilted in thought.

He looks like what I imagine Quinn would look like without the beard and longer hair. He's a few inches taller than Quinn and leaner. Still built solid, but not as bulky. He is stunning. Those freckles add character to his face, something the other brothers don't have.

He snaps his fingers as his green eyes light up. "The hospital. So you're the reason he ran out like his ass was on fire that day. I remember that skirt and those heels. Damn, I almost followed you out myself."

"Watch it," Quinn growls.

The brother throws his hands in the air, a mischievous smile crossing his lips. Oh, I can tell this one is a trip. He's not as reserved in his humor as Quinn is. Nope, this one is a live wire.

"Trenton's the name. Most of these folks call me Trent. Nice to meet you, gorgeous," he says smoothly.

"Nice to meet you, Trenton."

Quinn slaps Trenton's cheek twice. "If ya like yer bake, ya'll pick up yer tongue, ya will." Shoving pass his brother and taking me with him, he calls over his shoulder. "Don't make me say it again."

His brothers all laugh, including Trenton. I wrap my free arm around the one he has holding my hand. He gives a gentle squeeze as he walks me over to the kitchen island.

"This is my baby brother, the second youngest, Shane."

"Did ya really have to introduce me as the baby?" Shane asks in a voice that does not belong to a baby.

He has a slight accent, but not nearly as thick as Quinn's. I did notice that Trenton hardly has one at all. It reminds me that I've only picked up on Erin's a time or two. Mostly when she was frustrated with something.

"Aye, it's who ya are."

"Hi, Shane. It's nice to meet you." I chuckle.

"I think it's more of a pleasure for us. I haven't seen my brother look this happy in a long time," Shane says.

Unlike Trenton, I don't get the feeling that Shane is ribbing his older brother. I get the sense that he's saying it out of admiration. The glow in his eyes when he looks at Quinn says a lot. Shane is as handsome as Quinn and Trenton. He looks younger, but no less masculine or fit.

"Would ya like a stack?" the last brother asks from the other side of the counter.

"No. I'll be making hers," Quinn answers for me.

"What, ya think I'm going to poison the lass? Do ya see this?" He turns to Trenton and Shane.

"Aye, I do." Shane chuckles.

"I promised her I'd make her strawberry pancakes. Has nothing to do with the fact that yer feeding everyone burnt pancake," Quinn teases.

"Ach, I haven't served a single burnt—"

"Sorry, Uncle Kevin, mine were a little crispy," Conroy cuts him off.

"Ya fib, ya little...yer twistin' hay, ya are," Kevin says, narrowing his eyes at Conroy.

Conroy mock gasps, placing a hand over his heart. I can see the glee in his eyes. He looks to Trenton as if searching for approval. Trenton winks at him as a smile stretches across his handsome face.

"Me, starting trouble? I would never lie to you, Uncle Kevin," he says innocently.

"Whatever, I'm done here. Ungrateful lot youse are," Kevin grumbles, snatching up the plate he just stacked with bacon and pancakes. "I'm Kevin, by the way, and it's nice to meet ya. Good luck with yer boyfriend's pancakes."

"Nice to meet you too, Kevin." I laugh.

"I think Quinn is throwing shape for ya, lass," Shane says.

I take a seat on the stool Quinn pulls out for me. He leans to kiss my cheek before going to the other side of the island. When I turn confused eyes on Shane, he smiles.

"My brother is showing off for you," he says.

"I think it's sweet and romantic," Mckenna says from the table.

She looks like she has stars in her eyes. I grin, remembering how hard she tried to convince me to go out with her uncle. Her smile grows when she looks at me.

"You guys are so cute together," she says when Quinn reaches a strawberry across the counter, holding it to my lips.

I take it from his hand before I start to nibble on it. All eyes are on us; I don't have to turn to see them. I keep my eyes on the big man moving so easily around his kitchen.

"So yer a driving instructor?" Kevin says.

"Yeah, she's my teacher," Mckenna replies for me.

"That's Mommy's friend," Kasey says, looking up from the pancakes she's been devouring as fast as her little mouth will allow.

"You know Erin?" Trenton asks with the first serious face I've seen him make since I've met him.

"Yes, we go to the same yoga studio. That's how I became Mckenna's instructor," I say.

"Have you ever been seen around with our sister other than for the driving lessons?" he asks.

"We go for coffee or smoothies when we can," I say.

Quinn spins to look at Trenton. The dark look on his face has me edging back in my seat. Something tells me I don't want to piss Quinn off. I don't know what the two say in their silent conversation, but it's clear something passed between them.

Trenton leaves the room without another word, and Shane follows behind him. I look to Quinn for answers, but he's not looking at me. He appears to be trying to hold it together.

"You own the school. Is that right?" Kevin asks, drawing my attention to him as he turns on a megawatt smile.

I note that he has completely lost the slight accent I detected earlier. Kevin looks like Quinn, but there's something different about him. Maybe it's the hair. His is shorter and stands up neatly on top of his head.

"Yes, I own it," I say, but my eyes turn back to Quinn.

I can still see the tension in his shoulders. I want to get up and go to him, but I stay rooted to my seat. I'm not sure what happened that quickly. He was in such a good mood as he introduced me to his family.

"That must take up a lot of your time," Kevin says.

"Yeah, it can. I'm blessed to have a staff that can step in a lot," I reply.

Quinn walks over with a plate of pancakes and sausage, placing it down in front of me. When he goes to move away, I reach for his forearm, grabbing his attention. He turns back to look at me. I ask what's wrong with my eyes. Instead of answering, he leans to kiss my lips gently, then presses his lips to my temple.

"Eat before it gets cold. We'll get yer car and get ya home after," he says.

Turning to his brother, he says something so fast and muddled my head spins. Kevin gets whatever it is and nods. I can't help feeling a little rejected. I swallow down that feeling and turn to my plate. The sooner I finish, the sooner we can go.

CHAPTER 19

SO YOU REMEMBER

Alicia

I HAVEN'T SEEN QUINN IN THREE DAYS. NOT SINCE HE dropped me off to get my car and followed me home. He was silent the entire ride to the school's parking lot. My wheels were spinning, trying to figure out what happened to change everything.

I've given up since. Every morning I get a good morning text and another every night before I go to bed. I may or may not get one during the day. I know he has a business to run, so I'm trying not to take it personally. Yet, it's been super hard not to be in my feelings.

For someone who was chasing me down only days ago, Quinn sure has fallen off. I slam the car door as I get out of the vehicle. I'm just getting back from three back-to-back lessons. To say I'm in a stink mood is an understatement.

"I don't know why the hell I bother with men. This is exactly why I knew I should've stayed away from him," I mutter to myself as I walk to the front door.

I step into the school and freeze. Aidan and Tari are standing behind the counter with goofy smiles on their faces, while roses are covering my storefront. I mean, they are everywhere. Gorgeous lavender and white roses in gorgeous vases line the counter and the floor. I step in farther and can see a vase on my desk.

"Damn, girl. You must have put that *good* good on him," Tari says.

"You took the words right out of my mouth. Like, what did you do to him?" Aidan says.

"I didn't do anything."

"Oh please." Aidan waves me off.

I move to my desk, ignoring the two of them. Placing down my bag and tablet, I reach for the card sticking out of the top of the lavender roses. It's the only vase that's not mixed with both colors. When I open it, I can't help the smile I allow to tug at my lips.

> *I may not be able to be there, but my thoughts are. As soon as I get things squared away, you'll be in my arms, love.*
>
> > *Your man,*
> > *Quinn*

My face hurts, I'm smiling so wide. I bite my lip and think about our last kiss. Once I was on my front doorstep safely, Quinn planted a kiss on me I'll never forget. It was as if he tried to convey a million things in that single kiss.

"Look at that smile," Aidan sings. "What did he say?"

"None of your business," I say, leaning in to smell the roses.

"Ugh, you used to torture us with Giovanni this and Giovanni that. Now you have someone we want to hear about and you suddenly find a filter," Aidan gripes.

"I'm happy for you. Especially now that you can stop moping," Tari says.

"I wasn't moping."

"Yes, sweets. You were moping big-time." Aidan laughs.

"Whatever."

My phone rings as I sit. I smile thinking it might be Quinn. When I retrieve the device from my bag, I don't recognize the number flashing across the screen. The last time I answered an unknown number comes to mind.

Looking around at all the roses, I decide to ignore the call. Instead, I send it to voicemail and open up a text to Quinn. Biting my lip, I try to think of what to say. I could simply say thank you, but I want to come up with something a little more.

> **Me:** This was way too sweet. Thank you. Hope I
> get to be in your arms soon.

I chew on my lip, warring with hitting the send button. I'll be totally pissed if he sends back one of the short text messages he's been sending. At least, before he fell somewhat off the map.

Oh screw it.

I send the text and wait. I sit watching my phone for a few minutes, but a reply doesn't come. I twist my lips and sigh.

He's busy with work. The flowers were to let you know he cares.

I snatch up the phone and place it in my purse. Out of sight, out of mind. I'm not going to drive myself nuts waiting for a text. I have work to do.

I'm exhausted. The day seemed to drag on forever. I had to take out four more students before my day could wrap up. I've never been so happy to see my house in my life.

I was too exhausted to try to clear out the roses from the school. I only took the vase that was resting on my desk. I drag my tired body to the front door, juggling my bag and the vase. The door swings open before I can get my key out. Tari has that goofy smile on her face from earlier, causing me to side-glance her and narrow my eyes.

"O…kay," I drag out as she waves me into the house.

I stumble to a stop as I cross the threshold. White roses fill the foyer. On the table we keep in the center of the space is a vase filled with yellow roses. In front of it sits a basket and a gift bag.

I can't believe he did this again. The money he must have spent. Tari takes the roses from my hand and shoves me impatiently toward the table. I turn to her and make a face.

"Don't push me. Didn't you rush home to get ready for a date?" I gripe at her.

"That dude is corny. I cancelled. This is much more entertaining. Come on, I want to see what's in the bag. I've been waiting for over an hour now," she whines.

"Seriously?"

"Yes, open it," she replies, her eyes widening at me.

I wave her off, but move to the table. I reach for the card first, drawing an exasperated breath from Tari beside me. Ignoring her, I read Quinn's words.

I've admired my parents' relationship since I was a wee lad. Theirs is one that's built on a friendship. I've been thinking about you nonstop. I want to be everything to you, and I believe that starts with a friendship. The basket is my way of saying I hope you've had a good day, and if not, I want you to relax before we talk and you tell me all about it. The other gift is only the beginning of me spoiling you the way you deserve.

–Your Quinn

Oh, my God. I can't with this man. He does nothing the way I think he should. I feel the lock on my heart twist open slightly.

"Wow, that's…he's smooth. You're going to have to teach me what you did to him," Tari says over my shoulder.

I flap my elbows at my sides. "Give me some room, please and thank you." I laugh.

She places the heavy vase down next to the other one on the table and rests her hands on her hips. Ignoring her again, I reach into the pretty gift bag. I pull out a velvet box and my hand starts to shake as I open it.

My mouth pops open as the lid to the box does. Inside rests a necklace with a large single diamond pendent. It's stunning.

"Oh shit," Tari gasps. "You're going to tell me you didn't put it on him and pull his nose wide open?"

"I didn't do anything," I say as I stare at the necklace in awe.

"Girl, please. That is not a gift you give just any old girl."

"It's…wow. I can't keep this," I say almost to myself.

"Why not?"

"It's too much," I reply.

"Psssh, whatever. I wish I had someone that wanted to spoil me like that. We both know that's a first for you," she says.

"That's not true." I turn to her and frown.

"Any gift that comes with strings attached doesn't count. Everything that asshole Giovanni gave you came with multiple strings," she says.

"Okay, that might be true. Tari, he had to spend so much money on all of this. The necklace, the flowers. This is insane," I say as I look around.

"No, it's not. Like the note said, it's what you deserve. I think you're falling for him," she says with a smile on her face.

"I like him. He makes me laugh. He's nothing like what I expected, but I wouldn't say I'm falling for him."

"Ali, stop lying. Those words must taste like shit, because they're a whole lot of bull," Tari says and cuts her eyes at me.

I don't reply. In all honesty, Quinn chipped away at a lot of my resolve the night we spent together. It wasn't the sex, it was the moments in between. He spent the night making me laugh, asking me about my hopes and dreams, and allowing me to get to know him. It's one of the reasons I've been so disappointed that he hasn't called more. I want to talk to him.

"What's in the basket?" Tari coaxes.

Pushing aside the gift bag, I bring the basket closer to me. I start with the ribbon and organza wrap. My lips turn up as I see a ton of my favorite things. All things I told Quinn I love, during our night together. Pineapple- and vanilla-scented candles with the matching bath salt and oil, my favorite chocolate caramel candies, a bottle of wine, and an e-reader. I lift the e-reader and cradle it to my chest.

"Look, a gift card is taped to the back," Tari says. "Okay, not for nothing. He nailed this gift. It's totally you."

"I know. I can't believe he remembered all of this."

"Still think you're not falling for him?"

"Maybe just a wee bit." I laugh.

"Ugh, did you read that note with his accent in your head, because I did?"

We both laugh as I nod. I totally did. I wish it were his voice reading it to me. Reaching in my pocket, I check my phone. He still hasn't answered my text from earlier. With a sigh, I place the phone back into my pocket.

"I'm taking all of this and getting in the tub. It's been a long day and I'm tired," I say, collecting the basket and the rest of my things.

"Want me to order some takeout?"

"No, don't think I can hold my eyes open long enough to eat a thing," I groan.

"Good night, honey. See you in the morning."

She kisses me on my cheek and pulls me into a hug. I return it as best I can with my arms full. When she releases me, I drag my tired body up to my room.

Quinn's gift couldn't be more welcome. Drawing a bath is the first thing I do. I'm always grateful for the en suite in my bedroom; it's like my own private sanctuary.

I start some music and begin to strip out of my clothes. Once I'm undressed, I unload my basket on the bathroom counter. A smile splits my face when I remove two glasses. Engraved on one is *banphrionsa* and on the other is a word I don't know, *rí*. I sure did look up the spelling of princess on Google translate. It's the only reason I know what's printed on at least one of the glasses.

"Note to self, look up *rí*. You're so full of surprises, Mr. Blackhart," I murmur.

Quinn

Wiping the sweat from my face, I flex my back muscles. I'm coiled so tight, I can feel it in every cell of my body. My sweaty bare chest heaves as I flex my knuckles. I look at a shirtless Kevin, and he looks like I feel.

This is how we release aggression around here without taking someone's head off. Boxing in the ring of our training center at the office. I haven't been able to think straight much less focus since Kevin called to tell me he found some wanker lurking outside of Erin's house.

"Ya good yet?" Trent asks.

"Aye, barely."

"So we can talk about this now?" Kevin asks.

I walk over to the ropes and take the towel and water Shane holds up for me. Wiping my sweat off first, I then take a swig of water. I purse my lips and nod at Trent as I grind my teeth.

"Aye, go on. Explain to me what you found," I grunt.

"Moralez wanted to head over to Erin's to look at the scene for herself. When we arrived, the asshole was sitting in a car with his eyes glued on the house," Kevin explains. "We watched him instead of making ourselves known. He sat for a solid hour before I approached him."

"Why was he lurking outside our sister's house?" Trent grunts.

"According to him, some guy named Brunson calls him with jobs. This Brunson is connected to a few families and into all kinds of shit. But here's the part that makes my blood boil," Kevin says. "This guy, Duffy, was told to watch the house. If Erin or Cal showed up, he was to call it in."

"Ya should have shot him," Shane says dryly.

"Did ya look into this Brunson?" I snarl, ignoring my brother.

"I did. Some lowlife as far as I can see, but I'll be digging some more," Trent says.

"Where is this Duffy now?"

"Moralez called in a favor. We didn't want her name attached to this. We handed him over to the NYPD. They'll lose him in the system for a bit," he says with a smile.

"Find me everything I don't know about this Brunson," I say to Kevin and Trenton.

"Aye, we've got it," Kevin says.

I nod for Shane to follow me as I step out of the ring. I pull on my shirt and retrieve my phone. It's later than I thought. I see a text from Alicia, and my mind goes to where I'd rather be.

On top of needing to clear my head, I needed to get my temper under control before I head to Alicia's. I haven't held her in three days. That's three days too long, but I couldn't show up the way I had been when I learned someone was snooping around Erin's house. Not with the rage I had brewing within.

"How is she?"

"She's not in a shitty mood anymore, but she looked tired," Shane replies, already knowing who I'm referring to.

"So, she got the flowers and the gifts?"

"Aye, from what Jazz says."

"Send Jazz home. I'll take over for the rest of the night," I reply.

"On it."

Taking a deep breath, I close my eyes. I need to get this situation under control. Trenton has amazing instincts. When he gets a gut feeling, we act on it. When he asked Alicia about her interaction with Erin, I almost lost it.

We've been watching over her since. I won't leave anything to chance when it comes to her. Which has also placed my focus on finding a solid lead.

We are running our team too hard. Between pulling resources to find out who attacked Erin and Cal, having someone on my parents' house round the clock, our contracts, and now Alicia, we're wearing everyone out.

This is the first night in three days that I'm not chasing down a lead. Now that I have a grasp on my temper and the facts involving the trash that Kevin found outside of Erin's house, I have one person on my mind and one person only. It's time I bring a smile to my woman's face in person.

Alicia

That had to be the best bath I've ever taken. I finished the entire bottle of wine before I knew it. I was totally engrossed in the book I downloaded. I finally gave up on the book and the bath when the water turned cold and my stomach started grumbling.

After putting on my pajamas, I spent about fifteen

minutes trying to find my misplaced phone that was right under my nose. Not wanting to miss Quinn's text or call, I needed to find it before crawling into my bed. Once my phone was found, I flung my tired body across the bed with it clasped in my hand.

I'm too spent to walk downstairs to see what's in the refrigerator. My tummy has been protesting, but I haven't been able to peel myself up again.

The wine has my body relaxed and my mind drifting, probably having a greater effect since I drank it on an empty stomach. I'm almost off to dreamland when a tap sounds on my door. I groan into the mattress. Maybe if I ignore them, they'll go away. It's probably Aidan wanting to grill me about the flowers and the gifts I'm sure Tari told him about.

"What?" I whine when the tap comes again.

The door opens, and I get ready to tell whoever it is to go away. The sound of heavy footfalls causes me to flip over to look toward the door. My heart swells when I see Quinn standing in my bedroom.

"Hey, love. I've missed ya," he says.

I find enough energy to get off the bed and run to wrap my arms around his waist. His cologne welcomes me in right before his arms wrap around me. I don't realize how much I've missed him until he's holding me tight.

"What are you doing here? Who let you in?"

"I pulled up the same time as Aidan. I thought I'd bring ya something to eat, while ya tell me about yer day," he replies.

I look up at him with a smile, and he holds up the bag of food in his hand. The aroma of something delicious hits me, and my stomach groans in appreciation. I know what it is right away.

"Quinn Blackhart, are you trying to make your way to my heart?" I tease.

"Aye, ya have no idea," he says, dipping to peck my lips. "Come, let me feed ya."

He takes my hand, leading me to the bed. I climb on and he sits on the side, placing the bag on the nightstand. I study him while he bends to remove his boots. His hair looks damp as if he's taken a recent shower. He's wearing a plain black T-shirt and black jeans. His beard seems a little longer, not as short and trimmed as usual.

"You got my favorite?" I say as he scoots all the way onto the bed, placing his back to the headboard.

"Aye, lasagna and pinwheels," he says, reaching for the bag.

"Aargh, you're a lifesaver. I was so exhausted I had planned to starve in my sleep."

"Ach, we can't have that now, can we? C'mere," he says, waving me to take the spot between his thighs.

Crawling into the space, I settle in, my back to his front. He takes out a tray of lasagna and a wrapped pinwheel. I take the pinwheel from his hand, allowing him to open the tray and take a fork from the bag.

"Did ya save me any wine?" he says, kissing the top of my head.

"Not at all," I say around the dough and pepperoni I'm munching on.

"Are you langered, love?"

"If that means buzzed, then yes. I think I did get a little tipsy. I'd planned to go to bed after a call from my boyfriend." I snicker.

"Is that right?" he says, holding a forkful of pasta up to my mouth.

"Yup, wasn't expecting to see him."

"Glad he could make an appearance. How did ya like the roses?"

I turn my head up to look him in the eyes. I'm sure he can see how happy they made me. I still can't get over the fact that he did all that for me.

"You really didn't have to do that. Thank you. They were all so beautiful, but don't you think you went a little overboard?" I reply.

"Anything for my *banphrionsa*," he says, pecking my nose.

I feel my cheeks heat. That key twists in the lock again. On one hand, I want to slow this down to protect my heart. On the other hand, I'm falling faster and harder than I ever thought I could.

"You're not making this easy for me."

"What's that?"

"Nothing," I say, shaking my head. "By the way, what's *rí*?"

He smiles, showing all his teeth. Not for the first time, I note how his imperfections enhance his handsome face. Reaching up, I bury my fingers in his beard. He turn his face to kiss my palm.

"It means *king*," he says.

I burst into laughter. The wine probably making his words funnier than they truly are. His eyes bounce over my face.

"Are you calling yourself my king?"

"Aye, and one day I'll make ya a *banríona*. My queen," he says.

I lower my lashes and drop my head. Quinn shifts, placing the tray of food back on the nightstand. His arms wrap around me. When I don't look up again, he reaches to turn my face to him.

"Yer not wearing ya necklace. Did ya not like it?"

"I love it."

"Ya look tired. Do ya think ya had enough to hold ya over 'til the morning?"

"Yeah." I yawn. "But I'm not ready for you to leave."

His lips crush mine, delivering one of those drugging kisses. I push my fingers into his damp hair. He groans into my mouth, but breaks the kiss too soon.

"I don't intend to leave, love. Yer stuck with me for the night," he says against my lips.

"Oh really?" I smile.

"Aye, now get to telling me about yer day before ya fall asleep," he replies.

"That's easy. This is by far the best part of my day. You're right on time, Blackhart. Right on time."

"Always."

CHAPTER 20

NO BOYS ALLOWED

Quinn

"WHY DO YA LOOK SO NERVOUS?" I SAY AS I LOOK OVER at Alicia fidgeting in the passenger seat.

"You're taking me to meet your entire family," she replies.

"Ya already met most of them. It's just my ma and da."

"It's your fault I'm so nervous. You make your mother and father sound so amazing and scary. What if your mother doesn't like me?"

"That's not likely."

"Why not?"

I turn from the road to look at her quickly. Her eyes are worried, and she's gnawing on her lip. Reaching across the seat, I place a hand on her thigh. She covers my hand and laces our fingers together.

"It's hard not to like ya, love. Ya have a way of drawing people in," I reply.

"You're sweet, but you're also biased. You've been sleeping in my bed every night for two weeks. I can't trust your opinion," she teases.

"About that. Maybe we should go to mine tonight. I've been neglecting my duties as yer man," I say.

Her laugh fills the car. I stop at a light in time to turn to see the beautiful sight. She looks at me with sparkling eyes. Not able to help myself, I lean over to kiss her lips quickly.

"I forgive you. You've been exhausted by the time you arrive at my place. I keep telling you, you don't have to come spend the night every night," she replies.

"Ach, I can't seem to sleep without ya. I'd much rather pass out in yer bed than mine. Unless my arriving so late is starting to cheese ya off."

"No, I keep my phone next to my pillow for when you let me know you're on your way. I look forward to those texts. I'm sort of spoiled now too. I sleep better with you there. It's okay that we don't have sex when you sleep over," she says shyly.

"Hm."

"What does that mean? What's that sound for?" she says with a smile in her voice.

I pull up to the twins' school and park. Turning to Alicia, I cup her face. I lean in to give her a reminder of the heat we create. She moans when I suck her lip into my mouth.

"If ya feel like it's okay that I'm not shagging ya, we have a serious problem. I think I need to fix that."

She laughs against my lips. "I said it's okay. I didn't say I don't miss it," she says.

"Aye, we'll be going to my house this evening. I'll take ya to pack a bag after dinner."

"Are you changing your list mid-play, Mr. Blackhart? I do believe you rattled off our day this morning and you mentioned going to my place to end the night," she says with a smile.

"I've changed my list every day this week, and it's been yer fault every time," I tease.

Her fingers cup my jaw to massage my beard. I'm beginning to love when she does that. I think she does too.

"Careful, I might rub off on you."

"Tonight, I'm planning on it," I tease and lick my lips.

"You're just nasty." She laughs, pulling away from me.

I go to say something dirty, but Conroy opens the back door and hops into the car. He's wearing a frown that draws my attention. I turn to look into the back seat.

"What about ye?" I say to my nephew.

"I'm fine. It's Mckenna you should be asking about," he says with an attitude.

"What's wrong with yer sister?" I ask, unfastening my seat belt.

"She's boy crazy. Look, she's all in Jimmy Harrison's face," he replies, pointing out the window.

I turn in that direction to find my niece smiling up at some young punk. I'm moving to get out of the car before I can think about it. Alicia's hand on my forearm is the only thing that stops me.

"Quinn, baby, what are you about to do?" she asks when I turn to her, her gaze probing me.

"I'm going to have a talk with the lad and my niece," I say.

"What kind of talk?" she says warily.

"A wee chat."

"Oh, no. I hear it in your voice. Don't go embarrassing her. She's sixteen," Alicia pleads.

"Aye, she is. That's why she needs a wee yarn. She's too young to try to get off with boys. No, I'll be chatting with the two," I say tightly.

"First, babe, you need to calm down. I have no idea what

you just said. You can't go out there like that," Alicia says soothingly.

"He said he wants to have a little talk with her. She's too young to be kissing boys or making out or whatever," Conroy grumbles from the back seat. "Why'd she have to pick one of my friends?"

"*Quinn*," Alicia drags out when I try to move from the car again.

The back door opens and Mckenna jumps in. I turn my gaze from Alicia to my niece. She's smiling from ear to ear.

"We'll be talking about yer little friend," I say to Mckenna, causing her smile to drop. "I don't remember ya getting permission to be dating boys."

"I was only talking to him," Mckenna pouts. "We're just friends."

"Ach, it starts with just talking. No lad looks at his friends like that. Who do ya think yer fooling?"

"Thank you. I told her the same thing. I hear what the guys say about you when they think I'm not around. You don't listen," Conroy says.

"Can we not gang up on her?" Alicia says.

"We're not ganging up on her. We're looking out for her. There's a difference," I say.

"Can we just go?" Mckenna says as she slouches down in her seat.

"Boys only chase ya for one thing. Ya keep it to yerself and don't go giving it away to one of these little eejits," I warn.

"Sage advice. I think Mckenna and I hear you loud and clear," Alicia says.

"What's that supposed to mean?"

I narrow my eyes at her. She's glaring back at me. It's like that first day all over again.

"We're going to be late," she replies, turning to look out the passenger window.

"Yer pissed off?"

"We'll talk about it later."

I grind my teeth and buckle up. I turn to look at Alicia once more, but I hold my tongue and pull off instead. My grip on the steering wheel is tight enough to snap it.

The drive to the Golden Clover is a long one. Everyone in the car remains silent. This isn't how I wanted this evening to go.

Alicia

"Alicia, wait," Quinn says as I go to get out of the car.

When I turn, I'm greeted by concerned green eyes. I sigh, shifting back into my seat and close the door. I stare straight ahead as I purse my lips. The twins have already run into the restaurant.

"Why are ya so angry with me?" he asks.

I whip my head in his direction, and my eyes narrow on him. "Did you stop to think about her feelings? She's a young girl. Things are confusing and hard enough for her. She doesn't need her uncle she looks up to and her big brother ganging up on her. Or for that same uncle to embarrass her in front of a boy she likes," I snap.

He looks thoughtful. He runs a hand through his hair. I know he means well and I get that he wants to protect

Mckenna, but he can stand to be a bit gentler with her. She's such a sensitive girl, she reminds me of myself.

Reaching over the console, he cups my face and searches my eyes. I wrinkle my nose as I wonder what he's looking for. Leaning in, he places a soft kiss on my lips.

"My family will love ya. Ya have such a big heart. Yer right. I can be softer with the lass. I'll still be having a visit with the lad the next time he hangs out with Con, but I'll consider Mckenna's feelings," he says.

"You're impossible." I roll my eyes. "You pursued me relentlessly. Yet your niece can't even talk to a boy. What are you going to do if you ever have daughters?"

"First, I'm a grown man, not a boy. I take care of my responsibilities. I don't go chasing women to waste their time. Second, ya can bet yer pretty arse we're homeschooling and I'll have a shotgun ready for any little snot nose melter that comes sniffing around after our wee uns," he grumbles out.

I can't help the tiny smile that touches my lips. My head tilts to the side as I eye him. I don't think he realizes that he just referred to his future daughters as ours.

"I think it's sweet that you want to protect her. Just think about how you're doing it, Quinn. You can push her into making poor decisions if you're too hard on her."

"Ach, I said I'll be mindful."

"Good. Now come here. I think we need to make up after our first fight." I grin.

"Yer always fighting me," he teases, but takes my lips before I can retort. "Ya taste like caramel. Are ya sure yer not trying to get out of this date?"

"You're the one holding me hostage in this car," I reply.

"Aye, yer right. Maybe it's because I want to keep ya to myself."

He leans in for another kiss, but I dodge it as I laugh. He frowns, reaching to pull me closer. I block his hands and start to move to get out of the car.

"You will not have me making a bad first impression with your mother and father," I say.

"And ya won't be getting me clobbered. Don't ya move, I'll get yer door," he grunts, making his way out before me.

Quinn helps me out of the car. I take in the pub and restaurant before us. It's a lot bigger than I thought it would be. The sign on top has all the Irish charm I expected.

Turning to glance up at Quinn, I find a look of pride on his handsome face. His family means so much to him. I'm sure he's very proud of their business and accomplishments.

I smooth my hands down the front of my black T-shirt as my nerves return. Quinn told me to dress casually. I opted for gray jeans, a black T-shirt, and wedge sandals. Now, I sort of wish I found a better middle ground.

"Ya look beautiful, love," he whispers in my ear as if he can read my thoughts.

"Thank you," I reply.

His hand lands on the small of my back. The heat from his palm soothes me a bit as he leads me into the restaurant. I know I've met his brothers and Erin already, but I haven't been able to get over my nerves concerning his parents.

I'm also a bit nervous to see Erin. After all she's been through, I don't want to stress her unnecessarily. It's been playing in the back of my mind that she may not like the fact that I'm dating her older brother.

What if this is an issue? I don't want to ruin our

friendship, but I'm also falling for her brother. Quinn is stubborn, bossy, and at times he drives me bonkers, but he has treated me like the princess he calls me for the last two weeks we've been together.

When we enter, there is a hostess station right at the entrance. To the right is the bar, filled with high tables and bar stools. On the left are dining tables. The place has a welcoming feel.

"Quinn!" his brothers cheer.

They are all standing around the bar with drinks in their hands. There really should be a law against having them all in the same room together. I can see the women around the restaurant and pub ogling them. I don't blame them one bit. Although, I do scowl when I see a few turning in Quinn's direction.

"What are youse up to?" Quinn says as he moves us over to his brothers.

"Waiting around to see this," Trent says, pointing his mug behind us.

I turn to find a man with red hair that has grayed at the temples, walking beside a tall brunette. It's amazing how the man dwarfs the woman when she's so much taller than me. They are both very attractive, much like their children.

"Ach, she's such a wee thing, Quinn, but she's gorgeous, she is," the woman says.

She has me in a tight embrace the moment she reaches us. Surprised, it takes me a moment before I return the hug. Holding me out at arm's length, her eyes dance over me while a huge smile plays on her lips.

"I'm going to have such adorable grands," she says.

"Ach, Renny, don't ya think we should introduce

ourselves to the lass before ya go talking about grands? Yer sure to scare her off, ya are," the man says with a chuckle.

"I've been waiting long enough for Quinn to settle down and find someone, for Christ's sake. Aye, I've jumped the gun a wee bit." She laughs, cupping my cheek. "It's so nice to meet ya. I'm Quinn's mother, Renny."

"And this is my da, Teagon. Ma, Da, this is my girlfriend, Alicia," Quinn says.

"It's so nice to meet you both," I say.

"Lovely to meet ya too, lass. I haven't seen my boy smile this much since he was a wee lad," Teagon says.

"Really?" I say, looking up at Quinn.

His cheeks are a little pink beneath his beard. It's plain adorable. His brothers chuckle behind us, causing me to turn and stick my tongue out at them.

"You three leave him alone," I say to them.

"She's fallen to yer charms, Quinn. She's fighting yer battles for ya, she is," Shane teases.

Quinn wraps his arms around my waist and kisses the top of my head. When I look at up at his face, his eyes are twinkling with mirth, but he's frowning at his brothers. It's clear this family loves one another; it's hard not to feel the connection radiating from everyone.

"She's only defending me because she hasn't learned that I run the lot of ya," Quinn replies.

"Ach, ya run who?" Kevin says.

"I don't think I stuttered. Someone has to keep youse in order," Quinn says.

"Listen to ya. Alicia didn't come to hear all this naff. It's crap they talk, it is," Renny turns to me and says. "Save it for yer own time. Come on, lass. Erin wants to see ya."

Pulling me from Quinn's hold, she laces her arm with mine. Teagon comes to my other side, looping his arm through my free one. The three of us begin to walk toward the restaurant side. When we've put a little distance between us and the guys, Teagon leans over to whisper to me.

"We brought them up right, we did. Now the big fuckers act a maggot whenever the mood strikes them," he says.

"Aye, we love our boys, wouldn't give up a one, we wouldn't. But they've challenged us from the time they were in the womb, they have. Each and every one. Spent most my time clobbering their wee arses, I did," Renny adds.

"I'll still box one of them up if I have to," Teagon grunts. "Quinn ever give ya trouble, ya come to me. I'll set him straight."

"Thank the stars the last one was a girl," Renny groans as I snicker.

I love them. I wasn't expecting any of that to come out of their mouths, but the fact that they're so down to earth has relaxed me 100 percent. I know Aidan would go nuts over these two.

However, when we enter what seems to be a private room, my heart squeezes. The kids are all sitting around Erin, while she is sitting in a wheelchair. She looks so frail and fragile. Not at all like my yoga buddy I remember. The right side of her face tries to lift into a smile.

Quinn warned me last night that his sister may not be the way I remember her. I was expecting to see some of the effects of the shooting, but this is so hard to witness. Erin has always been so vibrant and full of life.

"Come, give me a hug. I can take it," she says, her words coming a little slow.

I rush over and wrap my arms around her as best I can with her in the chair. Her right arm goes around me limply. It takes everything in me not to burst into tears.

"It's okay. I'll be good as new in no time. I'm a Blackhart. We're tough," Erin breathes.

"That you are," I choke out.

I pull away and smile at my friend. Her eyes are glowing with the smile she's trying to force to her face. Quinn's arm wraps my waist right as Erin turns her eyes to him.

"I don't know why I never thought of hooking you two up," Erin says. "I totally see it now. Two of my favorite people."

"Everything happens when it's supposed to. I don't think I would have been ready before," I say shyly.

"You both look so happy," she replies.

"Oh, I did some shopping today. That might explain my mood," I tease.

Quinn's fingers tighten on my waist as he growls down at me. I throw my head back and laugh. It's such a relief to know Erin is okay with this.

"Tea will be served now that everyone is here," Renny calls.

"Tea means dinner," Quinn says when I look up at him questioningly.

"Alicia, meet my girlfriend, Danita," Kevin says, mirth playing in his voice.

I don't miss the scowl she gives him when he introduces her. It even looks like she elbows him on the sly. Kevin smiles as if nothing is amiss. I roll with it, holding my hand out to Danita.

"Hi, I'm Alicia."

"Nice to meet you," she says before turning to Kevin. "*Boyfriend*, can we talk?"

"After dinner, love," Kevin says, turning to walk in the other direction.

Danita follows him, muttering under her breath. I gaze up at Quinn with a questioning look, but he shrugs it off and leads me to a seat. I take one more peek in Kevin and Danita's direction to see them in an animated conversation.

Interesting. Do all the Blackhart men drive their women mad?

"Tell me more about yerself, lass." Renny's voice pulls my attention.

From that moment on, light banter fills the room as we eat and drink. With each moment that passes by, I fall for Quinn and his family more. I don't think I could feel more welcome.

Something clicks into place. I get a sense of finding something that I've been missing, but I don't look at it too closely for fear of it slipping away. Yet, a single word resonates deep within.

Family.

CHAPTER 21

WELCOME TO THE FAMILY

Alicia

Dinner was delicious. I've had such a good time tonight. The Blackharts are certainly a family that loves to laugh together.

I've been chatting with Danita and Erin. Quinn and his brothers took off a while ago. Wanting to stretch my legs and see where Quinn got off to, I make my way out into the main area of the Golden Clover. The restaurant looks to be winding down its night. Although the pub seems to be in full swing.

I spot the guys all sitting around a high table of their own. Teagon is behind the bar, looking right at home. I give him a small wave as I pass. He says something to the men sitting before him, and they all turn to lift their glasses at me.

My cheeks heat, but I return the gesture with another shy wave. When I get to Quinn's side, he pulls me right between his legs and places a hand on my ass and a kiss on my temple. He doesn't miss a beat in his lively conversation with his brothers as he does it.

"Yer not listening to what I'm saying," Kevin says. "The Shelby is a classic. A Mustang can get my blood pumping any day, but the Viper has better performance."

"I totally agree," I say. "Though with the right driver, a Mustang might surprise you."

All heads turn in my direction. I lift my hands and shrug. I could sit and talk cars for hours. It gave me cred with the guys on the track when I was younger.

I smile as I think about those days. I think my father wanted a son. I didn't mind. Once I fell in love with racing and tinkering with cars, it only made our bond stronger.

"I didn't open a driving school for nothing," I say.

"Do ya want to take my seat?" Quinn asks as he goes to get up.

"No, I'm fine here." I smile at him.

His fingers flex against my backside as he draws me in closer. I place a hand on his chest while I settle in for this conversation. The guys pull me right in. Kevin is happy to have someone on his side of the argument and becomes more enthusiastic as we begin to talk horsepower and twin engines.

"I never thought to ask ya about the kit on yer car," Quinn says in my ear.

"It was raining. I think you were more concerned with getting me home," I say with a shrug.

"Ya keep surprising me."

"Is that good or bad?"

"It's good, love. Very good," he says with a smile that transforms his entire face.

He leans down to peck my lips before we turn to reenter the conversation. My heart races the moment Trenton mentions a race track they go to. I'm all over going to join them, but I don't get to ask. Renny comes to steal me away.

"Come have a chat with an oul-doll and oul-lad, will ya?" she says.

"Sure," I say, turning to kiss Quinn's cheek before he releases me to follow his mother.

We go to a table in the far corner of the restaurant where Teagon is waiting for us. The waitstaff is busy cleaning the other tables around us. A young waiter comes over with three cups of tea before he hurries off.

"There's a wee bit of brandy in the tea, lass." Teagon winks.

"Thanks for the warning," I say and wink back at him.

"We believe in testing ya out the gate, love. If we knock ya on yer arse the first visit, we'll put the kid gloves on next time, we will." Renny laughs.

"Good to know," I say through my own laughter.

Quinn's laugh rumbles our way, pulling my attention. I can't help but smile when I see him and his brothers horsing around at their table. Quinn is such a different person around his family. I'm starting to appreciate the complexity of my man.

"Loud bunch, aren't they?" Teagon chuckles, giving me a little nudge with his elbow as he sits on my right side.

"They're just having fun. I wish I had siblings growing up," I reply.

"Aye, Quinn told me about yer losses. I'm sorry, love," Renny says, with a soft smile on her lips.

"Thank you. I think I miss them most during times like this. I would've loved to be able to take Quinn home to meet them," I say, staring down into my mug.

"Life is good at throwing us curveballs," Teagon says.

"Aye, it is. What's important is how we get up from those," Quinn's mother adds.

"I've certainly had a lot to bounce back from in my life." I snort, looking up at the two.

Teagon and Renny turn to each other, clearly having a silent conversation. In this moment, they remind me of my parents. I can see the love they have for each other and their children. It reminds me that I never had to question my parents' love for me.

I lower my gaze and stare at the table. I don't know how I missed that key factor in my relationship with Giovanni. Never once do I recall him looking at me the way my father looked at my mom.

"Alicia, can we ask ya something?" Teagon says, pulling my attention back to the present.

"Sure."

I take a sip of the tea, and sure enough, it packs a punch. I don't think my version of wee bit is the same as theirs. Yet I suck it up and take a second sip.

"I hope ya can appreciate how special Quinn is," Renny says. "I can see ya care about him, but do ya think ya can handle all that's our son?"

"Do you mean his OCD?"

"Aye, so he has told ya," Teagon says.

"He's a smart lad. I've never wanted him to feel different or odd. Still, he can drive ya batty when he's in one of his moods and can't let go of his need to grasp control through those lists," his mother explains.

"He also has a bit of a temper. Ach, he'd never harm ya, but he'll lose his shit if someone else tries to," Teagon says with a wince.

"I think I've seen a bit of that temper earlier today." I laugh.

"Oh, love. Ya haven't seen a thing if ya can laugh about it," Renny says, shaking her head, her lips pinching.

"Quinn protects those he loves, and when he feels they are threatened, he blacks out. Broke Erin's first boyfriend's nose for making her cry," his father says.

"Seriously?"

"Aye, I'd hate to see what he would do to someone that hurts ya," Renny says.

I place the addictive tea back on the table. I realize I've been sipping the entire time we've been talking. My cup is now only half-full.

"What makes you say that?"

"Ya don't see it, do ya?" she says, tilting her head at me.

"See what?"

"Our son is over the moon for ya," she replies.

"Aye, batshit crazy for ya, he is," Teagon adds with a bright smile.

"I've never seen him like this." Renny reaches for my hand and covers it with hers. "It's in the way he looks at ya. The way he gravitates to ya. Ya should hear how he talks about ya."

"I don't know. I think we're in a good place, but I don't think his feelings are that deep," I says as gently as I can.

They both burst into laughter. I mean, deep full-belly laughs. My face crumbles, and I purse my lips.

"Ya keep telling yerself that, love," Teagon says through his laughter.

"A mum knows her son," Renny says, patting my hand.

I turn to look toward Quinn. His eyes are already on me. When our gazes lock, he sends me a brilliant smile. I automatically return it with one of my own.

"I don't doubt that you do. I just think Quinn and I are taking our time," I say.

"Ya keep selling yerself that tale, lass. Just remember.

He'll give the last breath in his body to see ya happy. Be patient with him. Everything he does, he does out of love," his father says as his mother pats my hand.

I stare down into my empty cup. I don't know if their words are true. I'm falling for Quinn, but is it possible he has fallen for me too?

Quinn

"I like her," Trenton says as I stare across the room at Alicia.

"Aye, she's perfect for him," Shane says.

"I think so too," Kevin adds.

My heart swells. I love that my family has taken to Alicia. My parents seem to love her as I knew they would. She fits right in. I've watched her come out of her shy shell the longer she's been here.

My family has a way of pulling you in when they see you as their own. Alicia has become a Blackhart whether she knows it or not. That will help with checking off my list. I know exactly what I want my next step with Alicia to be.

"I'm starting to feel like I can't breathe without her," I muse aloud.

Low whistles sound around the table. I turn to look at my brothers. Pulling a hand down my beard, I try to figure out what made me tell them that. It's been on my mind, but I hadn't planned to reveal it to anyone.

"How are we doing with those leads and the laptop?" I say quickly.

All the smiles at the table turn to grimaces. Shane and

Trenton fall back in their seats and Kevin stiffens, crossing his arms over his chest. The question has definitely had the desired effect.

"The more I try to break the coding on the laptop, the more it's frying the damn thing. When the hell did Cal become a freaking computer genius?" Shane mumbles.

"He's been over yer shoulder enough," Kevin says.

"I've called in a few favors. I'm hoping to pull loose a few strings this week," Trenton says.

"Why does it feel like for each step we take, someone is two steps ahead in covering this shit up?" Kevin says.

"Aye, I get the same feeling. It's like being on a wild goose chase. None of it makes any fucking sense," I reply.

The table falls silent for a few beats. My mind starts to wander over the case. I begin listing all the information we have. Things we know and things we need to figure out.

It's in the middle of that list that my brain skids to a stop. I sit back in my seat and the thought takes wing.

"What if everything we've been chasing is bullshit?" I say aloud. "What if the crumbs we've been given are just that? Crumbs to keep us busy."

"That would make sense," Kevin says as he leans in.

"Let's start over. Wash the board clean. Shane, forget the laptop for now. I want ya in the street. Do what ya do best. Force the rats to us.

"Trenton, fill the holes. What have we lost focus on? Kevin, ya and the lass turn things up a bit. We've been too easy on these fuckers. I want this over. Find me who's lurking in the shadows on this. I have some doors I think it's time I start to kick in."

"Now we're talking," Trenton says, raising his beer.

CHAPTER 22

ON GUARD

Alicia

"I HAD A GREAT NIGHT WITH YOUR FAMILY," I say as Quinn turns into my block.

"I told ya they would love ya," he says with a smile in his voice.

"They're all so welcoming, and I can tell they love you. I can't explain it. They seem to all have a soft spot for you," I say.

"And I them."

I reach over to tuck his hair behind his ear. He turns his face to kiss my palm. I love it when he does that. My belly stirs with anticipation for the rest of the night.

"Should I only pack for the one night?" I ask, allowing my hand to fall to his thigh.

He groans when I start to massage his leg. Pulling in front of my house, he parks and lunges at me. I laugh into his mouth as he places a searing kiss on my lips.

"I'll have the kids this weekend, but yer welcome to stay as long as ya like," he says against my lips.

"Okay, I'll pack a few things real fast," I reply, but pull him back into another kiss.

My toes curl in my sandals. My whole body hums a song

for him. If Quinn were an ocean, his kisses would be like an undercurrent, dragging me in as I try helplessly to remain on the surface. I'm drowning in him, but I don't want to come up for air.

Unfortunately, his phone rings, interrupting us. Frustration rolls off him as he reaches for the device. His face tightens while he looks at the caller ID. I get a sinking feeling that we're not going to end the night the way we planned to.

I sometimes wonder how he deals with his job so well. Something always comes up to throw his lists off, but I've watched him adapt almost instantly on more than one occasion. When I think about it, it's like watching him rewrite his list in his head. It shows on his face, but he still makes the necessary changes.

"No, we'll all go," he says into the phone, confirming my suspicions. "Aye, I'm dropping her at the house now… No. Leave her where she is."

He rattles off a few more things so fast I can't make a thing out. When he hangs up the call, his eyes are conflicted. He looks quickly between me and the house.

"I'll be back as soon as I can. Go into the house and lock up. If Aidan is home, let him know I'm not there tonight," he says, leaning over to kiss my forehead before one last quick brush of his lips over mine.

"You'll text when you're on your way?" I ask, trying to hide my disappointment.

"Aye, but I don't want ya waiting up. I don't know how soon or if I'll be back. Go on, love. Get in the house," he says.

Hearing the urgency in his words, I hurry to get out of the car. I rush to the front door and get it open before turning back to look over my shoulder. Quinn honks his horn before his engine revs and he takes off.

I stare after him, wringing my hands. I don't like the feeling I have in the pit of my stomach. All at once, it hits me how dangerous Quinn's job is. Whether he's working security or investigating, it can get out of hand at the drop of a dime.

I narrow my eyes when something at the end of my block catches my eye. It's a black car with tinted windows. A light seems to flicker on the inside, pulling my attention. I don't recognize the car. This is a close-knit block. I know all my neighbors. I don't recall anyone getting a new car.

The Andersons' youngest daughter has a new boyfriend, but he drives a red car. Right as I get ready to shrug it off, the car comes to life and speeds off. A chill runs through me and the hair on my arms stand up.

"Hey, you," Aidan sings. "We were about to have a few drinks and have some girl talk. You down or is that sexy boyfriend coming over for the night?"

Turning to Aidan with a smile, I brush off the mystery car. I'm probably projecting my worry for Quinn. Shrugging it all off, I move into the house and lock up like Quinn told me to.

"I'll join you guys. I don't think he'll be back tonight," I reply.

Aidan nods and moves to place the alarm system on. Wrapping an arm around my shoulders, he ushers me into the living room where Tari is already set up. There's everything from vodka to tequila lined up on the coffee table.

One drink to calm my nerves. That's all.

Quinn

Maybe we won't have to send a message. It seems one has already come to us. Someone has set Danita's apartment on fire.

It's a good thing she doubled back to Kevin's tonight. She wasn't home, but her alarm was triggered and her neighbor called her with concerns about rising smoke and the other noises that came from the apartment before.

I pull up in front of Danita's apartment complex at the same time as Trenton and Shane. When I step out of the Jag, the first thing I take in is Danita cradling a large pit bull in her arms as she paces. The dog is almost as big as she is, but she's clinging to it tightly.

"*My home, my fucking home?*" Danita sobs as we draw closer to her and Kevin.

Firefighters are moving about as they get the fire under control. Kevin goes to wrap his arms around Danita as she rocks back and forth with her dog in her arms. The dog whimpers, and she kisses its head as tears roll down her cheeks.

Kevin whispers something to her and she nods. I've come to know this woman to be tough as nails. Seeing her like this has me ready to lose my shit.

Kevin looks up at me with an expression that matches the rage inside of me. This has been personal for all of us. Now, it's beyond personal.

"A warning," Shane says.

"Aye, but who the fuck are they to warn *me* of anything?" Kevin seethes. "I'm going to rain hell on their heads."

"We have to figure out who *they* are," Trent grunts.

"Something tells me that won't be hard. We must have triggered their attention. They're letting us know they're coming," Shane says.

"Aye, maybe, but if so, that's their mistake. We never warn that we're coming. We just fuck shit up and move on. It's time whoever this is learns who they've been fucking with. Change nothing, the plan I gave ya at the pub is the course we should have been on. I want to make sure we rattle the right nest," I say.

I look around again. Something nags at me. I've yet to put a finger on it.

Danita lifts her head and looks me in the eyes. I've seen that look before. Yet, I also note the veiled look in her depths. I've had the feeling that Danita has secrets, but this is the first time I've felt like they affect my family. She closes off before I can dig.

"Sunny is the last piece of my abuela I have left, if he had gotten trapped in there…if I had lost him," she sobs. "I'm going to fucking gut them. Do you hear me?"

"Aye, love. We hear ya," Kevin says, kissing the top of her head.

A blind man would be able to see that Kevin hasn't been pretending to be Danita's boyfriend. I don't know how far things have gone between them, but that line has been crossed in his mind a long time ago.

I narrow my eyes, wondering if that's such a great idea. I'm missing something. I start to list the things I know about Detective Moralez. Perhaps it's what I don't know that I need to focus on. Which means I want her where I can see her.

"There's plenty of room at my place for ya to crash," I offer.

"I think she needs some time; she'll be staying with me. The house is about finished. I'll start to settle in this weekend," Kevin says.

"Grand, but ya both can still stay at my place tonight if ya like." I pause to think, pulling my keys from my pocket. "Or ya can go up to the cabin for a night or two."

My cabin upstate is the perfect place for Danita to cool her head and gather her thoughts. The drive alone is enough to allow her to pull it together. It will also give me time to refocus and start putting pieces together.

Kevin nods and catches the keys I toss to him from my ring.

"I'll take ya up on that one," he says.

"Trenton, get the boys out here. See if ya can find something we can use," Kevin demands. "I'll call Dugan to see if he can buy us some time."

"Already on it," Trenton replies.

CHAPTER 23

SURPRISES

Alicia

QUINN HAS BEEN MIA AGAIN SINCE THE NIGHT HE dropped me off. He calls to let me know he's still breathing, but I haven't seen him in a week. Although, I get a gift delivered to my door every morning.

Always two dozen roses and a gift. I've gotten a bracelet, earrings, the purse I had been eyeing online a few weeks ago when he come over, and the list goes on. His attention to detail when it comes to me is amazing.

Still, the one thing I want more than any of these gifts is to see his face. I want to spend time in his arms. Last night was the longest conversation I've had with him ever. Hearing his voice rumble in my ear for hours only made me miss him more.

I was surprised to find out he's not even here in New York. I'm starting to adjust. The more I learn about him, his life, and his profession, I get that there will be times when he has to go away for work. At the moment, I'm a bit frustrated and missing him.

I kick the copy machine and growl. It hasn't done a thing to me, but I think I'm losing my mind. I miss Quinn so much, I can smell his cologne. I think I'm losing it until I see two hands land on the copier on either side of me as big arms cage me in.

I spin and look up. A smiling Quinn looks down at me. A yelp leaves my mouth, and I jump into his arms. He doesn't hesitant to capture my lips and hold me up, placing my butt on the copy machine.

He kisses me so thoroughly, my panties are soaked through within seconds. It's definitely been too long. I twist my fingers in his hair as I hold him to me and start to grind my hips.

"Ach, I missed ya too, but ya have customers out front. I don't think we'll be able to be that quiet." He chuckles.

"What are you doing here? I thought you were in Boston," I pant.

"Aye, I was. I just got back and came straight to see ya. Can ya take the rest of the day? I have some place I want to take ya," he says with a boyish smile.

I eye him warily, wondering what he's up to. It's still early. I haven't been here more than an hour. A quick glance at the clock tells me it's been even less.

"I don't have any classes or lessons today, but I planned to help out here in the office and work on the app," I say, thinking out loud.

"App?"

"Oh, I've been tinkering with some things. You know to bring in more streams of income. I have one for the school. It's in the early stages, but I think I have something," I say with a shrug.

I leave out the part about the app being for race car drivers. I'm still not ready to share that secret.

"Do ya know that ya amaze me?"

I don't answer; I just give him a dreamy look. I've truly missed him. I inhale, filling my lungs with his scent.

"The office won't fall apart without me for the day," I finally say.

Honestly, I was supposed to take the day off anyway. I was going to work on the app from home. I came into the office to get my mind off him.

"Grand, let's go. I have a full day planned."

I go to hop down from the copy machine, but Quinn has my waist in his grasp as he places me gently on my feet. Before taking off to get my purse, I wrap my arms around him and squeeze. Quinn returns the embrace, holding me a bit longer.

Something shifts as we stand here. When I take a look within myself, I see the key hasn't just turned in the lock. The door to my heart is sitting wide open. I turn my head up, and the eyes looking back at me are revealing that vulnerability that makes me so trusting of him.

"What?" he asks as I stare at him.

"You're not what I expected, Quinn. I…I like spending time with you," I say.

He cups my face and runs his thumb across my bottom lip. I smile. He's making one of his list. It's written all over his face.

"There isn't enough time in the world for me to spend with ya, love. But my thoughts are always with ya," he says.

I nearly let the words slip from my lips. Instead, I bite my tongue and break away to get my things. I say a silent prayer in hopes that I'm not a fool for falling in love with a Blackhart.

Quinn

"I haven't been to the city in so long," Alicia says as we enter Central Park.

"And ya have never been to Central Park in yer life," I say.

"I was wondering if you remembered me saying that."

"Aye, I do."

I love the light that brightens her brown eyes. I've missed her more than she'll ever know. Talking to her last night, I knew I had to get home to spend time with her.

I've been hot on the trail of a guy who I think will lead us to the big fish we want. Davis was one of the last numbers dialed in Cal's phone. We thought it was a first name until Shane found a Lo Davis in one of the files Danita gave us. It's an alias, but it led me to a guy in Boston.

Scott, one of our team managers, traded places with me. He'll be able to keep an eye on Davis while I'm here helping the family and running things at the office. I'll also be able to get back to spending time with Alicia.

"What are we doing here?" she asks excitedly.

"I'm taking ya on a tour of Central Park," I tell her.

"Really? Babe, seriously?"

"Aye, love. We'll be spending the day checking this off yer bucket list," I reply.

"But aren't some of the attractions closed this time of year? Like the gardens and isn't the castle being renovated? I really wanted to see those."

"I have a few friends who did me a couple of favors. We have our own escort for the day. We'll get to walk the gardens too," I say and wink at her.

Wrapping an arm around her and tucking her into my

side, we make our way to our waiting carriage. I never knew a horse and buggy could bring such joy. Alicia bounces in place when I stop in front of it.

"I feel like I'm in fairy tale," she sings.

"We're only getting started," I say, holding out my hand to help her up into the carriage.

When we're both seated safely, she snuggles into my side. The lazy stroll of the horses guides us into a content silence. The city may be moving fast around us, but we're in our own space and time as Alicia eyes the sights in wonder.

"Quinn?"

"Aye, love."

"Thank you."

I shift to look down at her face. She gives me that breath-taking smile. The one that stars in my dreams.

"For?"

"For being you. For not giving up on chasing me, and for all of this. I'm glad I got to know you," she says.

I stare back at her, wondering if I'll scare her away if I tell her that I love her. I'd do anything to bring a smile to her face. When I get reports back that she's safe but looks sad, it tears me apart.

I'm doing all I can to make my family safe again and that includes her. However, I don't think the time is right to tell her how I feel. While I can see Alicia opening up to me, I'm not sure if her wounds have healed enough for her to love me the way I've fallen for her. So I make the decision to hold my words for now.

"Yer welcome."

Alicia

I've almost blurted out *I love you* a million times today. This has been the best date I've ever been on. Not just the planned-out details, but every bit of the date has been amazing.

Quinn took me to the Belvedere Castle, which we shouldn't have had access to. We went to the Kerbs Boathouse. We played a game of chess in the Chess & Checker House. We took a stroll through the Mall and Literary Walk. Then, I got to see the Conservatory Garden, and we had a picnic lunch in Sheep Meadow.

One of my favorite parts was our walk through Bethesda Terrace. A light rain shower started right as we wandered through, making the Minton Tile Ceiling seem so much more majestic as we ran in for cover. Quinn held me close as he whispered stories of his childhood visits to Ireland.

I've crossed one thing off my bucket list, but I've added Ireland in its place. Quinn makes it sound so magical. I can't wait to visit it for myself someday.

Now, as the sun sets and the stars begin to light up the sky, we're riding the carousel. Central Park is its own place of wonder. I've been fascinated by it for years, but never made the trip.

I truly feel like I've spent the day in the middle of a dream. Being in this dream with Quinn has been icing on the cake.

"This is so…" I say, shaking my head as Quinn stands beside my horse with his arm around my waist.

The wind blowing through my hair, music and laughter surrounding us. I'm thrown back in time to when my father would take me to the fairs. My eyes fill with tears, but they're not tears of sorrow.

Yes, I miss my mom and dad, but this moment is reminding me of all the good times I have to be grateful for. For once, I'm seeing that I truly can make new happy memories.

I place my head against Quinn's chest and sigh as I look out at the stars. His warm embrace tightens as he holds me in that protective way of his. I feel treasured and cared for.

Closing my eyes, I inhale the scent that is Quinn and commit this moment to memory. Someday, I'll tell my little girls of the man who made one of my dreams come true just because. I know with Quinn, I won't have to hear about what he did for me later on.

I don't want to stop relishing the heat that's coming from Quinn. The ride comes to an end way before I'm ready. He rubs his hand up and down my side, and I force myself to lift my head.

"Where to now?" I ask expectantly.

"We have a suite at the Ritz-Carlton. I thought we could spend the night in the city. Room service and the rest of the night in," he replies.

I look at him, a playful smile on my lips. Quinn's eyes fill with lust, and my heart starts to race. He has been such a gentleman all day. I'm ready to get him behind closed doors so he can have his way with me, and I with him.

"I don't have anything to sleep in. I guess that means you're going to have to keep me warm tonight," I say.

"I've taken care of everything ya need, but if ya prefer to sleep nip, I'm all for it," he says.

"Nip?" I laugh. "Is that naked?"

"Aye, nude. I've been wanting to get ya naked since I walked in on ya kicking that poor machine," he says.

"Ugh," I groan. "You saw that?"

"Aye. I don't know what the thing did to ya."

"It didn't do anything. I was frustrated and missing my boyfriend," I say.

"Frustrated?" He eyes me curiously.

I lower my voice and look up at him through my lashes. "Yes, sexually frustrated and really missing my boyfriend. I mean, really, really missing him and super sexually frustrated."

Quinn lifts me from my horse and sets me on my feet. He has my wrist grasped in his hand, leading me off of the carousel. Our ride is waiting for us. Quinn helps me inside the carriage and murmurs something to the driver before hopping in next to me.

Taking out my phone, I move closer to him. I go to take a picture of us, but Quinn plucks the phone from my hands. Holding the phone out, he snaps the picture for me. I turn and kiss his cheek as he takes another. Turning his face, he nips my lip, then deepens the kiss. All while continuing to snap way.

"I guess having long arms has its benefits." I laugh.

"Aye, it does," he says, pressing his forehead to mine.

Rubbing the tip of his nose to mine, he takes a picture. Kissing my forehead, he snaps one more. I turn to the camera, and this time he kisses my cheek.

"Let me see," I say, taking my phone back. I swipe through the photos and beam with happiness. "We do look cute together. I love this one."

It's the one with him rubbing our noses together. He nods, tapping at my phone to send the picture to himself. I look at him curiously when he takes his phone out.

"What are you doing?"

"Changing my profile status. When are ya going to accept my request?" He turns to me with a pointed look.

"In my defense, I didn't know who Milo was at first."

"Ach, Milo is my middle name."

"Well, when I figured it out, I was still avoiding you," I say, trying not to laugh. "Then, I forgot you sent one."

"The profile is mostly for family. We don't make our profiles public because of the job."

"Makes sense," I say.

I open the app to accept his request. Almost instantly a notification comes through announcing I've been tagged as *in a relationship*. I click on Quinn's profile to see that not only has he posted the picture of us, he made it his profile pic.

My phone lights up with another notification. I laugh when I see it's Renny commenting on the photo. I show Quinn and he groans.

"She really wants more grandbabies," I say.

"Aye, not just more grands. She wants them from me," he says.

"Clearly." I chuckle.

"Don't encourage her," he says as I go to reply to her comment.

"What? I'm only going to say thank you."

"To what? Her calling us a gorgeous couple, or her telling me to shag you and give her grands," he teases.

I roll my lips to keep from laughing. She didn't put it as nicely as he did. Renny is not afraid to say what's on her mind at all.

"Go on, get it out. I'm already embarrassed," he says, causing me to laugh. "Only my mum would be on social media typing: *My son and his bird are hot as fuck. Get off of here and go make me some grands to spoil, loves.*"

I laugh harder. "But, babe, she's so cute."

"Ach, sure she is," he mutters and shakes his head.

We stop across from the hotel, and Quinn helps me out of the carriage. He clasps my hand and we make our way across the busy street. I smile as Quinn places himself between me and the traffic. Always in tune with my safety.

It doesn't take long for him to retrieve our key or for us to get up to our room. The suite is huge and breathtaking. I feel like a princess as I walk in and look around.

"Make yerself at home. I'll order room service and then we can relax," he says as he picks up the menu.

"Room service can wait. Why don't we wash off the long day first," I say with a seductive grin.

Quinn tosses the menu down and heads in my direction. I'm over his shoulder the moment he reaches me. This time, instead of fussing, I laugh and go with the flow.

CHAPTER 24

BUBBLE AND CHILL

Alicia

"Aye, ya can laugh at me all ya want. There are just some things that should never touch," Quinn says as I crack up at him.

We've been relaxing in a bathtub filled with bubbles. My back to his front, his arms around me, and his thighs thrown over mine, caging me into all that is him. I've never felt more secure in my life.

"It's food. You put it on a plate to eat it. I've watched you place more than one thing on a fork at a time," I say.

"Ach, no, ya haven't. Not to feed myself. Maybe when I share my food with ya, but that's because I was trying to avoid this," he says good-naturedly.

I think of all the times we've eaten together. As I picture the methodical way he eats, I realize he's right. I've never seen him mix his food.

"Oh, my God! You're right."

"Aye, I always am," he teases.

"Whatever. Let's not get ahead of ourselves, big boy." I snort.

"Name a time I've been wrong," he says as he buries his face in my neck.

My eyes close. I can't think of anything else as his mouth latches onto my skin. A small moan leaves my lips, and I squirm beneath the water.

I forget what we were talking about moments ago, but my smile doesn't leave my lips. Reaching behind me, I push my hand into the back of his hair and start to massage his scalp. He groans and sighs, kissing a trail down to my shoulder.

"You like that?"

"Aye," he replies, nipping my ear.

We fall silent, enjoying the moment. He takes a lazy trip up my sides with his hands, avoiding my breasts that ache for his touch. He's been building the anticipation since we entered the tub. A touch here, a caress there. I'm on the verge of bursting into flames.

"Tell me something about ya parents," Quinn says as he traces the tops of my breasts with his fingertips.

I shift, causing the water to splash a little. I don't answer right away. Instead, I glide a hand over the bubbles and watch as they separate and come back together.

"My mom was from Brooklyn and my dad was from Texas. A real life gun-toting cowboy. He was a rancher before he came to New York and fell in love with my mom. I was in awe of that. My dad being a Black cowboy. You know how people make it seem like that's not possible," I say. "I loved looking at the pictures of him, his brothers, and friends. They were the real deal."

"You'll have to show me those sometime," he says.

"I haven't looked at those in years. I used to ask him if he missed that life. He'd tell me no. Shoveling shit would never hold a candle to the treasure he found in the city. I believed him, but I didn't. I know he loved me and my mom, but I think he left a piece of himself back home in Texas."

"Ya never went to visit?" he asks.

"No." I shake my head. "My dad was the baby. His brothers had him by ten to fifteen years. All but one of my uncles died before my dad. I didn't meet him until after my father passed. They all fell out over Daddy leaving to move here and marry my mom. Apparently, they were counting on him to help run things.

"I met him at the funeral, but that was it. He offered me to come to Texas, but this is my home. I had the house, and I'd already been accepted to college here. We tried to stay in touch, but I think it was too hard for him."

"I'm glad ya stayed," he says next to my ear.

I turn my head to look at him. Quinn crushes my lips with his, coiling desire in my belly. I turn onto my knees to wrap my arms around his neck. My dripping wet breasts press against his hard chest.

We both release the hunger that's been building. Quinn glides his hands down my back to cup my backside. I shiver in his hold, wanting—no, needing more of him.

He doesn't disappoint. Deepening the kiss, he reaches for my thighs and pulls me to straddle him. Thank goodness for the large bath tub, I don't think I can wait any longer. Quinn cups one of my breasts as he breaks the kiss. His head lowers and his mouth wraps around my aching nipple.

My hips start to grind on their own, greedy for what's to come. The pleasure is mind-numbing. I don't have a single coherent thought. I reach between us for his length, knowing having him inside me is the only way to put out this fire.

I start to lower onto him, causing him to lift his head and my nipple to pop free from his mouth.

"Wait, let me—ah, fuck," he rasps.

My head falls back, and I start to ride him slowly. His hands grasp my hips and his forehead drops to my collarbone. I lace my fingers into his hair, wrapping my other arm around his shoulders.

I've missed this feeling more than I thought. I've always been so shy and insecure about sex, but Quinn makes me want to release a part of me I never knew was there. He lifts his head and I lower mine to look at him.

The desire, awe, and passion I find spur me on. Unfolding my leg, I plant the pad of my foot on the floor of the tub, followed by the other leg. Placing my palms on his shoulders, I start to alternate between bouncing and rolling my hips.

"Fuck," he breathes through his teeth.

His grip tightens, his leg lifts as he shifts his hips to thrust up into me. I start to cry out in pleasure. Each thrust brings a bite with it that sends a cocktail of confusion through my senses. My belly coils with the signs of my first orgasm.

"Quinn," I whimper.

"Riding my cock like this is going to get ya in all kinds of trouble. Yer not as innocent as ya want me to believe. Show me what ya really want, love," he says huskily.

I bite my lip and nod. I stand, allowing him to slip from my body. Lifting my right leg, I place my toes on the edge of the bathtub behind his shoulder, angling my pussy into his face.

Quinn wastes no time, his face is buried in my folds as he uses his hands to help support me. Boy, do I need that support. My cries fill the bathroom as his tongue creates figure eights through my lips. I thread one hand in his hair and the other in my own. The brush of his beard against my inner thighs is an added push to the edge.

My orgasm takes hold of me and locks on relentlessly. I feel like my heart and soul are being ripped from my body. My legs start to tremble, and I swear I'm going to crash into the water.

However, in one swift motion Quinn raises to his feet, lifting me into his arms. I wrap my legs around him lazily. I link my arms around his neck as his lips seize mine.

Carefully, he steps from the bath. We're moving to the bedroom as my body continues to quake in his hold. My back hits the mattress softly while his body covers mine.

He breaks our lip lock to start moving down my body, dropping a trail of kisses as he goes. When he gets to my belly, he pauses to give attention to my belly button. He circles his tongue around it, before dipping inside.

Bowing my back off the bed, I focus my gaze on the ceiling and grasp the bedspread. He licks his way back up to my right breast to torture me some more. I look down when I can sense him hovering, but no longer touching or licking.

His eyes are on my face as his breath fans across my mound. Goose bumps rise and I quiver. The intensity of his look alone is enough to trigger another round of multiples. He splays his hand on my stomach and glides up slowly.

"What would please ya most, love?" he asks in a deep rasp. "Tell me how to unlock that goddess I see waiting for me. She wants more than for me to fuck her. Ach, but she needs more than for me to make love to her."

I scrunch up my face. I don't know how to tell him the things I really want, but he's right. I want something in between.

"You were holding back last time," I say timidly. "As… as if you would scare me off or hurt me. I want that, what you're hiding from me. I'll give you her if I can have him."

I watch his eyes light up with something dark. His tongue peeks out to drag across his lips. I'm getting my first true look at Quinn. The shield he's been holding in place to protect me falls to the ground, forever shattered.

I fail to hide the thrill that consumes me. My heart and body recognizes that we've found our perfect match. Resolve fills me. I can trust Quinn with all of me, I can give him what I've never felt right giving to another.

I lift, pushing at his chest until he turns onto his back. Straddling his stomach, I cup his face and kiss him. It's not one of our normal hungry kisses. No. I place a little extra into this one. Taking his tongue into my mouth, I mimic what I want to do to him.

He opens his mouth to me as I suck and bob, pulling deep groans from him. He roams my back and butt with his hands. Wanting the real thing, I start to move down his body. Slowly, I lower, leaving a trail of openmouthed kisses.

When I get to the crest on his chest, those piercings call to me. I shift to lick across his right nipple, circling the piercing. His moan of approval guides me to the left one to repeat the action. I blow, relishing the goose bumps that rise, loving that I have this effect on him.

I take my time to trace his tattooed chest with my tongue. Reaching for my own breast, I pinch my peak, sending a bolt of sensation to my core. Quinn shifts his weight beneath me, drawing my attention. The look in his eyes as I play with my breast turns me on so much, I slide my hand down my body to find my nub.

I begin to rock my hips against my hand, soaking my fingertips. His jaw works as if he's doing all he can to keep from pouncing. His loss of control is my gain, and it feels so powerful. To have him look at me this way gives me confidence to do what I'm longing to.

With my gaze locked on him as I look up through my lashes, I lift my wet fingers to his lips. He sucks them into his mouth, making a show of cleaning them. Pulling my hand back, my fingers pop free from his lips with a wet sound.

"Ya taste delicious, love. Taste it," he commands huskily.

I reach between my legs to coat my fingers again before lifting them to my own lips. A smile turns up the corners of my mouth as I place them inside. I hum around them, licking each one clean.

Wanting to know how he tastes, I finish my descent. I settle between his legs, wrapping my fingers around his throbbing length as best I can. A tentative flick of my tongue rewards me with a burst of our flavors mixed together. I take him in greedily.

It's awkward at first, but the more he starts to rock his hips and his groans fill the room, the more I get into it. I allow my saliva to coat him as my hands and mouth work together. His hand lands in my hair, and I reach to lace my wet fingers over his. It's a plea for his guidance to bring him more pleasure. His eyes narrow on mine and understanding fills his gaze.

"Ah, yer doing just fine, love," he groans.

I smile around him, but hollow my cheeks. The wide-eyed expression I receive drives me forward me. I swirl my tongue around him on my next pass and the reward is more than gratifying. I'm convinced I've got this.

"Fuck, fuck, fuck," he bellows.

His stomach caves, his knees bend, and his toes curl. He makes a gorgeous sight as his head falls back and he pushes his free hand into the front of his hair. His hand in my hair tightens, creating a tingle in my scalp.

I double my efforts. When I feel him swelling in my mouth, I relax my throat and take as much of him as I can. I start to gag the first time, but I'm no quitter. I try again and again until I'm sure Quinn is no longer speaking English.

"Alicia," he roars as his seed shoots down the back of my throat.

I blink in surprise as the warmth fills my mouth and throat. I hold it for a moment before deciding to swallow. It's salty, sweet, and hot, but what's scorching hot is the look on Quinn's face.

"C'mere," he beckons.

Climbing up his body, I straddle him again. His places a hand behind my neck, tugging me into his demanding kiss. I'm surprised when he guides my hips over his already-recovered erection.

"Quinn," I breathe as I sink onto him.

"Show me," he coaxes.

I nod and release all my inhibitions. My heart is full. I want this, and I want it with him.

Here goes nothing. Careful what you ask for, Quinn.

Quinn

Her eyes lock on mine and she lift her arms above her head as she starts to rock and roll her body over mine. My shy girl is gone. In her place is the vixen I've been eyeing on the inside of her.

A seductive smile touches her lips as she drags her right hand down her left arm. She sets the rhythm and tempo we move to. I don't thrust up into her to dominate. Instead, I rock my hips slowly with short strokes to add to her pleasure without taking away from her moment.

I'm well aware that I'm watching her find herself. It's the most beautiful sight I've seen in my life. She claims another piece of my heart as she does.

"Yer so gorgeous, love," I say as I watch her face twist in ecstasy.

Her eyes lower, she sucks her lip between her teeth, and her arms fold over her head. It's as if she's trying to hold onto her body to keep from leaving it. I understand the feeling.

Rising, I glide my hands up her sides, over her arms, until my fingers intertwine with hers. I allow my lips to tell her the long list of words that come to mind when she's in my arms. Her heat gushes around me, causing me to harden and moan into her mouth.

Like in the bathtub, she plants her feet into the mattress and her hands on my shoulders. Only this time, she leans back as she takes me into her body over and over. My gaze falls to her breasts bouncing. My jaw ticks. I'm not going to be able to hold back much longer.

"We made a deal, Quinn," she breathes. "Her for him."

She doesn't have to ask twice. In a single breath, I have her on her back with both of her legs over my right shoulder. My hips roll into her body, taking this slow, building the explosion I want to come.

"Yer so wet. Are ya ready, love?"

"Ready?" she pants, confusion in her voice.

"Aye, do ya think yer ready for me?"

Her hands reach over her head for purchase. She's going to need it. She has given me permission to unleash the beast that's been in waiting. She might want to take that back when I'm done.

"Yes, yes, please," she pleads.

"As ya wish."

I grasp the tops of her thighs and start to pound into her tight, fat pussy. The more her walls squeeze around me, the deeper I thrust. She arches her back off the bed, pushing her breasts toward me. She thrashes her head from side to side, but it's the look on her sweat-soaked face that drives me.

"Damn, Quinn. That's what I need, baby. That's the shit I've been wanting," she sobs out. "Yes."

The sexy look in her eyes and her dirty little mouth have my balls tightening. I swirl my tongue in my mouth, savoring her flavor that's still lingering there. Having her bare herself to me has something primal rising on the inside of me.

"Fuck, I can give ya this all night, love. Yer pussy is so good. I'm going to fuck ya into next week," I grunt.

"Please."

I reach for a handful of her hair and tug her head back. I lean into her. My thrusts keep hitting their mark. Not breaking my stride once as she soaks my cock.

"You're mine, Alicia. No one else will ever touch ya like this again," I breathe into her ear.

"Baby, no one ever has," she whimpers. "You're the only one who's made me feel like this."

I crush her lips, reaching between us for her clit. I'm so close and I need her with me. My thumb circles her nub, and she goes off like a rocket, her mouth opening on a silent scream. I lock my arm around her legs to keep her from getting away from me as I give a few more thrusts and explode inside her.

As I throb within her heat, I remember she climbed on top of me in the bathtub before I could say something about a condom. Once inside of her bare, it's the only way I want her. I think to say something about it, but her tiny snores reach my ears.

"Don't give me up so fast, love. It's going to be a long night," I whisper in her sleeping ear.

CHAPTER 25

UNSAFE

Quinn

"I NEED TO GO ACROSS TOWN THIS MORNING," I say, pecking Alicia's lips after she rinses the toothpaste out of her mouth. "I'll take you in when I get back."

"Okay," she says. "Wait. I need to get to the school early. I can take an Uber."

"Ach, no, ya won't," I reply.

Jazz has been watching over Alicia. However, this morning Jazz will be coming with me. I thought Alicia would be here in the safety of my home until I returned. I don't want her going to the office by herself. There's too much going on.

She frowns, placing her hands on her hips. "Why not? I need to get to work."

My jaw tightens. I don't want to lie to her, but I don't want to alarm her by telling her that I have my team watching her. I have to make this meeting this morning.

"I'd feel better if ya wait for me to get back," I say.

"How long are you going to be?"

"I don't know yet." I blow out a frustrated breath.

"Would you feel better if I drive one of your cars?"

"No, I want to know ya arrived safely. Driving one of my cars doesn't ensure that."

"Babe, I seriously have a ton of work to do. I need to get into the office early. With the system crashing unexpectedly, taking that one day wrinkled things more than I anticipated. I have payroll, scheduling, and I need to check on one of the cars that one of the instructors texted to complain about," she says.

I pinch the bridge of my nose. Running through my list of where everyone should be this morning, I hold up a finger and pull out my phone to make a call.

"What's up, Quinn?" Trenton answers.

"Aye, Trent. Can ya come take Alicia to work for me?"

Really? Alicia mouths at me. I don't response. I'm not allowing her to drive in on her own. If Trenton takes her in, I can head back to her after my meeting.

"I can be there in an hour, but I need to head to that job by nine," he replies.

"She'll be ready."

"Did you handle that meeting with your connection? How far out is that?"

"No, I'm on my way now," I say. "It's in Massapequa."

"Do you want me to see if I can switch out with someone to stay with Alicia until you arrive?"

I twist my lips and think about it. If I leave now, I can get back in time. Jazz can resume her station then.

"No, I'll take care of it. Get her to the office," I say.

"Got it. I'll be there," he says and hangs up.

Alicia stands before me with her arms folded across her chest. I can see in the flare of her nostrils, she's annoyed with me. I wrap my arms around her, pulling her into me.

"Humor me, love," I say, brushing my lips against her forehead.

"Sometimes you make me feel like a baby who needs a babysitter. I know how to get myself to work," she mumbles.

"You're not a baby, but I…I want to make sure you're safe," I reply, avoiding those three words I don't have the time to deal with this morning.

Last thing I want to do is send her running from me. We've had three amazing nights together. This still doesn't sit right with me, but I know how important her business is to her. I was lucky to get the day she gave me.

I've been to the office two nights in a row to pick her up after hours. I know she's dedicated to catching up on things turned upside down at the school. I rock her in my arms until her eyes start to soften.

"Go to work." She sighs. "We'll talk about this later."

Giving her a crooked smile, I dip my head for one last kiss before releasing her. Only the kiss turns into a long heart-pounding, lip-searing kiss. When I break it, I have to take a moment to think.

"*Is breá liom tú.*"

I've held the words in long enough. This way she can't run, but I've said them before they burst inside me. I have no doubt that I'm in love with Alicia.

"What does that mean?" she says with the stunning smile.

"I'll tell you later. Have a good day, love."

Alicia

"Thanks for the ride, Trenton," I say as he pulls into the parking lot of the driving school.

I have laughed the entire ride. Trenton is hilarious. Although I was annoyed with Quinn for insisting that I have a chaperone, I did enjoy getting to spend a little time with Trenton.

"Anytime," Trenton says with that mischievous smile of his. "And I'm waiting for you to start calling me, Trent."

"Okay, okay, I'll try to remember that. Why do I get the feeling you give your woman lots of trouble," I tease.

"Me? Never. I'm always a gentleman, and I take care of my woman." He chuckles.

Whoever his woman is, she's a lucky one. That dark hair and those freckles have a charm of their own. It doesn't hurt that his green eyes are always sparkling with some playful secret. Honestly, Trenton is a sweetheart beneath it all.

"Sure, that chuckle says everything." I shake my head. "See you later."

"Hold on, I'll park and walk you in," he says.

"Don't worry about it," I say. "I'm going into the coffee shop."

He frowns, looking exactly like Quinn. He looks at the clock and chews on his lip. I know he has to get to his assignment. I rush to get out before it turns into a big fuss.

"I want a bagel and frappe," I say as I wave.

"Later, sis," he calls after me.

I head for the coffee place across the lot from my school. I turn to find Trent watching me enter the front door. I wave and he nods, but still doesn't leave. I laugh and go in.

The place is pretty empty, allowing me to place my order quickly. I decide to sit and finish my breakfast while clearing the emails that are my first task for the morning. Fifteen minutes later, I cross the lot to the back entrance of my shop.

My key in hand, I get ready to push it into the lock, but I pause mid-motion. Something isn't right. The door is sitting slightly open.

I take out my phone to text Aidan and Tari to see if they have arrived. Last we texted, they were both still at the house. Tari replies quickly, informing me they're leaving.

My heart begins to race. I dial Quinn before I can think twice. On autopilot, I back away from the door and look around. My car is still parked in the lot. I head for it as I wait for Quinn to answer. It only takes him two rings.

"Are ya all right, love?" he asks right way.

"No, I think someone broke into the school. I don't know why I called you. I should be calling the police," I say in frustration with myself.

"Ya did right, love. Don't go inside. I'm sending Trenton back, and I'm on my way," he says tightly.

"Okay—"

My reply gets cut off when the sound of screeching tires draws my attention. I have just enough time to jump out of the way. My phone flies from my hand, sliding under the car, and my purse spills onto the ground. I try to reach for the phone, but from this side of my car, I see the black car backing toward me.

"Oh, my God!" I scream.

I scramble to my feet and grab my car key from the ground. I don't have time to reach my phone. I unlock the car and jump inside. My car roars to life as I smash the ignition button. I whip out of the spot before the other car can switch into drive and smash into my driver's side door—barely.

I do the one thing I know I do best. I drive. My hands are

trembling, but I ignore that as I maneuver out of the parking lot onto the street. A glance in the rearview tells me this person is right on my bumper. These Long Island streets are mostly single lanes. I need to get somewhere where I can move.

Making a quick decision, I pop out into oncoming traffic. I have a split second to step on the gas and pass the two cars to get back in the right lane and not crash head on with the Mack Truck headed for me. I gun it and zip into the right lane as the truck blasts its horn at me.

"Hell yeah, Ali," I holler, adrenaline pumping.

I look around, forming a plan. Quinn said he was going to Massapequa this morning. I don't know how, but I know I need to get to him. A quick turn and I start to pick off small blocks, hoping to lose the car and to make my way to Route 27.

"Shit, sorry!" I call as if I can be heard. I barely dodge an old lady in the middle of the street. "I have to get off the residential blocks. This dude is crazy."

I dart for the street that will dump me onto the service road, the black car is so close. I grit my teeth and step on the gas. I don't have time to pause for the stop sign. The dealership has a clear path from its side entrance to its service road exit. I'll have time to see the oncoming traffic before I enter it.

Decision made, I fly through the lot so fast the cars rock as I pass. I see a truck in the right lane and three cars coming in the left, but I can't stop for them. I press the button dropping my BMW into sport and I take it.

I fly across the front of the truck into the lane with the three cars, ignoring their protesting horns. I've lost the car for now, but I know it's not over. I pull onto the highway as soon as the entrance comes into view. Just as I thought, I don't get to breathe for long. The car is behind me, closing in.

"Quinn! I need you," I sob.

Quinn

I'm losing my fucking mind. Jazz and I were already on the way to the school. Jazz's car is there already.

All it takes is a split second. I know this. Why didn't I tell Trenton to stay with her until I arrived? I knew I never should have let her go in until I returned. I felt it in my bones, and I still let her go.

"Where is she?" I bellow at the phone.

"Tapped into her car's app system. She's on the move. The locator has her moving northwest. Fuck, southwest. Damn, she's moving fast. Quinn, I think she's trying to get to the highway. Head for Route 27," Shane replies in frustration.

"Smart, love," I murmur to myself. "Trenton, where are ya?"

"Heading for 27. I'll head east," he replies.

"Aye, I'm heading west. Kevin, ya take west with me from yer location," I command.

"Already on it."

I punch my steering wheel, wishing I'd driven the Jag this morning. No matter, I push the fuck out of this pickup truck. Alicia's screaming voice playing in my head is driving me forward. I have fire blazing through my veins.

Thank God for my genius brother and his fast thinking. I'll follow my woman to the pits of hell to rescue and protect her. If I can find her, I'm there. Fuck, that it's not an *if*. My heart will lead me to her.

"She's on 27. Head west, past Bayshore," Shane calls.

"Got it," I say, dodging in and out of the two-lane traffic.

"I'm on the highway heading east," Trenton replies.

"This traffic is bullshit," Kevin growls.

That it is. I get to the turn for the service road and blow through the light as it turns red. I almost flip my truck over turning so fast.

"Easy, boss," Jazz says as she holds onto the passenger handle.

"Keep an eye out for her car," I demand.

"Stay out here," Jazz warns. "If you go inside, we'll get locked in."

I grind my teeth and nod. We won't be able to see certain strips of the highway that elevate, but she's right. If we get onto the highway, it could be worse.

"Holy fuck!" Trenton's voice comes through the line. "She can drive. Quinn, she's between Exit 40 and 39, moving fast. Woohoo, baby girl!"

"Aye, get yer ass on this side, Trent."

I floor it. When her blue BMW comes into view, my heart thunders in my chest. She's dodging in and out of lanes with a black car hot on her heels. The windows of the black vehicle are tinted. I can't see the driver or if anyone else is in the car.

"I'm going to fucking kill ya," I snarl when the car gets right on her bumper.

She's locked into the outer lane, and I can't get to her. There's fence and railing blocking the way onto the highway. I feel so helpless. There isn't an entrance for me to get on in sight.

A roar rips from my chest. Right when I think I'm going to lose it altogether, a car in the right lane opens up for her to slip through. Alicia takes the opening, but the cars don't close rank fast enough to close off the other car. It gets through and gives chase.

Cars start to clear the way, moving off to the side of the road. Finally, I see the entrance coming up. I step on the gas, demanding the truck move faster. Just then a yellow Camaro and black Viper fly past.

"We're on it, bro. Let's box this motherfucker in," Trent says.

"Well, shit. Aye, she'll be retraining the staff," Kevin's voice comes through.

I'm speechless. I can't believe what I'm watching the woman I love do. She's trying to give me a coronary and impressing the fuck out of me at the same time.

"Hot damn," Jazz whispers beside me. "She's my new shero. Now that's Black Girl Magic."

"Is she driving into oncoming traffic?" Shane says through the line. "I'm trying to get a live visual, but from the app, it looks like she's driving into oncoming traffic."

"Aye, that she is," my brothers and I reply in unison.

Alicia

He's going to drive me into the back of this truck. It's going to

decapitate me. I'm not dying like this! Not now. I finally started
finding myself and happiness. God, help me.

Panic seizes me. I whip my head back and forth as my
gaze bounces around. I can't go left or right. Looking in the
mirror at the view behind me, cars have pulled to the side of
the road to watch this unfold. Other cars are still coming,
but there's an opening.

As my mind races to figure out what to do, Trenton's
yellow Camaro appears in the mirror. Then, in the distance I
see a black-and-silver pickup truck speeding in my direction.

"Quinn!" I cry out in relief. "You got this, Ali. Your man
is coming for you. Just get to him."

The black car bumps me, pushing me toward the back
of the truck in front of me. Making a hard right, I turn into
oncoming traffic, darting onto the slim shoulder and barely
avoiding a car in the lane. My heart is pounding as I call on
all those Sundays I spent with my dad on those race tracks.
I thank my lucky stars I was the substitute for the son my
father always wanted.

I weave in and out of the cars heading for me. Drivers
start to freak out, making it harder to counter them, but I
focus and dodge them, outmaneuvering the stunned drivers. When I get to Quinn, I spin into a sharp U-turn and get
behind him. I know he's heading for the car that was chasing
me.

"I hope he catches you and fucks you up." I pout and
tighten my hold on the steering wheel.

Popping out to Quinn's left side, I pull up beside him. I
frown when he starts to slow, but I slow with him. His door
opens and he jumps out of the still-moving truck. A woman
slides into the driver's seat, while Quinn jumps into my car.

"Go," he barks once in the car with me. "Follow Trent and Kevin. I want that fucker."

He pulls a G19 Glock and cocks it. My eyes widen, but I take off. It feels good to be the one chasing and not the one being chased, but I drive just as hard.

Beside me, Quinn is breathing like a raging bull. I realize that Kevin must be in the black Viper. They're coming up on the car that was chasing me, but the highway has opened up to stoplights and cross streets. This asshole has too many options to get away.

"Not on my watch," I fume and gun past Trenton and Kevin.

The car turns to switch directions, heading back east. I bang the turn hard. Sirens blur, signaling the police are coming, but I don't stop. Trenton and Kevin are behind us.

Quinn makes a rumbling sound in his chest, rolling the window down. He sticks his huge frame out the window, resting his butt on the windowsill. The first shot fires and the back tire blows out. The second shot blows out the back window.

Pissed off and needing my own outlet, I step on the gas and ram the back of the car. Quinn jerks and grunts, causing me to brake and reach for him. But he has already steadied himself. Coming to a full stop, I watch as Quinn pulls himself out of the car.

"Quinn," I call, but he's headed for the car that has spun out and crashed. "Quinn!"

I go to get out of the car and follow after him, but it slams back shut and a jean-covered butt sits against it. I scowl as I look at Trenton's back pressed to my car. I turn to crawl out the other side. However, I'm met with angry green eyes.

"Leave him be," Kevin says. "He won't hear ya. He's too far gone."

With that, Kevin turns his back and sits his butt on the other door. I fold my arms over my chest and fall back in my seat. My mouth drops open and my eyes nearly pop out of my head when I focus on Quinn. He's holding a guy up by the throat with his gun shoved in his mouth.

"Oh, my God," I cry out. "One of you stop him. He's going to kill him."

"He'll be fine," I hear Trenton say through the glass.

"The police are coming," I say in exasperation.

"It's handled," Kevin says.

"So I'm just supposed to sit here?" I gasp.

"Yup," Trenton says.

"Aye," Kevin grunts.

"Grr."

CHAPTER 26

ANGRY BEAR

Alicia

I CAN'T STOP PACING. TRENTON BROUGHT ME HERE TO the Golden Clover after Quinn was placed in cuffs and put in the back of a squad car. Kevin tried to reassure me that Quinn would be out as soon as he made it to the station. I call bullshit.

We've been here for an hour and Quinn hasn't arrived yet. My nerves are shot. All the adrenaline has worn off and the reality of the situation has set in. Someone broke into my school and tried to kill me.

"They're going to total your car," Trenton says as he gets off his phone.

"I don't care about the car. Where's Quinn?"

"He should be here soon. Although, I think you may want to give him some space for a while. He's pretty pissed," he says with concern in his eyes.

"At me?" I ask, holding my mouth open.

"We told you to stay in the car. Getting out to argue with the cops didn't help the situation. We had it under control," he says pointedly.

"That guy tried to kill me. He should have been the one in cuffs, not Quinn," I say.

"Yeah, and he would have been the only one in cuffs if you stayed in the car."

"Aye, ya don't listen," Quinn's voice barks, causing me to turn.

I run at him, flinging myself into his arms. He lifts me, and I bury my face in his neck and inhale him. His embrace is stiffer than I'm expecting. I lift my head to look into his eyes.

His jaw works and he won't look at me. I slide down the front of his body and take a step back. I place my arms around my middle protectively.

"Let's take this into the back room," Kevin says from behind Quinn.

Turning, I follow Trenton into the room we all had dinner in the night I met Quinn's parents. Trenton offers me a seat, but I don't want to sit. Instead, I keep my eyes on Quinn and the rage rolling off of him.

"If they tell ya something, it's for yer safety," Quinn bellows.

I snap my head back. I don't know what I was expecting when he arrived, but this wasn't it. I drop my arms and stand straighter.

"I'm not a child. I was trying to help you."

"Ya would have helped me just fine by listening—" He cuts his own words off, closing his eyes and tugging his hair. "I watched a man chase ya down and try to run ya off the road. I heard ya screaming through the phone, love. I was not in my right mind when the police arrived. What do ya think was going on in my head when that officer put his hands on ya to hold ya back away from me?"

"Oh," I murmur.

"Aye, oh."

"What's the plan?" Kevin asks.

"What did ya learn at the school?"

Quinn turns to the woman who took over driving his truck. I noticed her when they arrested Quinn and put my car on the tow truck. She looks familiar, but I can't place her.

"Nothing was taken. Most of the damage was to her desk and the register," she says.

"The family is on lockdown. I'm taking Alicia up to the cabin for a while. Narrow this down while I'm gone," Quinn says.

"What happened to the guy?" Trent asks.

"Beats the fuck out of me. The boys were planning to hand him over, but someone got him out of there before they could," Kevin says tightly.

"What?" Trent snarls.

"Aye, it looks like our friends on the force are shrinking," Kevin replies.

"Which is why *everyone* is on lockdown," Quinn says.

"Hold on, hold on," I call out, waving my hand in the air. "I'm not leaving to go anywhere. I have to get to the school to find out the damage. I need to replace my car, and I have to get my work done. I'm not going to let one nut ruin my business."

Collective groans sound around the room. Quinn's eyes take on a crazy look, but I stand my ground. He moves toward me like a big angry bear.

"*Quinn,*" Renny's voice rings in warning. I hadn't noticed her enter the room.

He lifts a hand to hold her off, not taking his eyes off mine. I tilt my head back as he stands over me. I bring my hands to my hips.

He's not the boss of me.

"I didn't know I said this was up for discussion," he says in a low voice.

"Yup, you done lost your ever-loving mind," I snap. "Quinn, I'm not your child. I have a life and a business to run."

"A business that was broken into. A business that I need to make sure is secured. Until all of that is taken care of—"

"You don't have to make sure of anything."

"Yes. I. Do," he rumbles.

"I'm going home."

"No, love. No one is going back to your house until I have this under control. When I say everyone is on lock-down, I mean *everyone*," he says.

"Renny, come get your son before he can't have children," I say, narrowing my eyes at Quinn.

Quinn

She does my head in. I don't know whether to kiss her sense-less or strangle her. I haven't placed my lips on her because I know I'll devour her when I do. I want that to be a private moment, but it's taking all my restraint.

I also want to refrain from telling her this is all my fault. That being with me put her life in danger. Yet, she's always fighting me on something. Discounting what I tell her for her own good.

I can't deal with it right now. My need for control is through the roof. I grind my teeth as I look down at her.

"Maybe ya should take a dander to cool off, Quinn," Ma says behind me, I can hear the humor in her voice.

"I don't find this funny. Not one bit," I say.

"Yeah, it sort of is. She's this tiny little thing, but I swear she's about to hand you your ass," Trent snorts.

I close my eyes and start to count backwards. I go back to my list of priorities. That's my guide to getting this all under control.

"I'm going home," Alicia repeats.

"No, yer not."

"Why the hell not?"

"Because I need to know yer safe. Because there are people out there targeting my family, targeting ya. Because I love ya," I bellow.

The words are out before I can catch them, but I don't care. I grab Alicia and kiss her the way I've wanted to since I walked in and saw her safe. She locks her fingers into my hair, holding on tightly. She returns the kiss with as much vigor as I give.

"I think that settles that." Trent chuckles.

"I love you too," Alicia whispers when I break the kiss.

I search her eyes as her words sink in. I smile down at her. The calm I've been trying to grasp all day settles in. I place my forehead to hers.

"Say it again, love."

"I love you, Quinn, but I'm going to kick your ass if you keep bossing me around."

"Ach, I need ya sa—"

"You need me safe, and you've been holding things back from me. Explain to me—like I'm your woman—what's really going on. When you do, I'll go wherever you need me to be," she replies.

"Fair enough," I breathe.

"Quinn?"

"Yes."

"Thank you for coming to save me," she says softly.

"Oh, love. Ya never had to worry about that. I was coming for ya."

"About that. How did—"

"We need to have a long talk," I groan.

Alicia

"You've had someone watching me for how long?" I ask after Quinn finishes telling me all that's been going on.

Everyone cleared out to give us a little privacy. I think I've entered a state of shock. I can't believe someone has been watching me and reporting to Quinn.

"Jazz has been watching over ya since the day ya met my brothers. After Trent asked ya about how much time ya spent with Erin," he replies.

I lick my lips, not really sure how I feel about this. I'm still processing. I scratch my head and nod.

"Okay, so you think it's best to leave for a little while. How long is a little while?"

"We can go to the cabin for a few days. I need the distance. I'll be able to think clearer once I step out of the box. But ya won't be returning to the office until we can rearrange a few things. A week or two," he says.

I groan. "Two weeks, Quinn. I have a business to run."

"Aye, I know, love. After looking at the pictures, I'd say the repairs to the shop will take a day or two as long as supplies are available. Ya have said before that ya can work remotely. I'll bring in a few guys to help Aidan as ya and Tari work from home for now," he says.

"Why does Aidan get to go in but not Tari and I?"

Quinn pulls a hand down his face. I can tell he's losing his patience as much as I am. I'm trying here, but this is my life. I'm not going to up and leave my business to fall apart.

"Love, ya have to know I did a background check on him and Tari. I know Aidan is a blackbelt and licensed to carry," Quinn says.

"I'm not going to touch that one," I say, shaking my head. "Okay, a week or two. I'll work remotely. God, I have to get the system back up so I can rearrange the schedule. I have enough drivers if I bow out for a while."

"Shane will help with your database. He'll have it running in no time," he says reassuringly. "I'll still bring in two office workers."

"Two weeks," I repeat.

"In two weeks, we'll figure something else out. I'm not making promises. When it comes to ya safety, I'll do what's best first."

"Hm," I grunt, making the sound he always makes.

CHAPTER 27

GETAWAY

Alicia

My heart is pounding. It feels like it's knocking against my ribcage. My body buzzes with aftershocks. Quinn took me far beyond the realm of bliss and ecstasy.

"I love ya," he says, looking into my eyes.

I'm not sure if it's because of the car chase or the fact that we've professed our love, but something has changed. His green gaze gives me a sense of a deeper connection. His touches are more tender and sensual.

"I love you too," I pant.

As I come down from my climax, I melt into the king-size bed. It's bigger than the one in his home, swallowing me as I relish in the cocoon Quinn has built around me.

He rolls onto his back, taking me with him, causing me to snuggle into his warmth. Lifting my hand, I begin to trace the crest on his chest.

I hadn't stepped fully into the cabin before he pounced, carrying me to the bedroom. This is the first time he has let up in hours. Honestly, I'm grateful for the distraction. With all the things Quinn told me, I'm not sure how I feel about it. My instincts so far have been to avoid it.

Under different circumstances, this would be such a

romantic spot to get away to. The beautiful mountains. The fresh air. We're out here in our own little world. Yet, the real world is lurking—out there and in the back of my mind.

"You know we can make the best of this," I say, lifting my head to look up at him.

He runs a hand over my messy hair. I've given up on it by now. Quinn doesn't seem to mind either way.

My fingers go into his beard, massaging his jaw. He looks tired and stressed, which is understandable. He has had so much on his shoulders.

"I thought ya wanted to get some work done," he replies, wrapping his other arm around me.

"I did, but we both deserve a moment to just process for a few hours. This place is beautiful, let's not waste it. Tell me something I don't know about you yet."

He brushes a lock of hair behind my ear. I search his face as his thoughts play across it. Some of the stress leaves his features as a smile lights his eyes.

"As a wee lad, I loved doing origami when I wasn't being my mum's little helper. She could get me to focus on origami for hours. I made my first crush a dozen origami flowers for Valentine's Day." He chuckles.

"I think that just made me a little jealous." I laugh.

"Don't be. She tossed them to the floor and stepped on them. Broke my wee heart."

"Oh, no," I pout.

He kisses my lips softly then shrugs. "I got over it."

"You were probably such a cute little boy," I say, running my hand through the front of his hair.

"Depends on who ya ask. My mum probably thought I was a little terror."

"A cute little terror and apparently sweet. You've always been a romantic," I say.

"Ach, a wee bit. My da would give my ma flowers all the time. I did what I knew," he says thoughtfully. "Where'd ya learn to drive the way ya do?"

I burst into laughter. I've been waiting for this question. Trenton wasted no time asking.

"Remember I told you my dad met my mom when he came to New York from Texas?"

"Aye," he nods.

"Daddy loved cars. He was in New York for an amateur race car tournament. My mother was a part-time model to pay for her undergrad. She walked past Daddy's crew and that was it. Love at first sight.

"My dad opened a garage to restore cars and support Mommy through law school. I spent a lot of time with him on the weekends. Going to the track was one of the things he did with me and Aidan. I took to the sport. I went from go-carts to amateur racing," I say with a wistful smile.

"But ya don't know how to fix cars?" he says with curiosity clear in his voice.

"You're thinking of the night I broke down? BMWs nowadays are mostly run on computers. I can actually build an engine if I wanted, but newer foreigns are different from the cars my father worked on. Besides, you were the one who came bossing me around, wanting me to pop the hood in the rain. It was pouring cats and dogs, and my only flashlight was on my phone that died. You assumed I couldn't figure it out on my own. I was fine with letting roadside get her on a flatbed until the next morning," I say.

"I do make a lot of assumptions, don't I?" he says, giving me a lopsided grin.

"Mm, I think we both have. I've also omitted a lot when you ask questions," I say with a mischievous smile. "But to answer the original question, I haven't been on a track in years, but I've still got it. My app is actually to start working with amateur drivers."

"Full of surprises. Well, now I have two things to thank your father for someday," he says.

I tilt my head, looking into his eyes. I love this man. I don't know how he managed to make his way into my heart, but he has carved a huge place for himself.

"What's the first thing you want to thank him for?"

"Co-creating the love of my life."

Tears sting the backs of my eyes. "I wish he could have met you."

"Aye, but he will. I'll be following ya when ya get yer wings. If I have to swallow all the holy water in the world, I'll be following my angel wherever she is," he replies.

I just stare at him. Sometimes the things that come out of his mouth leave me stunned. It's like night and day from what I'm used to.

"What?" he asks, concern filling his eyes.

"Nothing," I whisper, lowering my head.

He cups my face, lifting it to his view. I hold his gaze but I remain silent. I'm not ready to reveal the thoughts that are circling my head.

"When yer ready, I'll listen. I'll always be here to listen."

"Yeah, I know," I say as that fact sinks in.

Quinn

Alicia stirs in her sleep, snuggling into my side. I sigh because I don't want to leave her, but I have some work I need to do while we're here. I would never leave my brothers to do all this on their own. I just needed to get away to clear my head.

I pull the sheets up over her, kissing the top of her head. I climb out of the bed and I pad to the front of the cabin where I left our things. I grab a pair of sweats from my bag and toss them on.

Taking my laptop to the office, I get set up to work. It's late but Shane doesn't sleep. I know he'll answer my call.

"What about ye?" Shane answers the call.

"Wish I could say *grand*. Did ya find the driver?"

"Ach, no. The address was bogus," he replies.

I massage my jaw as it works. This is not what I wanted to hear. Closing my eyes, I roll my shoulders.

"Do you have the phone I lifted?"

"Aye, Kevin gave it to me. There are calls to one number, but they're both burners," Shane says.

"Fuck. I need a break."

"We'll get one. I'm sending the financials ya asked for. Do ya really think yer onto something with this?"

"I hope the fuck not. But I'm not leaving any more stones unturned," I reply. "Have ya gotten Alicia's database up?"

"Aye, she can log in as soon as she wants. I restored everything and gave her a new firewall. Quinn?"

My eyes pop open. I don't like the sound of that. I know he's about to tell me something I won't like.

"What?" I snap.

He sighs heavily on the other end. I brace myself for

what's to come. My grip on the phone is already tight enough to break it.

"Her system didn't crash. It was corrupted. Someone did this," Shane replies.

"Are ya fucking kidding me?"

"No." He sighs. "I tried to track it, but it links to one of those cloaked IPs. It's pinging from India, but that's bullshit."

I shove a hand in my hair. I want to toss something across the room. First, Danita's place, now this.

My head is ready to explode. He's still not telling me everything. I can hear it in his voice.

"What aren't you telling me?"

"Cal had an apartment. Someone cleaned the place out before I dug it up. This shit is getting weirder by the minute," Shane says.

"It's time to put an end to this. First, I want hourly check-ins when someone isn't at the house. Second, school has let out. The kids will have to cut back on their outings—"

"Ma isn't going to like that one bit," Shane grumbles.

"Da will take care of that. I'll talk to him."

"Ha! Ya know that's a load of shit, but good luck to ya and Da."

"We'll handle it. She'll want the chisellers safe, as much we do," I say, rubbing my forehead.

"We'll have answers soon, Quinn," Shane says. "I feel it. Something will give."

"Aye, it better."

CHAPTER 28

LESSONS LEARNED

Quinn

"WHERE ARE WE GOING?" ALICIA ASKS AS I LEAD HER through the trail behind the cabin.

"We're almost there," I say.

Alicia spent the morning getting all of her work done. She said it was much more efficient now with Shane's help. I was happy to see her smiling and less stressed.

Since her work for the day is complete, I want to address something that's been on my mind. I don't come up here as much as I used to. I bought this place to have somewhere to get away and decompress. Every now and then, Kevin would come up with me and we'd find ourselves out here in the woods.

The silence and seclusion worked just fine for the two of us. Sometimes, I think my brother would come along to keep an eye on me. My sister has been up here a time or two. I brought her on this same path to do exactly what I plan to do with Alicia.

"If I didn't know any better, I'd think you were walking me out to dig my own grave," she teases.

"I only bury bodies on Tuesdays and Thursdays."

"I believe you." She snickers.

"Ach, I'm wounded."

She laughs louder, making my heart swell. I love that I can bring that laughter and a smile to her face. She may not be smiling after she learns why we're out here.

This is a necessity for my sanity. I'll be able to sleep better at night. I only hope I can get her to humor me without a fight.

"Are we having another picnic?" she asks excitedly as we stop at our destination.

"Not quite," I reply, placing down one bag and taking the knapsack off my back.

I unzip the bag and take out the pistol I packed for her to use. When I lift my eyes to see her reaction, she has a smile on her lips and her hands on her hips. Not the response I thought I would get.

"Nice, a G17," she says slyly.

"What have ya not told me this time?" I say, returning her smile.

"You have one more thing to thank my dad for," she says. "If we weren't on the track, we were at the gun range."

"So you know how to use this?"

"It's been a while, but…" She shrugs with a cheeky grin.

I lift a brow. I have to see this. From her nonchalant response, I know she's playing me for a stook. However, when it comes to Alicia, I'm no fool. I think she could take over the world if she set her mind to it.

"Okay, girly, show me what ya got," I toss her the words that she once told my niece.

"Don't you want to run through your checklist?" she challenges.

"If you insist—"

"Oh, God, no. Give me that," she groans.

I give a hearty laugh. When I hand over the firearm, she inspects it thoroughly. I go to set up the targets I brought in my other bag. When I make my way back to Alicia, she's aiming and gauging the shot.

"I hit them all, you're making me dinner and pancakes in the morning," she says, looking over her shoulder at me.

"Ya hit them all, I'll give ya anything ya want," I say and wink.

"Yum, I just added something else to my list," she says as her eyes roll over me from head to toe.

She winks back at me before turning for the targets. I put eleven bottles up, ten yards away. In the order they're lined up, she destroys each and every one. I feel the smile that covers my face. Alicia does a little dance, shaking her hips. She turns back to me and wiggles her brows.

"You see that, big boy? I've still got it." She throws her arms in the air and does another wiggle.

"Aye, ya do." I grin.

"To be fair, I've been hiding my gun magazines when you stay over." She laughs. "I was told it was unladylike to be interested in guns."

Moving closer, I pry the gun from her fingers and place it on safety. It's tucked back into my bag before I tug her into me. I didn't know I was missing something until I found her.

"Who cares about the eejits who told ya that? Yer perfect the way ya are. I want to know all the things that interest ya," I say.

"In that case, I'm more obsessed than interested in cars and guns. I also have a baseball card collection," she says sheepishly.

"I think I love ya more, the more ya open yer mouth," I say before I take her lips.

————————————

Alicia

Hinder croons through the speaker about the lips of an angel as I watch Quinn build a fire in the fire pit. I burrow down into his sweatshirt to snuggle into its warmth. It was warm during the day but the temperature has dropped tonight. Today has been great. I've almost forgotten why we're here.

My current view has gone a long way in helping me get lost in this world we've built. Quinn's arms flex and his back muscles play beneath his T-shirt. His jeans give me a delicious view of his ass and strong thighs.

"Grand, that'll keep us warm," he says when the fire roars to life. "Now for our s'mores."

"*Woohoo*, s'more!" I cheer.

"I would fall for the lass that's a little nutty," he says, shaking his head.

"Me? Nutty? Quinn, you did a background check on me," I scoff.

He groans, taking the seat beside me. "Ach, are we going back to that?"

"Big baby." I laugh as he pouts at me.

He leans in to peck my nose. "Yer big baby and don't ya forget it," he says with a sexy grin.

My own smile takes over my face as I lean my head on his shoulder. We fall into a comfortable silence as our marshmallows toast. I'm lost in thought when I hear Quinn grumbling.

"What happened?" I ask.

"I gave ya the graham crackers. Where'd ya put 'em?" he asks, looking around at the things we brought out with us.

"Oops," I say, biting my lip. "I might have put them down when I went back for the Bluetooth speaker."

He purses his lips at me. I have to roll mine to keep from laughing. He actually called off a list of things we needed to carry out. It's why I went for the speaker. I just forgot to pick the crackers back up.

"Sorry?"

"Here, hold this. I'll go get them," he says, shaking his head at me.

"Love you," I call after him.

"Sure ya do."

I chuckle as I watch him go. It's not like he has to go too far. He's probably just annoyed with my scattered and forgetful behind.

My cell buzzes in my pocket. I talked to Aidan and Tari earlier. They're getting settled in at Renny and Teagon's. I'm not expecting to hear from them again tonight. Shifting the marshmallow sticks to one hand, I pull the phone out. It's a text.

Unknown: Where are you, bitch?

I grit my teeth and glare at my phone. The message is from an unknown number. I look up at the house ready to tell Quinn, but something halts me. It's the thoughts that I've been holding at bay.

For the last thirteen years of my life, I've been a victim.
Before my parents died, I was so fearless. I took life head on.
I was always shy, but I took chances. I had a backbone.

Having to run for my life brought that back to me. So
did being able to shoot with Quinn today. It reminded me
of all the times my father used to tell me not to lie down for
anyone.

Anger fills me as I think of someone trying to take that
from me again. I won't go back to being everyone's doormat.
Quinn can't fight all my battles.

I roll my lips. I don't think I'm going to tell him about
this. He has enough on his plate. Besides, I'm here with him.
I'm safe. I go with my gut.

Me: Kiss my ass.

I send the text back and tuck the phone into my pocket.
My chest puffs out. I'm not playing anyone's punk ever
again. Those days are over.

CHAPTER 29

FUTURE TOGETHER

Quinn

AFTER SPENDING THREE DAYS AT THE CABIN, WE'VE BEEN back home for a week and a half now. I want to go back. This house is overcrowded, and I can't find a moment to think to myself. Ma and Da have the biggest place, and it makes more sense to have everyone together until we get this under control, but it's driving me to drink.

"Uncle Quinn, can I go to my friend Torey's house?" Conroy stops me in the hall to ask.

"I heard Kevin tell ya no. What makes ya think *my* answer would be any different?"

"Fine," he mutters and stomps away.

I roll my eyes. That kid is going to make me kick his little arse. I know he's not being straight with us. He's hiding something.

"Do you know if I'm still having my birthday party?" Kasey asks Alicia.

I stop in the threshold of the living room to watch as Alicia brushes my niece's hair, while Molly brushes Alicia's. The three are content in their own world.

"As far as I know, you are," Alicia replies.

"Good because I've been so excited. All my friends

are invited," Kasey gushes. "Will you help me pick my invitations?"

"Sure, honey." Alicia chuckles. "When your mommy wakes, we'll see if she's up to doing some planning."

"Yes!"

"I want to help," Molly says.

"Of course. You're a part of the squad. We're riding together," Alicia says.

Molly tosses her arms around Alicia's neck and squeezes tightly. Alicia reaches to return the embrace. Molly's face lights up.

"I'm one of the cool kids," she says proudly.

"You sure are, sweetheart."

My chest pangs. I can't wait to see her with our babes. The girls, including Mckenna, have been following her all around the house.

"Are we still going to bake cookies?" Kasey asks.

"Yeah, I want to bake cookies," Molly cheers.

"Shh, we don't want your uncle Quinn squashing our plans," Alicia whispers.

Clearing my throat, I step into the room. The girls start to giggle and Alicia looks like she's been caught with her hand in the cookie jar. I told the girls they weren't going to bake cookies until they cleaned the room they're sharing.

"We were about to go clean that room, and then we were going to make those cookies," Alicia says innocently.

"Aye, sure ya were, love," I say as I give her a knowing look.

"We were. Promise," Kasey says, holding up her little hand with her fingers crossed.

"Ugh, you're supposed to hold your crossed fingers behind your back," Molly groans.

"*Oh*," Kasey draws out.

"Babies." Molly sighs as if she's so grown up.

Alicia covers her mouth as she laughs behind her hand. I reach to pull her out of her seat and into my arms. She buries her face in my chest as she laughs, while the girls start to argue among themselves.

"They're all going to drive me to drink and ya aim to help them," I whisper to her.

"But they're so cute. I'll clean the room. Let them bake the cookies. *Please*." She gives me the saddest pair of puppy eyes.

"Ach, that's not fair, love," I murmur.

She places her arms around my neck as she lifts on her toes. I peck her lips and place my forehead to hers. She had everything she wanted before she asked.

"They'll clean their own room, but they can bake the cookies after you and I go for a little walk. I need to get some fresh air," I relent.

"Yay!" Alicia says, turning to the girls to give them high fives. "You start cleaning. We'll make cookies as soon as your uncle Quinn and I get back."

"Oh yeah!" The girls sing and dance.

I chuckle at them and Alicia as they do their victory dance. The girls strut out of the room like they've won some great prize. It's good to see them happy.

"Yer rubbing off on them," I say as I wrap my arms around her from behind.

"Is that a bad thing?"

"Not at all. We all love ya," I say into her neck.

"Uh-oh," she says, turning in my arms. Her gaze searching mine. "What's going on?"

"Nothing, come on," I say, lacing her fingers with mine.

We walk out of the house and start on a quiet walk. This is just what I need. The stress melts as I have my woman at my side.

Alicia

He might be silent, but I can hear his brain talking. The gears have been turning with each step we take. I'm not sure if I should interrupt or not.

"Ya will be returning to the office on Monday. Three days a week for now. Someone will take ya in and they will bring ya home. Is that fair enough?" he says into the silence.

I've been waiting for this talk. The two weeks have come and gone. Things have been running smoothly without me, which has helped me to relax and work on my plan to branch out and expand.

"Thank you for sort of asking." I chuckle. "I think I can work with that if you feel it's best. The place has been fine without me. You were right. This is how I planned to run the place when I first opened. Working from home hasn't been that bad."

"Ach, if ya don't count the house full of madness," he groans.

"There is that." I laugh.

We fall silent again. Quinn lifts my hand to his lips. I look up at him and smile. He's looking straight ahead, but I can tell he's deep in thought again.

"How many babes do ya want?" he says out of the blue.

I jerk my head up to look at him. He's watching me closely. Those green eyes pierce me. I feel like he's trying to strip me bare right here on this street.

"I...I don't know. I used to want three when I was younger, but Gi—Things changed," I reply.

His lips tighten. He caught my words before I swallowed them. I try not to mention my ex around him. Heck, if I can help it, I don't mention my ex at all.

"Would ya consider more now?"

"I guess. I haven't thought about it in a while," I say.

Wrapping his arm around my waist, he brings me into his side. Resting my head on his chest, I sigh contently. I had been convinced I only wanted one baby because it was Gio's idea to have a small family. Now that Quinn has brought it up, I would love to have more than one kid. I love the big family he has. Being an only child has its pros and cons. For me, more cons.

"We'll start with three. I'd like to have more, but three is a start," he says.

I lift my head to look at him again, he's watching just like before. Stopping midstride, I turn to face him. I stare at him as my thoughts whirl.

"Aren't we moving kind of fast? I mean, babies usually come after marriage. You know?"

"Ach, are ya forgetting my list, love?"

I bite my lip as my brain works. It takes me a minute before it clicks into place. I gasp and step back. I'm unsettled for a moment.

Am I ready for that kind of commitment?

When I look at the Quinn, the answer is clear. It's jarring but it's the truth. I can run from it or embrace it. Fact is, he's going to pursue me until he has what he wants. Why deprive us both of our happiness?

"That's what you changed on your list. You went from making me yours to making me your wife?" I say slowly, making sure I truly understand what's going on here.

"Aye." He nods. "Relax, love. I'm not proposing today. Soon enough, but not today."

"I...I...Wow," I breathe. "Okay, yeah. We'll start with three."

His face breaks into the most endearing smile I've ever seen on him. It's like the sun has risen all over again. I leap into his arms and wrap around him.

"I think we're both nuts." I laugh into his neck.

"Maybe, but yer the only person I want to be nuts with," he replies.

CHAPTER 30

STOLEN MOMENTS

Alicia

"Quinn," I whisper as he thrusts into me.

It's been three weeks at the house with the family. Finding time to be alone is a gift. Time to be intimate is something that has to be stolen, like right now.

"Shit, I want to taste yer pussy one more time, love. Come for me so I can taste it," he pants in my ear.

With Quinn's insatiable appetite, once a night isn't enough. Besides, for the last week, he hasn't been in bed at night. Duty has been calling.

"We can't stay in here that long." I panic. "You said we'd be quick."

"Ach, I did, but that was before I got inside ya. I can't stop. Do ya feel how hard ya have me?"

"Quinn," I chide.

"Saying my name isn't helping, love." He chuckles darkly.

I go to chastise him some more, but he dips his legs and shifts angles. I turn to look over my shoulder. His face and chest are covered in sweat. His T-shirt was tossed on top of the washing machine long ago, along with my shirt.

He slaps my ass as he pumps into me from behind, causing me to cover my mouth with my hand as a yelp tries to burst free. Leaning forward, he licks his way up my spine. My eyes roll and my body shakes. This will be my fourth orgasm since he locked us in the laundry room.

I really need to remember not to play dress up with the girls again. They talked me into wearing the pencil skirt that's now bunched up to my waist and the black-and-silver heels on my feet. Actually it was the girls, plus Aidan and Tari. They were responsible for packing my things that were brought here. Those two knew this would happen.

"Aye, that's my girl. Come on that cock. Ya know it's yers," he says.

"Quinn, I can't," I whisper-plea as he rocks through my orgasm.

"Aye, ya can. I'll show ya," he replies.

Grasping handfuls of the skirt around my waist, he pulls me to him as he thrusts inside me, hard. My teeth start to chatter. I hold onto the sides of the washing machine, but it's useless. He has me lifting onto my tiptoes.

"I love ya," he says against my neck before sucking the skin into his mouth.

"Argh," I cry out.

He shoots his hand up to cover my mouth. My cheeks heat. I've been trying so hard to be quiet. I can't believe I just did that.

"That good?" He chuckles.

I nod as I explode around him. Tugging my head back, he removes his hand to cover my mouth with his. He kisses me deeply as he pulls out. My legs are jelly as he slips from my body.

"I'm not leaving this room," I pant.

"No one heard ya," he says with humor lacing his voice.

"Bullshit."

"We could always stay here and I can give ya something for that dirty mouth," he teases.

I turn and pin him with a glare. "We did that already."

"Aye, we did. I wouldn't mind doing it again." He grins. "Especially if I get to go down on ya again."

"Seriously, how long have we been in here? It doesn't take this long to go to the bathroom. I was supposed to be joining game night," I whisper, looking around for my panties.

"We'll get to game night," he says, walking over to me with a towel.

He squats before me, tapping my thigh for me to spread for him. I open as I watch him wipe between my legs and clean me up. Once I'm clean, he arranges my skirt and stands. Tossing the towel aside, he tugs the cups of my bra back up.

I turn so he can help me back into my shirt sleeves. When I face him again, he works on the buttons. Looking around the room, I still don't see my panties.

Quinn pulls his shirt back on as I move around to see where the heck they went. I try to smooth down my hair as I rack my brain for what could have happened to my underwear. I turn to a whistling Quinn, eyeing him suspiciously.

He digs into his pocket and pulls the lacy panties from inside. They dangle in the air between us as a grin turns up his lips. Bringing them to his nose, he inhales deeply.

"Would ya be looking for these?" he says.

"Boy, if you don't give me those."

"First, I'm not a boy. Second, they belong to me now. If you don't want me to nuck ya kex, don't take them off in front of me," he says slyly.

"Ugh, whatever, you freak."

"Yer freak, love." He chuckles.

I palm my forehead. Why do I even bother? His lips brush the top of my head as cheers fill the house.

"Sounds like they started game night without us," he says with mirth.

"I told you," I pout.

"Come, love. I'll get ya to the family before ya burst into tears."

The bananas thing is, I do feel like I'm going to burst into tears. I'm not this damn sensitive. I guess it's because I promised Molly and Kasey we'd be a team tonight. They were so excited.

Quinn tucks me under his arm and unlocks the door. We step out and run right into Trent. From the smile on his face, he knows what we were doing. My face couldn't be more heated. I turn and bury it into Quinn's side.

"Don't even, if ya want to live," Quinn growls.

"What? I've got nothing," Trenton says.

I peek up to see him with his hands raised in surrender. Quinn grunts, and we head toward the family room. My eyes close when Trenton's words hit my ear.

"You might want to go to your room first. Your shirt is inside out, Quinn, and there's something on your skirt, Ali," he says through barely contained laughter.

"Kill me now," I mutter.

Quinn

"Dugan says he needs time. He'll contact us in a few days,"

I tell my brothers as we sit around my parents' dining room table.

"It's about time. He better be coming with something worth hearing too," Kevin says.

"That's for damn sure," Trent adds.

"So, the financials were clean on Dugan? You don't think he has anything to do with this?" Shane asks.

I sit back and fold my arms over my chest. I combed through those records a million times. If there was something dodgy about them, I would have found it.

"The financials were clean as a whistle. There's nothing stink about our boy's bank accounts. Now, if ya ask me if he's hiding something or knows more about this shit, I'd tell ya, yes, he does," I reply.

"It has to be big for him to keep it from us. Dugan has come to us anytime he has something he doesn't want his boys on the force touching. We're always there to put our necks on the line. Why all this cloak-and-dagger shit when it comes to family?" Trent says in frustration.

"I get the feeling we're missing something," I say.

"Yeah, you're not alone," Kevin says tightly, drawing my attention to him.

I tilt my head as I study my brother. That reminds me. I want to look into Danita's files a little more closely. That has just moved to the top of my list.

"Cal is showing some signs of becoming responsive," Trenton says.

This has me sitting up. I've been hoping he'll wake. Then we can get all the answers we need straight from the source.

"Don't get your hopes up. It could be nothing," Kevin says.

"How long until we know?" I ask.

"Don't know. Listen, Quinn. We can't bank on Cal. He could wake and still be useless if he doesn't remember anything," Kevin says.

"I know," I grunt.

Danita walks by with a beer in her hand, catching Kevin's attention. His eyes follow her as she walks out the back door. I'm sure she's going to join the others in the guesthouse.

"You guys need anything else?" he asks, getting to his feet.

"Nope," Trenton scoffs.

I wave him off as he starts after her. It didn't matter if I did need something. His brain is already elsewhere.

I study Kevin as he walks away. His words play in my head. *You're not alone.* He knows something he hasn't told me yet. I know him too well to believe differently.

I'll give him time. This family is as important to him as it is to me. He wouldn't hold back anything that would put anyone in danger. That I know for sure.

Alicia walks through the door as Kevin walks out. My attention has officially been redirected. I bank my list for peeling back the mystery between Kevin and Danita for later.

"Never thought I'd see the day two of ya lost yer noodles over a lass." Shane chuckles.

"Ya will learn someday," I call over my shoulder as I start for Alicia.

"Never," he scoffs.

"Ha, I have two grand that says ya will."

"Yer on," he calls.

Ignoring him, I wrap my fingers around Alicia's arm. She looks up at me with sleepy eyes. Closing the small distance between our bodies, I tenderly kiss her lips.

"Ya look knackered. It's been a long day," I say.

She yawns, trying to shake the sleep off. Giving up, she places her head on my chest instead of trying to speak. The sag of her body tells me everything.

"Time for bed, love," I say before lifting her in my arms.

She lifts her arms around my neck. "Have I told you I love you, Blackhart?"

"Aye, love. Ya have." I chuckle.

She nuzzles my throat, planting a soft kiss there. Her tiny snores reach my ears before I make it to our bed. As I undress her and get her tucked in, I think of how much I want to do this for the rest of my life.

Aye, time to add shopping to the list, Quinn.

I strip down and climb in beside her, pulling her body into the warmth of mine. Placing a kiss on her forehead, I settle with a smile on my lips. It most certainly is time I secure our future.

In every way possible.

CHAPTER 31

CAN WE TALK?

Alicia

I'VE BEEN SO IRRITABLE ALL DAY, AND THAT'S SO UNLIKE me. Maybe it's because I've never been confined like this. Sure, I get to go to the office three times a week, but that's all I get to do without a chaperone.

Heck, I would love the extra time my new schedule has placed in my hands if it came with freedom. I miss coming and going as I please. I'm tired of trying to convince Quinn to let me go shopping or even to spend more time at the office. Anything to get out of this house more.

That never goes over well. I'm not ignoring my safety. I'm just...I miss my normal life. I would kill just to be able to get into my car and drive to the store for a pint of ice cream. I'm going stir-crazy.

My phone buzzes and I bare my teeth. I have to roll my neck before reaching into my pocket for it. This could be the other reason I'm so short-tempered and ready to jump down everyone's throat.

Unknown: I'm coming for you, bitch.

I get at least ten of these a day. I still haven't told

Quinn—it would be a distraction from the things he should be focused on. Like getting everyone back to their own lives.

Me: Bite me.

I shouldn't even reply to these stupid text messages, but today I've been going right back at them. I'm tired, I'm cranky, and I want to be left the hell alone.

"Fucking jerk," I mutter as I shove the phone back into my pocket.

I start to think. Maybe I should take my phone to one of the guys. Not Kevin, his temper is as bad as Quinn's. Shane is more laid-back and he seems to be the go-to tech guy.

He's been gone a few days, but I'll give the phone to him when he gets back. Maybe it will actually help with their case.

"Ugh, what did I come down here for?" I say as I look around the kitchen.

That's another thing. I'm always forgetting something or losing stuff, but lately I'm plain useless. I have to look down to see if I remembered to put on pants. If forgetfulness is truly a sign of genius like that article I read says, I'm blowing Einstein out the water.

"Hey, Auntie Ali," Mckenna says as she enters the kitchen.

I turn to give her a warm smile. She just started calling me that and now the little girls do too. It tugs at my heart every time.

"Hey, honey. What's up?" I say. Opening the refrigerator, I grab the grapes I came for before I forget my purpose all over again.

"Can we talk?"

I turn to see her looking around cautiously. I know that look. I'd get it anytime I wanted to tell my dad something I didn't want my mother to know. My mother was so much stricter on me than my father. He had a gentle way with me. Something like what Mckenna needs—in my opinion.

"Sure," I say, rounding the counter, waving her to follow me to the back deck.

We both walk out and claim a lounger to sit on. Some vitamin D might do me some good. I've been cooped up in that house much too long, and it's only my first full day off this week, three more to go.

I wish we could have spent more days at the cabin. After I got my work done, we spent most of our three days in bed, only coming up for food and bathroom breaks.

"What are you smiling about?" Mckenna giggles.

"Huh? Oh nothing," I say as my face heats.

"You were thinking about Uncle Quinn. That's the same look you have when you look at him," she says.

I shove a few grapes in my mouth in response. I didn't think I was that transparent. Although, Aidan and Tari have been teasing me about the same thing. I chalked it up to them being silly until now.

"Have you seen Tari this morning?"

"Oh, yeah, she went out with Scott. She needed lady things, and no one here has the stuff she uses. That was totally funny. She growled at Uncle Kevin and Uncle Trenton when they said they'd go for her." She giggles.

"Sounds about right." I laugh.

Tari gets kind of unbearable during that time of the month. Which reminds me. I need to check my supplies.

We usually start around the same time. I pause for a minute to ponder that. Actually, I'm usually first.

Um, there are a lot of women here. My cycle could have gravitated to one of theirs. I totally believe in that. It happened when Tari and I moved in together. I'm sure I'll start soon. That's probably one more reason I'm so crabby.

"Poor Scott. He got yelled at too," Mckenna says.

"Oh, no, he's so sweet." I laugh.

Scott works for the guys. Their team seems to be pretty nice, although the guys can be intimidating. Most of them are over six feet and look like they spend a ton of time in the gym. I don't know why I thought Quinn's entire staff would be Irish.

His team is actually quite diverse, including a handful of females. They are totally badass. I like Jazz and Bridget after getting to know them.

"How old were you when you first had sex?" Mckenna asks, pulling me from my musing.

I snap my head up from my grapes. I want to find the nearest exit and run. I had a feeling she would want to talk about boys or her girlfriends, but I didn't think she'd go straight there.

Quinn will kill me. Yup, she's trying to get me murdered. Someone help me.

Quinn

I turn the corner just as Mckenna asks the question. I'm still out of their sight, but I can see Alicia and Mckenna clearly from where I stand. Alicia looks like she's going to bolt, while my niece looks desperate to have her new friend answer.

I've seen the way Mckenna looks at Alicia. She admires her and wants nothing more than to have her approval and friendship. It makes my heart swell to see my family take to the woman I plan to marry.

However, I don't know how to feel about this. My muscles lock to keep me in place. Alicia said to be more gentle with the lass. Storming out to tell her she's not having sex until she's thirty isn't so gentle.

"I'll be honest. I was actually twenty," Alicia says nervously.

I sag in relief. Still too young for what I had in mind for Mckenna, but much better than I feared. I was fifteen, but the girl was a senior in high school. I know for a fact that at least two of my brothers were younger than that when they lost their virginity.

"Really?" Mckenna says with wide eyes.

"Yeah, not that I didn't have boyfriends who tried to pressure me. I got a lot of pressure." Alicia rolls her eyes.

"Yeah, I bet. You're gorgeous and you have a great body," Mckenna replies.

"Thank you," Alicia says shyly, her hand going to her belly.

My lip curls back. She still thinks something is wrong with that body I've come to love. It makes me want to strangle those eejits for making her question the skin she's in.

"Uncle Quinn is lucky. I can see how much he loves you," Mckenna says, looking down into her lap. "My boyfr…the boy I've been texting says he loves me. He's been asking if… you know. If I'll be ready soon."

I take a step forward ready to demand her phone, so I can find this lad and batter him. No sixteen-year-old niece of mine will be losing her virginity. Conroy learned his lesson the hard way last year, bringing a girl to my house when he didn't think I'd be there. He'll be keeping it in his pants as well.

"Oh, Mckenna, I'm going to tell you what I wish someone had told me." Alicia's words halt me.

"Okay." My niece nods expectantly.

"Just because someone says they love you doesn't mean it's true love. Not the kind of love that's deserving of your most precious gift. Sex can be an amazing thing, but with the right person. Outside of that it's…hollow.

"When you find out you're not in love with that person or that they were never truly in love with you, it leaves this void. It's like…like they took something you'll never get back. We're human, we crave intimacy, but once we fulfill that craving, the void is still there if not filled with the actual emotion behind that craving—love. Do you understand?" Alicia says softly.

"I think so. It's like craving your favorite chocolate during that time of the month. It's not the sweets you crave, it's the comfort," Mckenna says.

Alicia chuckles. "Yeah, I guess you can say that. Listen, don't be in a rush. Your uncle once told me I was impatient. At the time, I thought he was totally wrong. Now, I think he may have been right. I was in such a rush to find someone to love me.

"It was when I stopped looking that love found me. Even then, I took my time and this time I know it's the right love for me," she says.

"Yeah, I don't think I love him. At first, I was kind of excited that he said it, but…he doesn't look at me how Uncle Quinn looks at you or how Dad looks at Mom. It's more like how Uncle Quinn looks at steak. I don't want to be steak. I want to be you," Mckenna says softly.

"Oh, my God, you're about to make me cry. But you're right. I forgot about how my dad looked at my mom. If I had thought of that, I could've saved myself some heartache," Alicia says.

"I hope you guys get married. It will be so cool to have you as my real aunt," Mckenna gushes.

"We'll see." Alicia chuckles. "I don't know how far down the list that is."

"I'm sure you're at the top," Mckenna says. "Hey, did you know he makes Christmas lists and Con and I always find them?"

I lift my brow, but a smile comes to my face. Alicia handled that just fine. I think she did a better job than my brothers and I could have done.

My phone vibrates in my pocket. So much for stealing a moment with my heart. I take one more look at Alicia and the smile on her face as she laughs with my niece.

"Yer right at the top of the list, love," I say to myself, before answering my phone and turning back the way I came.

CHAPTER 32

TAKE A RIDE

Alicia

I STOMP DOWN THE STAIRS, MY HANDS SHOVED INTO MY hoodie. It's hot as hell outside, but Renny has the AC blasting throughout the house. It's like an ice box in here.

This isn't helping my mood at all. I've been buried under the covers trying to stay warm, but I've had enough of staring at the ceiling. I need some warmth and something to do.

My app is done; I can launch it once all of this is over. Which means I'm out of tasks to do at home at the moment. Call me wacky, but I never thought I'd long so much to be teaching a sixteen-year-old to drive.

I think about going out to the guesthouse with Tari, but she needs her space for the next few days. I don't think my current disposition will make for good company anyway. I head for the front porch to at least get warm for a little bit. Maybe the fresh air will help me think clearly.

I sit on the front steps and sigh in relief. The sun beaming down on me is more than welcome. I tilt my head back and close my eyes as my bones start to thaw out.

Sweat starts to bead on my neck and upper lip in no time, but I'll brave the heat and sweat for a while before going back into that human refrigerator. My mind starts to travel to the thoughts I'm having a hard time keeping a lid on.

While content with my relationship, I still have some soul searching to do. It's time I pull the Band-Aids off and start to address these festering wounds. I twist my face up as I peek into the pain. I miss my parents so much, but I know they wouldn't want me to hurt this way.

"Ach, why do ya look like someone stool ya puppy?"

Opening my eyes, I find Quinn staring down at me. His eyes are filled with concern. He takes the seat beside me as he searches my face.

"A lot on my mind," I reply.

"Care to share?"

"I…I don't know just yet," I say and shrug.

The pain is only beginning to settle in. I don't think I can talk about it at the moment. Not without falling apart. That would only draw the attention of everyone. This isn't something I want Quinn's entire family to witness.

"Fair enough," he says, rubbing my back.

His touch warms me, soothing some of the tension away. I lean into his shoulder and absorb his strength. I can finally admit Quinn has been a part of the whole.

As I heal myself—even just the tiny wounds—he's been a soothing beam to the hurts. I needed that. Not for him to make things right. No, that was my job, but it's still nice that he makes the healing process less abrasive by just being him.

I guess they're right about opposites attracting. Quinn's organization and attention to details is exactly what I need as I piece things together within. He might be teaching me something after all.

"I think it's time I get ya out of here. Go change, we're going for a ride."

"What?"

"Ya heard me. We're getting out of here," he says with a gorgeous smile.

"Where are we going?"

"Anyone ever tell ya, ya ask too many questions?"

"Fine." I laugh.

"Ach, ya know what. Pack to spend the night," he says.

I do need a change of scenery. Matching his smile, I stand and head back into the house. I smile some more when I walk up on Renny and Teagon smooching in the hallway. They are adorable and sweet.

"Nothing to see here, lass," Teagon says as I pass by snickering.

"Grandma, Molly won't share the dollies with me." Kasey enters the hallway, ruining the private moment completely.

"For Christ's sake, didn't I tell ya two to play nice and give me and ya grand a few minutes?" Teagon says.

Renny laughs at her husband. "Come, love. Let's talk to yer sister before the lot of ya turn yer grandpa completely gray."

"You and grandpa are always kissing. It's disgusting, you know. You can pass germs," Kasey says.

"Ach, ya mind yer wee business," Renny chides.

I cover my laughter with my hand and run up the stairs. This is what goes on all day. No moments are private. It's not all terrible. I've had plenty of laughs, but it's hard to think with someone always around. I think it's my only-child syndrome kicking in.

Yes, I need out of here for a while.

Being that it's so warm, I put on a tank top and a pair of

leggings. A long ride in the car could get sticky. Yet, Quinn turns the AC on in the car like his mother does in the house. Thinking of the temperature in the house, I shudder and grab a jean jacket just in case.

I make quick work of throwing an outfit for tomorrow, plus nightie and matching panties into a little bookbag I pluck from my things. A few toiletries and I'm ready. I dart out of the room with excitement rolling through me.

When I return to the front steps, I come to a halt. Quinn is straddled over a motorcycle. He looks sexy as hell with the black-and-silver machine between his legs. He has on a leather jacket that gives him a drool-worthy bad-boy look.

"Where'd that come from?" I ask as I move to his side.

"We all have one. We keep them here in the second garage. I haven't ridden mine in a while," he says thoughtfully.

"I…um…are you sure you don't want to take a car?"

"Alicia Rhodes, are ya going chicken on me?" he teases.

"No, I'm not a chicken," I reply, squaring my shoulders. I pull on my jacket and place the bookbag on my back. "Give me that helmet."

"C'mere," he coaxes. I move closer, eyeing him warily. "It'll be fun. Ya will love it. I promise."

Instead of placing the helmet in my outstretched hand, he places it on my head. Holding my hand, he steadies me as I throw a leg across the bike and settle in behind him. The smell of Quinn and leather envelops me right away. It's both comforting and enticing.

I wrap my arms around him and press my chest against his back. His hand lands on my thigh and I squeeze my legs around him on reflex. He chuckles before lifting up to bring the bike to life.

I release a squeal of excitement. It's like the thrill of driving a car on the track. The energy that courses through me comes up from my toes and moves through my scalp. It's the best feeling ever. Freeing and empowering all at once.

Just what I needed.

Quinn

My woman has been moody, and I think it's my fault. Her work and friends are her life. I made it so Aidan and Tari are with her, giving them a place to safely stay in the guesthouse. Yet, working remotely, with only a few days in the office, and not giving lessons is taking its toll. At least, that's the conclusion I've come to.

I can't allow her back at the school full-time just yet, but keeping her locked away at my parents' when she's not at work is wearing her nerves thin. I decided to take the day off to do something about it.

This is also my secret reward for the way she handled Mckenna yesterday. I'll always be eternally grateful for the conversation she shared with my niece. I think Mckenna will value it as well because of who it came from.

I forgot how much I love riding on the back of a bike. The sun bright in the sky, the salty breeze blowing through my hair and in my face, the vibration of the engine beneath me, and having Alicia wrapped around me—are all the things I need in this world. I think it's what we both needed.

We pull up to the beach house my parents used to bring us to when we were kids. The same one I brought the kids to when the family brought Erin home from the hospital. Although they were a pain in the arse that weekend, I have a lot of fond memories of the place.

"That was so much fun," Alicia says as I help her off the bike and remove her helmet.

"I told ya, ya would love it," I say, returning her bright smile.

She palms my face to kiss my lips. I chuckle at her excitement. I guess she truly did need some time out of the house.

Spinning in a circle, she takes in the private beachfront property. It's a bit windy, nothing like the scorching heat back at the house. Her hair blows in her face, making her picture-perfect. I take my phone out to capture the moment before it's too late.

"What are you doing?" She laughs.

"Yer gorgeous, love. Yer face is glowing," I reply.

She sticks her tongue out at me as I take a few more pictures. Soon it turns into a little impromptu photoshoot. I burst into laughter when she crosses her eyes and touches the tip of her nose with her tongue.

"C'mere ya," I say, lifting from the bike and pulling her into my arms.

I get lost in devouring her mouth. The stress that has been emitting from her is replaced by happiness. It's infectious. When I pull away, I take a long look at her.

This isn't the woman who was lost in her head earlier. Something has been going on with her, but in this moment, she seems carefree. This is the way I always want it to be.

"What now?" she says breathlessly.

"Let's go inside and get a few blankets. We can sit on the jetties and watch the waves," I reply.

"That sounds amazing. The views coming here were breathtaking."

"Aye, ya haven't seen nothing yet."

"Lead the way, handsome," she says.

I place my arm around her and lead her into the house. I start for the closets upstairs to find some blankets, but the grumbling of Alicia's stomach stops me in my tracks. I turn back and give her a questioning look. She makes the cutest face at me as she holds her belly.

"I didn't eat much of my breakfast this morning," she says shyly.

"Ach, then off to the kitchen it is. I had the kids here not too long ago. Let's see what survived," I reply.

"Do you come here often?"

"No, Erin brings the kids a lot. I stopped coming here as much as I used to after my teens," I say. "Bringing the kids here this summer was my first time in years."

"It's very nice. You guys have great taste in property," she muses.

"They never look this way when we purchase." I chuckle. "My father is a bit of a penny pincher. He'll watch for a deal and good bones. Then, we all pitch in to polish it up. Sure, we hire contractors, but we do as much as we can too. I remember hammering my first nail here."

"Really?"

"Aye, it was only one. I was still a wee lad, but it was the first family home I got to put my stamp on," I say of the fond memory.

"You guys have some of the best stories," she says with bright eyes.

"Ma and Da have told ya enough of them. I still can't

believe they showed ya pictures of me in the bathtub." I wince.

"Oh, my God. Those were so adorable. You hugging your little duckie. Come on, Quinn, you have to admit that was totally too stinking cute," she coos.

"Whatever ya say, love."

"Your prom pictures were my favorite," she says mischievously.

I spin from the open refrigerator. I had no idea my parents showed her those. I hate those pictures.

Alicia's head falls back as she laughs, her cheeks glowing. It's hard to be angry when I see her like this.

"Your mom said you'd have that reaction," she says through her laughter.

"I thought I was one of the members from that rock band, Nelson, I did," I say, shaking my head at myself.

"Your hair was so long." Her eyes scan me from head to toe. Sucking her lip into her mouth, she leans forward. "It was kind of sexy."

"Ya think so?" I give her a questioning look. I close the refrigerator door and move to the island she's sitting at.

"Yup," she says as I tower over her.

I dip to kiss her soft lips. As soon as I deepen the kiss, her stomach growls again. I pull away, chuckling.

"I can make ya a quick PB and J," I say. "Most everything else needs to thaw. I'll take something down to make us dinner."

"Sounds good," she replies. "We should hurry up anyway. It looks like a storm may roll in, and I really want to go out there. It's so beautiful."

She turns to look out of the windows longingly. The

panoramic view does make for an enticing sight. I almost forgot how serene this place can be.

I make us a couple of quick sandwiches. While Alicia eats hers, I go to find the blankets. I can't help getting a little nostalgic as I move through the house and see the pictures on the walls.

My mind drifts to being able to bring our own little family out here. I'll have to add it to the list of things we'll do once we start to have babes. I have already added the cabin to that list.

With blankets in hand, I return to find Alicia with the same pensive look on her face as when I found her on the front steps of my parents' home. I stop to lean against the wall and observe her. Whatever is nagging at her is deep. There's a mixture of sorrow and longing in her expression.

I don't want to push, but I ache to make right whatever it is. I can't force her to talk, but I'm hoping time here will cause her to open up. I think her reluctance earlier had something to do with the overcrowded house.

She turns as if sensing me, and her face lights up. Pushing off the wall, I move to her and kiss her forehead. Her eyes close and she exhales.

"I don't know how you do it," she whispers.

"Do what, love?"

"Every time I tear open a wound, you come to sooth the burn away," she says. "You're always on time. I didn't know I wanted or needed that."

I let her words sink in. As I see the sorrow hovering in her gaze, I vow to always be the chaser to the bitter pills life gives her to swallow. I also take note of a new strength in her. She may not have acknowledged it yet, but I see it clearly.

"Always," I say. "Come on, let's go."

She hops down from the stool and laces her fingers with mine. As we step out of the back door, the salty air whips at us. There will be a storm. Something to cool off the hot day. Although it's always cooler here by the water.

We walk out to the jetties, and I lay out one of the blankets before placing my leather jacket over it. I sit, tugging her down between my legs. Using the other blanket, I wrap us both in its warmth.

"This is perfect," she whispers.

"Aye, it is," I reply, tightening my arms around her.

CHAPTER 33

STARS AND LIGHT

Alicia

I wake to find the bed next to me empty. I was exhausted after my shower. I put on my nightgown and fell into bed face first. Quinn was on a phone call at the time.

So much for me trying to seduce him when he was done. I lift a hand to my head and my scarf is gone. I can imagine the sight he walked in on when he did come into the bedroom. I sit up and look around the dark room. Glancing at the clock, it's not that late at all.

I get up to go in search of Quinn. When I get downstairs, the house is too quiet, so still I know Quinn isn't here.

Looking out of the panoramic wall of windows, I see a large figure sitting out on the jetties. Our time out there earlier was serene. We didn't talk much, but it still felt good to have the time alone.

I grab a blanket to wrap around me and head out of the back doors. I smile as I get closer, and Quinn comes into view. His hair blowing in the wind as the stars shine down on him is a gorgeous sight.

He turns and the dark look on his face brightens with a smile. He reaches out a hand to help me up, settling me between his legs. I shift the blanket from my back so he can wrap it around the both of us.

"What are you doing out here?"

"Ya were sound asleep. Didn't want to bother ya. Thought I'd come out here to think," he says.

"About the case?"

"Aye," he says, his words coming with a hard edge.

"That doesn't sound good," I reply.

"Never is when you have to be the bad guy."

I turn my face up to look at him. He's staring off into the distance. His jaw is tight and his eyes are hard.

"You'll do what's right," I say.

He looks down at me and kisses the tip of my nose. "Wish it were that simple."

He lifts his gaze up to the stars. I turn to follow suit. The rain never did come earlier. Yet it's starting to look like the clouds are going to roll in again, leaving their mark this time. Still, the twinkle of the stars is enough to shine through and make the night look majestic.

In the silence that falls between us, my thoughts start to roll in just like heavy clouds. The reason we've been staying at his parents' home, all the things that led me to my current state. It has all been piling up and begins whispering in my ear.

"I think I gave up control."

The words burst from my lips when I can no longer keep them in. Sitting out here, engulfed in his embrace has given me the strength to move forward full steam. In this moment, I latch onto the listening ear he has always promised me.

I can no longer ignore the enormity of what happened that day. Someone chased me down. My life was in danger. Yet, that's not the most significant part for me. I start to speak aloud the thoughts that have been looming in my mind.

"I feel like I allowed myself to be victimized. I turned into a scared, abused rabbit after I lost my parents. I took the scraps that were handed to me and never asked for more," I confide.

I don't say it, but I think that's why I resent being hidden away at the house. I'm tired of being the victim. I want to face things head on. I'm tired of running away.

"But ya know yer stronger than that," Quinn replies.

"Yeah, I know that now. I mean, that's not me. At least, once upon a time it wasn't me. I used to have so much confidence. My dad was so proud.

"Because I was Black and a girl, I had to be fierce to drive in the amateur circuit. Guys would make remarks and try to intimidate me all the time. Until I demanded respect," I say more to myself than Quinn.

I gained many friendships from standing up for myself. It broke my heart when it all came crashing down. I took a break when mom turned for the worse. It was some time before me and Dad could make our way back to the track after she passed, and then, he was gone and I couldn't step foot on the track without falling apart.

"Ach, I can believe that. Ya were ready to kick my arse the first day we met." He chuckles in my ear.

"I left an entire life behind when my parents passed. I think that included the core of who I am," I say, swiping at my tears. "It's a harsh reality to realize you don't like the person you've become."

"It's an even nastier one to hear the woman ya think is perfect say that." His voice is thick with pain.

I take in a deep breath of the salty air. It fills my mouth and lungs with the taste of the ocean as it opens my chest. It brings with it a new epiphany.

While my mother and father are no longer here with me, I'm still breathing. I'm still in the land of the living, and if I do nothing else, it's my duty to live my life to the fullest and make them proud.

I lean forward and turn my head to look up at him, and Quinn brushes a whipping strand of hair from my face. Those eyes look right into my soul. It's like watching him reach a hand in and pull my truth free. His words are only the vehicle that revelation rides in on.

"Don't look at what was lost. Look at what was gained. Yer the most beautiful woman I've ever met on the inside and out. The butterfly never goes back for the cocoon, love. It flies away in all its glory, never to look back again," he says softly.

I sit silently, allowing his words to sink in. Have I been spending all my time looking back? Maybe I have.

"The broken girl…that's not me anymore. I don't want to continue to live in her shadow. I don't want to look behind me."

"And ya don't have to. It's time ya free yerself. Only way ya can gain control is if ya take it," he says.

I frown as my eyes drop to his throat. I try to put the pieces together so that I can grasp the full picture. When my eyes lift back to his, mine are filled with tears of frustration.

"I don't know where to start. How do I take back control?"

"Stop selling yerself short. Ya already have, love."

I give him a wobbly smile. Reaching up, I tuck a lock of his windblown hair behind his ear. He turns his head to kiss my hand.

"Quinn…" I go to tell him about the text messages I'm still getting, but the tenderness in his eyes stops me.

I don't want to lose that look, and I think it's time I do exactly what he said. I'm going to take control. I'll talk to Shane about it, just to make sure it's not connected to their case. I don't know what it is about the texts. I just don't feel like they're connected to Quinn and his family.

If Shane proves my instincts right, I'll handle it on my own. Quinn has so much on his shoulders. I don't want to add this.

"What is it, love?"

Instead of answering, I lean in and kiss him. It doesn't take long for him to take over the kiss, consuming me in that way he does. An ache starts to build in the pit of my stomach.

I smile as I listen to the waves crash. They're creating a symphony of their own, and I decide we should dance to it. Reaching between us, I tug the drawstring of his sweats free.

My tongue flicks against the roof of his mouth. Quinn moans and cups my breast, kneading it in his palm. Once I have the string loose, I twist a little more to help him push his pants down his hips.

With my back still to him, I plant on his shoulder as I shift back to straddle his hips. Lowering again, I hover over his erection. I spit in my palm and reach to massage him.

"Alicia," he says tightly.

He bunches up my nightie, uses his other hand to push my panties to the side as his fingers find my wet center. We work each other slowly to the rhythm of the waves. When I feel my climax approaching, I grab his wrist to stop him.

Holding the damp fabric of my panties to the side, I

slowly sink onto his waiting length. His hands lift to my breasts as my back presses to his front. I let everything go. It's just me, Quinn, and the miles of ocean before us.

"I love ya," he says in my ear.

My mouth falls open as I rise and fall, but I can't form words. I cover his hands and our fingers link together. Neither of us seem to notice the clouds rolling in.

Quinn is too busy kissing and licking at my neck. The waves start to crest faster and harder. I lift my gaze to the sky as my chest heaves.

My pace increases to match the waves. I lower each time they crash against the jetty we're perched on. Water starts to spray against us, but we don't stop.

"Yes, baby," he groans in my ear. "Let go, love... Ah."

"I—" I gasp as he thrusts into me, swallowing my words.

His hands go to my side, grasping my ribs. I continue to ride him, circling my hips once to pull a groan from his chest. I feel him beginning to swell inside me.

The sky darkens and the waves increase. The taste of sea salt sprays into my mouth. The front of my nightie is completely damp and not from my sweat.

Quinn tugs my head back. "Come with me, *banphrionsa*," he says huskily in my ear.

His lips cover mine, always taking and giving. He spills into me as my walls spasm around him. The waves crash, soaking us, and the sky opens to shower down on us.

I can't help it. I start to laugh. It's the most freeing moment of my life. Quinn looks at me like I've lost it before a breathtaking smile takes over his face. He rubs his nose against the tip of mine.

"I'm going to be okay."

"I know ya are, love," he says with such conviction.

"I love you."

"Is breá liom tú."

"That means 'I love you.'" I laugh, as I remember him saying the same words as we stood in his bathroom that morning.

"Aye. I do. Let's get ya inside."

CHAPTER 34

SOMETHING'S NOT RIGHT

Alicia

I FEEL LIKE SHIT, AND I'M A LITTLE TERRIFIED OF THE reason why. Excited and terrified. I don't know if Quinn wanted those babies now or later, but I think Renny will be getting her grands sooner than we all thought.

After watching Tari tear into Aidan this morning for messing up some files in the school's database, it clicked. The foul mood, not being able to remember a damn thing, and my period still hasn't started. Checking my calendar confirms that I'm late.

I haven't said anything to Quinn. He has enough going on. To be honest, I'm still in denial.

"Quinn's the first guy I've ever had unprotected sex with," I say to Tari and Aidan.

"You really think you're pregnant?" Tari whispers.

"Yeah, it would make sense," I say in the same hushed tone.

Aidan stands staring with a goofy look on his face. "A baby," he breathes like a big dope.

Tari chews on her lip, the wheels turning as she looks at me. I only told them because they've repeatedly asked me if I'm okay since I stumbled from the bathroom to my desk. I'll admit, I felt like I might faint and vomit at the same time.

I blurted the words out as I burst into confused tears. I don't know if I'm coming or going today. This is the first lag in business we've had all day, and I'm grateful for it.

"I want to be sure before I say anything to Quinn," I say.

"Okay, okay, the best way to be sure is a test. We can get one of those from the store," Tari says.

"I'll go," Aidan says excitedly.

"Oh, no, you don't," Tari and I say in unison.

Aidan sags his shoulders and pouts. "Why not?"

"Because you'll jump on the phone and call Quinn as soon as you're out the door. You think we don't know you're his little snitch?" Tari says.

"Me?" Aidan places a hand to his chest. "The nerve. I've never been a snitch in my life."

"Boy, please," Tari says, waving him off. "I can go."

"Aren't you supposed to be fixing that schedule?" Aidan says with an evil grin.

"I wouldn't be fixing it if you didn't royally fuck it up in the first place," she snaps.

I palm my forehead. I really do enjoy not being here every day. I never realized that these two make my head hurt all the damn time until now.

"Enough." I sigh and go to take a seat at my desk.

The bell over the door rings, announcing a new customer. Tari looks at me then at the front. Throwing her hands up, she stomps off to attend to our customer. Two more walk in, ending our small break in flow. However, I let Tari handle them all. I still feel queasy.

"I can get you some crackers, ginger ale, and those tests," Aidan whispers. "You know you want to know for sure. I promise my lips are sealed."

"Fine," I groan, reaching for my purse to get some money.

"Oh, no, this is on me. My first uncle duty," he gushes.

I laugh at him and his excitement. I think I'm still too far in denial to get excited yet. I watch him run to his desk to make a list for the store. It makes me think of Quinn.

"Where are you going?" Tari asks when Aidan tries to breeze past her and the last customer she just finished with.

"I'm going to the store," he says and keeps moving.

"Not without me," she sasses, following him out the door.

I place my head down on my desk and give a short laugh. "You poor baby. Your mommy has twisted friends," I murmur.

I lift my head and really let that sink in. I'm going to be someone's mother. I'm having a baby. My palms get sweaty as I place them over my belly.

"Oh, my God. Your father is going to lose it. I can kiss this place goodbye. He's going to lock us in the house from now on." I chuckle. "But if it means you're safe, I'll do it."

That realization hits me. I'm ready to take a step back from this place and run it from home like I have been these last month or so. I want to focus more on my app and flesh out some of my other ideas. Things I can do as a mom.

The bell at the front door chimes, drawing my attention. I get up to attend to the customer but stop in my tracks as the person who just entered my business comes into view. All at once, an all-consuming rage rushes through me. My veins fill with white-hot fire.

"You," I fume.

"Hey, Ali."

CHAPTER 35

IT CLICKS

Quinn

"Hey, boss, good to see you," Bridget says as she and Q walk into the office.

I grunt and nod.

"That's not a good sign," Q murmurs and steers clear of me.

The place is the most lively it's been in months. It seems like everyone's in the office today. I've been sitting at my desk with my arms folded across my chest, watching and running my lists through my head.

"Conroy," Q sings, pulling my nephew in to kiss his cheek, causing him to blush. "How are you, sweetie?"

"I'm good," he says, his voice cracking and his blush deepening.

"Anyone see Uncle Kevin? I need to talk to him," Con calls out.

"He and that detective are on their way up. They were having a pretty heated conversation in the parking lot." Q shrugs.

Just then Kevin and Danita walk in. I narrow my eyes at them. I've spent the morning looking at Danita's background check.

The first time I combed it, I missed a simple rippling in the information, a gap that makes no sense to me now. It's the kind of thing that's meant to be missed. The kind of thing that makes my wheels spin.

"Kev, I was just looking for you," Shane calls through the office.

I'm no longer in the room. It's as if I'm watching from above. My lists are about to match up. Gaping holes are plugged and questions are answered as I watch the people before me.

"Fuck," I roar, and the room freezes.

"What the hell?" Kevin says, looking at me like I've lost my noodle.

"Ya've been right under our noses," I say as I lift to my full height. "How many lies have ya fed us? I want the truth and I want it now," I bellow.

"Shit," Danita says, rubbing her forehead.

"Quinn, it's not what you think," Kevin says, holding up his hands. He turns to Danita. "And this is the shit I warned you about."

"And I told you, the less you know, the safer everyone is. I need the files on that laptop."

"It's my fault," Conroy rushes out.

We all whip our heads his direction. "What?" Kevin and I say in unison.

"Dad told me to keep scrambling the computer if anything happened to him. I have a laptop that I'm frying the other one from. Every time you try to get in, the scrambled files come to me," he continues to explain. "I grabbed all the stuff from the apartment too.

"I…I cut school one day and climbed in the back of

Dad's truck. He was so pissed at me. I didn't know…I…I wanted to spend time with him. When I popped out of the car, shit got crazy. I fucked up. That was the day he met up with Detective Moralez.

"Dad was freaked. He kept saying he had to fix it. I think they came for him because of me."

"Shit, kid," Danita breathes and tugs at her hair. "It's a little bigger than that. None of this is your fault."

"Explain," I bark.

"Go on. We trust everyone in this room with our lives," Kevin says. "I'm more than ready to hear this."

Danita starts talking. "Nothing is as it seems. I'm FBI. I was planted on the force. I've been on this case for years. I'm so deep undercover, I don't exist anymore. Which is how this whole mess started. Cal stumbled into my case around the same time my handler went missing.

"I had no one to pull me out of this mess, and I was desperate. I have a few of the low-level guys dead to rights, but Cal was so damn close to getting me the guys calling all the shots. Cops, judges, cartel, this case is my resurrection.

"If anyone in that precinct figures out who I am, I'm dead, and no one will ever know the difference. Danita Moralez doesn't even have family to mourn her. My family is in Puerto Rico, probably already visiting a grave with my real name on it. A year turned into two, and two turned into three and now…I need that laptop, Con," she breathes.

"This is what you've been hiding from me?" Kevin says, looking like his head is about to explode.

"Look at what happened the last time I told someone," she says, emotions taking over her voice. "I've caused your family enough trouble."

"And the fire?" I ask, narrowing my eyes.

"Unrelated," she says, lifting her chin.

"You sure?"

"Yeah, she's been getting notes on her car," Kevin says tightly. "Different problem. I'll be handling that one."

"Hm," I grunt.

Different problem. That seems to be a theme. *Nothing is as it seems.*

I latch onto the words as more pieces fall into place. Ignoring everyone, I sit and bring my computer to life. I open the file with Alicia's name on it.

"What is it?" Trent asks as he comes over to my desk. "I know that look. What are you thinking?"

"I never looked at Alicia's background check. I only plucked her address and phone number," I say as I comb through the file, waiting for something to jump out.

"You don't think her attack had anything to do with this?" Trent says in understanding.

"No," I grit out. I freeze when I find the blemish I'm looking for. "Son of a bitch."

"What?" Trent says.

I can't believe I missed what was right under my nose. I've drawn her so far into my world, I neglected to see the one she already had. This is all on me.

It's an old trick that dirty developers use all the time. Two attorneys willing to turn a blind eye at the table. Usually the homeowner is so far behind on the mortgage, they agree to sign the property over, thinking they can save their home, only to have it pulled right out from under them. In this case, it looks like someone pulled a deed and lieu right under Alicia's nose. Signing her signature and all.

"Alicia said the marshals put her out of her home. If yer evicted for a foreclosure, ya sure as fuck wouldn't have a fucking signed title or deed transfer," I bite out.

As soon as the words are out of my mouth, my phone rings. I look to see it's Jazz. My heart drops into my stomach. I know I'm not going to like this call.

"Boss, some chick walked into the school five minutes ago. She looked like a normal customer. I'm so sorry, Quinn. Shit, I need back up. I can't get a clean shot," Jazz rushes.

"Fuck," I bellow, already on the move with my team at my back.

CHAPTER 36

RESCUE

Alicia

"WHAT DO YOU WANT?" I SNARL AT THE BITCH STANDING in front of me.

She rolls her eyes at me in disgust. Her face is twisted as if she smells something nasty. You would think I was the one who tried to ruin her life instead of the other way around.

"You always thought you were better than me," she says, her words dripping with contempt.

I jerk my head back. I have no idea where this is coming from. It's a news flash to me.

"You were like my very own sister. I never treated you as anything but. If I had, you had," I snap back.

"Bitch, please. You can save that shit. You and your uppity-ass mama. She got that law degree, and y'all left me behind like shit on the bottom of y'all shoes," she says.

"Excuse me? First, say something else about my mom and I'm going to beat that fake ass off you like I should've done after I lost my house," I threaten. "Second, have you lost your damn mind? My parents invited you over every other weekend. You were at my house every Christmas. You were never left behind."

She scoffs and moves beyond the front counter to get

closer to me. I ball my fists at my sides, forcing myself not to lunge at her. I don't think I'll ever get over what she did to my life.

"What, you found your backbone now?" She cackles. "You ain't been gangsta in years. Letting dudes run over you. Talk shit to you. You not about to whip my ass."

"Heaven, you know what your problem is? Your mama give you a beautiful name, but you're an ugly person. Your heart is as black as coal. You have to be the center of attention. Even if that means picking on someone who loves you to get it," I say with my fists tight.

"Oh, please. I saw Gio first. He was going to holler at me. Then here you come. Miss. Entitled, high saddity, my mommy and my daddy died and I need some attent—"

I lose it. One minute she's talking, the next, I have her by her weave, punching her in her head. I told her not to talk about my parents. I said I wouldn't be the victim anymore. I don't even know where the strength comes from, but I drag her ass around the shop, whipping it like she stole something.

"I told you to keep my mama's name out your mouth. I moved on with my life. Why you got me in here acting out of character?

"You stole my money, had me standing in the middle of the street, confused, embarrassed, and in tears as they took my house from me. That wasn't good enough? I let you have a pass. I should've whipped your ass then. But no, you still fucking with me and for what? Some dude I'm not even with?"

"Help!" she screams. "Get her off me!"

I freeze at the sound of a gun clicking. The hard metal is shoved into the back of my head. My chest is heaving as I calculate if I can beat the brakes off both of them and take the gun. Heaven starts to struggle, causing me to release her.

I toss the tracks I ripped out of her head at her. My tongue slides over my teeth in satisfaction as I look at her beat-up face. Her eye is already swelling.

"Man, we don't have time for this," a male voice says behind me. "Get the money wired into your account, and let's get this over with before her crazy-ass boyfriend finds us."

"Money?" I seethe.

"Yeah, bitch. I know they left you all that money. You owe me. I had to live like a bum while you were living all high and mighty. If your family thought so much of me, why didn't y'all take me with you? Y'all knew my mama wasn't shit. If I was like a daughter or a sister, why didn't they leave me any of that money?"

I vibrate with anger. I swear I'm going to beat her ass again. My rage consumes me until I start to shake with it.

"I gave you fifty grand, you crazy-ass nut. That's how you went and got those boobs and that dumb-looking ass. You lived with me anytime you needed a place to stay. This shit is about some money?" I say in disbelief.

"Well, yeah, that and Gio. I mean, you don't do nothing with it. You bought that house and then started acting like the rest of the money doesn't exist. I had those fake-ass papers drawn up and hired dudes to act like the marshals. Then Junior set up the deed thingy, but that place costs too much to keep up," she says as if I'm the crazy one.

"Are you kidding me?"

"It was easy. I couldn't get to the big accounts you had in that estate name, so I stashed the money from the mortgage and the other bills I wasn't paying. I've been using that to live in that nice-ass house.

"One way or another I'm going to get the life I deserve. If it weren't for you, I would have bagged Gio first. This could have been my life without you. I had him wrapped around my finger from jump, anyway, feeding him all that shit to say to you and your low-ass self-esteem," she says nonchalantly.

"You sound so crazy. He had nothing to do with me buying that house or building my business. Oh, my God, you can have him. You two deserve each other," I growl.

"Please. He still hung up on you. Shit, I thought fucking him would secure the bag for me and help me until I could sell that place. But all he does is bitch and moan about you leaving him. Ugh. Fucking disgusting." She sucks her teeth.

I can't even process all of this. Like, I'm hearing it, but I still don't understand it. I've moved on with my life.

"So what now? Why are you here?"

"You love that dumbass Gio. You'd do anything for him. And for whatever reason, he's obsessed with getting you back. He really thought I was going to help him break up you and your new boyfriend. Like that's going to last anyway." She laughs. "Gio got all pissed off when we tried to scare you a little."

"Wait, what?"

"Benny here was the one driving the car." She snorts. "Gio has been fucking me and giving me money since you broke things off. I told him I'd help him get you back if he kept the money coming.

"He got all paranoid and angry because you could have

gotten hurt," she scoffs and rolls her eyes, making air quotes as she says the last word.

"Wow."

"I wish you had. It would have saved me a lot of trouble," she huffs.

"How? Aren't you after the money?"

"I always have a plan B, sis. If you're dead, everything comes to me. I had you sign some papers way back. It was my last-resort insurance." She smiles.

"Wow…just…you're twisted."

"Whatever, a few of my friends have Gio. Imma need you to come up off that cash if you want my friends to let him go untouched. The cash or Gio, boo. You choose," she says like she's so proud of herself.

I widen my eyes. She's off her rocker. She can't possible believe this crap. I'm not handing anything over to save Gio. Especially now that I know he was fucking this vile, disloyal, entitled-ass heifer. Damn, he really wasn't shit.

"Aidan was right about you," I scoff.

"What did that faggot have to say about me?" She pulls a face.

My jaw tightens. I'm going to beat her ass for that one too. She has always talked shit about Aidan behind his back. I should've been broken her jaw.

"He said you're one stupid b—"

The lights go out before I can finish my words. I drop to the floor and kick out behind me. A loud yell fills the room, telling me I hit my target. I scramble to get to the front exit.

I don't get far before someone grabs ahold of my hair. The backs of my eyes sting as they yank back. I try to fight but their hold is too strong.

"Damn, I can't believe I got myself into this," the guy says behind me.

Quinn is going to fuck you up. And I'm going to watch.

Quinn

"Quinn, what the hell is going on?" Aidan demands as he and Tari rush up to me, Kevin, and Bridget standing out of sight in front of the shop.

From this angle we can see into the mirror inside the school, but they can't see us. My skin feels like it's going to burn off my body as rage consumes me. That motherfucker has a gun to my woman's head. I'm going to tear him apart.

"Someone's holding Alicia hostage," Bridget bites out.

"That's that bitch Heaven," Tari growls.

Aidan goes to rush past me, but I grab his arm and tug him back. No one's putting Alicia's life in danger. We're getting her out without a hair on her head harmed.

"Stand down, Aidan. Ya'll get her killed," I snarl.

He looks back at me with tears gathered in his eyes. "She's pregnant," he chokes out. "I shouldn't have left her alone."

"What did ya just say?" I seethe.

He reaches into the bag he has in his hand, pulling out a pregnancy test. My knees almost give on me. I want to roar with anger, but I bite it back and hold my focus. That's my whole world inside that storefront. The woman I'm going to marry and our child.

I close my eyes. I never wanted to take Alicia's sense of

normalcy from her workplace. It's why Jazz never goes into the school, only watching from the outside. I was okay with that, knowing how protective Aidan is of her.

"We need to get in there," Tari sobs.

"We have this," I say tightly. Talking into the communicator to my team, I say, "She's carrying my babe. We do this as clean and safe as possible. Get those lights off now."

"Aye, move on three, two, one," Shane says.

I signal for the team with me to move in as soon as the shop goes dark. A second team is around back at the parking lot entrance. My team follows me to the front door.

I slip in the front door, feeling Bridget and Kevin behind me. We move as a unit into the shop.

"Get off me," I hear Alicia yell.

"Hold her," a female voice follows.

I squint into the darkness. The generator kicks in right as I locate the targets. The guy with the gun to her head now has Alicia by the hair.

The female I'm assuming to be Heaven moves closer to the two. It looks like someone got a hold of her and rearranged her bake. Her eye is swollen and her lips look like they've seen better days. Her hair looks like a rat's nest, and her clothes are in tatters.

"We're walking out of that door with her," Heaven says.

"Ach, that would be a negative," I respond.

Sirens sound in the distance. I tilt my head at a now-alarmed Heaven. She looks with wide eyes from the sound to my crew with me.

"Dude, I didn't sign up for this shit, man," the guy says as his face turns red.

My gun is trained on his head. He goes to release Alicia,

but Heaven pulls a gun from his waist and aims for Alicia's head, moving behind her.

My team holds their positions. Our goal is to keep Alicia and the babe safe. That's exactly what we'll do.

"Shit," Heaven cries out as the sirens get closer.

The wanker with her bounces with indecision before turning to take off out back. I ignore them both. My eyes are on my woman. She's calm and collected. I can see her confidence in me. I look down to her stomach and nod. She gives me a small smile.

"How are ya, love?" I say to Alicia.

"I'm good, babe. I'm going to whip this bitch's ass, though," she says matter-of-factly.

"Ach, we have a problem."

"What's that, honey?"

"I don't shoot or hit women. I mean ever," I say.

"Is that right? That is a problem. Are you sure there are no exceptions?"

"Ach, no. Remember the girl I made the origami roses for?"

"Yes, I do."

While we talk, Heaven starts to have a meltdown, rocking back and forth behind Alicia. Meanwhile, my girls are moving into formation. Bridget has eased two steps left every time Heaven rocks right.

"Well, love, she didn't just toss them to the floor and stomp on them. She slapped me. Ma taught me never to hit a girl, so I stood there and took it," I say.

"Is that right, baby?"

"Aye, but I gained four friends that day."

"Did you?"

My eyes narrow. I see Heaven about to lose it, but I'm not worried. My girls always have my back.

"Enough," Heaven screams. "What the fu—"

"Shut up," Q snaps as she shoves her gun into the back of Heaven's head, cutting off her words. Willow steps up to her right, Jazz is to her left, holding their guns to her temples. Bridget moves in and snatches the gun from Heaven's hand.

"The Carter girls have had my back ever since," I say. I holster my gun and open my arms. "C'mere, love."

Alicia rushes to me, jumping into my arms. I hold her so tight, I might break her. Her body trembles in my arms and I squeeze tighter.

"You're always on time," she whispers.

"Always."

EPILOGUE

OUR PEACE

Quinn

"QUINN, I'M TIRED." ALICIA SIGHS AS SHE WADDLES forward. My hands splay her huge belly as I walk behind her.

"I know, love," I say, kissing the back of her head. "My boys are giving ya a go. Just humor me for a wee bit longer."

"Fine, but I want poke after," she huffs.

I chuckle. "I'll get ya as much ice cream as ya want."

"Did you leave the radio on in the car or something?" she asks as we get closer to the garage.

Jodeci's "Love U 4 Life" drifts toward us. I bite my lip and smile. I don't answer as I stop in front of the door that leads out to the garage.

We've fallen comfortably into our life. Alicia lives with me now, and I wouldn't have it any other way. My list is almost complete. This is the last step.

"Open the door," I say into her ear.

She opens the door and the music gets louder, but her shriek drowns it out. I give a deep laugh. I haven't seen her move this fast in months.

"Happy birthday, love," I say as I lean on the doorjamb to watch her.

"Quinn," she sobs, turning to me with tears.

"Do ya like it?"

"Are you kidding me? A mustang? Oh, my God, Quinn." She turns back to the silver-and-blue car I had custom made for her.

She moves to the driver's side and peeks inside. My lips twitch as she geeks out over the car. She still hasn't seen her other gift. I push off the doorway to see if I can help her.

Alicia

I can't believe he did this. I touch the big red bow on top of the car and shake my head. My car was never replaced after the chase. We talked about getting me a bigger car for the twins. Not a sports car. This says he totally gets me.

"I thought we were getting me a truck?" I say as I turn to him.

He opens the door and takes my elbow to help me inside. With his help, I get my butt and all this belly inside. I don't know what to look at first. All the detailing and features are calling for my attention. As Jodeci plays, blue lights dance across the dashboard. I run my hands over the steering wheel.

"Oh, my God, you even customized the shift knob. Look at the pony. This car is so sweet," I squeal.

I reach across to touch the stitching of the custom seats and squeal again.

"You put Ali on the headrests? Quinn, this is everything!"

I look back to the dash and turn the car on. It roars to life and I do a happy dance. Quinn gets into the passenger seat and I can feel his eyes on me. I turn to him and beam. I'm still sniffling from my surprised tears.

"Alicia?"

"Yeah, babe?" I say like a big goofball.

"How is it ya noticed every detail of the car, but ya still haven't noticed the four carat diamond ring right in front of yer face?"

"Huh?" I look at him, confused.

Quinn reaches to finger the ring hanging from the rear-view. My mouth drops open. It's gorgeous. I cover my face and start to sob.

Quinn wraps an arm around me and kisses the top of my head. "Does that mean yes, love?"

I nod. Lifting my head with trembling lips, I cup his bearded face and kiss him passionately. My fingers bury in his beard as I relish the feel of it.

"Yes," I say and chuckle. "I want to love you for life, Mr. Blackhart."

"Grand, *banríona*."

He takes my lips and kisses me thoroughly, placing his hand on my belly. The babies move as if they know it's their dad reaching for them. My heart swells with so much love.

"Hold that thought, love," he says as his phone rings. He grins at his phone and places it on speaker. "Aye, Kevin. What about ye?"

"Something's not right, Quinn," Kevin says quick. "She hasn't called. Something's not right."

I can hear the pain and anguish in his voice. I lift a shaky hand to my lips. Just when I thought everything was starting to settle.

"Ach, hold tight. I'm on my way."

ACKNOWLEDGMENTS

This book! Yes, this one right here will go in the records for so many reasons. While not the first book I've ever published by far, it's the first of many other things for me. My first with Sourcebooks, my first in the Blackhart Brothers series, the list can go on and I believe it will grow. I put my heart and soul into every book and this one wasn't any different. I love Quinn and Alicia.

I want to thank my husband for being there through all of the madness that goes on while I write and publish. He is truly the voice of reason around here. This is a house of much laughter, which usually ends up with us both laughing at me. Thank you for reading every book I send you and for being honest each and every time.

I want to thank my readers that have come to treat me like family. Thank you for your support, encouragement, and love. Every email, message, review tells me that I've touched your life in some way and that's an honor for me. I humbly thank you for spending time in the worlds I build. You all make this journey so much sweeter. Thank you for spending hours in my head.

Big thanks to my author friends. Those willing to text me for support. Those that guided me in my choices. Those that have just been there to cheer me on. My LIRW family, you know who you are. Thank you for making sure I didn't drop the ball.

Thanks to my new Sourcebooks family for welcoming me in. I'm excited to see where we go. Good vibes and awesome books are our future.

Ultimately, none of this would be possible without my Source. I'm doing the most in my career and I know for a fact I could not do this on my own. God has been with me every step of the way. Without his Grace there would be no Blue. Thank you, Lord. May I continue to walk in your presence and demonstrate your Glory.

On to the next! Kevin! I'm so freaking excited about book two!

ABOUT THE AUTHOR

As a young girl, Blue's mother introduced her to the world of love and creativity through movies. Once she got her hands on books, an authoress was born. A story here, a few songs there, but she actually didn't complete a manuscript until 2009. Blue is now an award-winning, bestselling author of over forty contemporary romance novels and novellas.

The self-proclaimed hermit was born in Far Rockaway, New York, but is now a Long Island resident with her loving and supportive husband. The two work round the clock creating music and characters. There is no shortage of laughter or creativity in their home.

THE ONE FOR YOU

Secrets come to light and lovers learn to heal in this steamy series by bestselling author Roni Loren

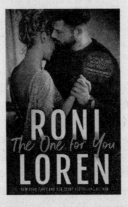

Kincaid Breslin is a survivor. She doesn't know why she got the chance to live when so many of her friends died when prom night turned into a nightmare, but now she takes life by the horns and doesn't let anybody stand in her way.

Ashton Isaacs was Kincaid's best friend when disaster struck all those years ago, but he chose to run as far away as he could. Now fate has brought him back to town, and Ash will have to decide what's more important: the secrets he's been hiding, or a future with the only woman he's ever loved...

"Absolutely unputdownable! Roni Loren is a new favorite."

—COLLEEN HOOVER, #1 *New York Times* bestseller, for *The One You Can't Forget*

For more info about Sourcebooks's books and authors, visit:
sourcebooks.com